EVERYTHING YOU LEAVE BEHIND

A NOVEL

WESTON HAYES WALKER

Published by River Grove Books
Austin, TX
www.rivergrovebooks.com

Distributed by River Grove Books

Design and composition by Greenleaf Book Group
Cover artwork by Forrest Scott Walker. Cover design by Greenleaf Book Group
Back cover image © Adobe Stock / Arlenta Apostrophe

Publisher's Cataloging-in-Publication data is available.

Print ISBN: 978-1-966629-73-3

eBook ISBN: 978-1-966629-74-0

First Edition

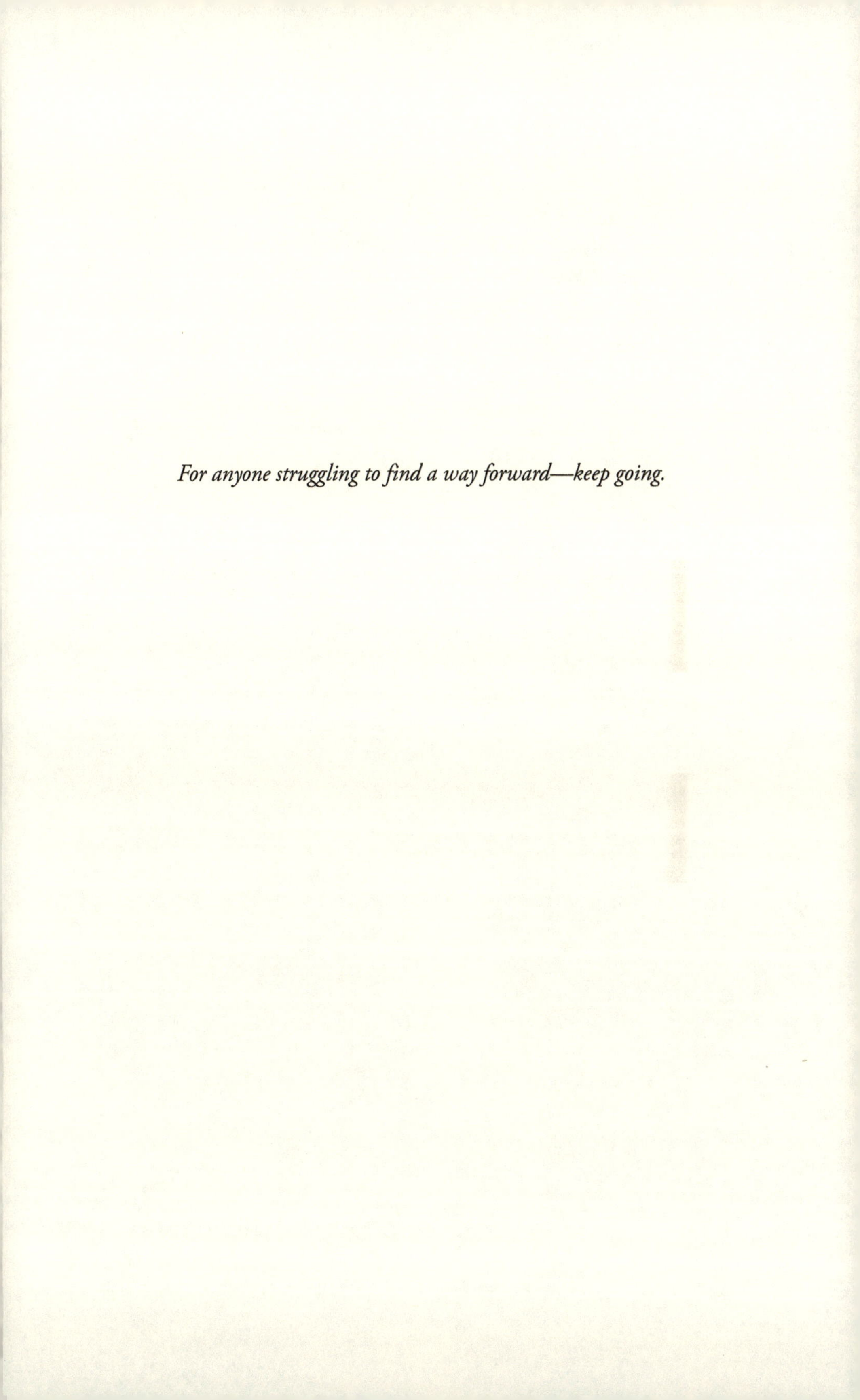

For anyone struggling to find a way forward—keep going.

CHAPTER ONE

The morning of January fourteenth started like any other for Vincent Palmer. As the winter sun struggled to rise from its prolonged slumber, the clock flipped from 5:59 to 6:00 a.m. and the opening salvo of Metallica's "Enter Sandman" began to emanate from the battered iPhone lying on his bedside table. The volume steadily increased until Vincent was forced to acknowledge this new day, and he scrambled to turn off the alarm before Lisa started complaining, once again, about how obnoxious his alarm choice was. Managing to cut the alarm before his wife was pulled away from her dreams, Vincent quietly shuffled over to the bathroom to begin his daily routine.

Just like every day for the past ten years, he started the shower and turned on his handy waterproof bathroom radio. And, just like every day, he was greeted by the sound of Elliott Montgomery, the local shock jock, who was announcing: "Today is Friday, January fourteenth, and here's the news you need to start your morning . . ."

Clouded by his early morning fog, Vincent had completely forgotten until that very moment that today was his birthday.

He had despised his birthday since the first grade, and he was particularly dreading this one. Forty-five. It sounded so . . . middle of the road. Young enough to be considered lively by his elderly relatives, but too old to be considered a peer by his younger coworkers and neighbors. His birthday felt like an unwanted reminder that he hadn't come close to accomplishing anything noteworthy in this life that once seemed so full of possibility. He'd spent much of his youth dreaming big, at different points imagining a near-future version of himself making it as a professional baseball player, successful businessman, artist, or even a local politician—all things he'd felt interested in and passionate about at various stages of his life. But events had never seemed to work out the way he'd imagined, and this birthday felt like a painful signal that any chances he had to change that fact were long gone.

Sulking in the shower, he reflected on what this day represented. Setting aside his thoughts of now-distant friends and loose acquaintances sending him shallow well wishes in thinly veiled attempts to show they gave a shit (when he knew they didn't), he chose to journey down a much darker path this morning. After forty-five insignificant years on this planet, was there anything left to live for?

Why *hadn't* he jumped off a cliff yet?

There were the obvious reasons: His wife and young daughters would be devastated, and it was likely that a handful of friends he'd made over the years would have a tough day if he were to turn up dead. Those had been reason enough to keep moving forward in the years since his mom's unexpected passing, when his mood really seemed to take a turn, but they didn't seem to have the same power over him they typically commanded. Sure, it made him feel terrible to think that others would have to suffer because of his selfishness, but what about him? Having to keep up appearances while crumbling within left him constantly exhausted. Lately every breath he took felt like a punishment. Wouldn't they be happy if they knew he'd found some peace in choosing to opt out of this agony?

As the water gently massaged the back of his scalp and neck,

Vincent allowed himself the indulgence of imagining how he could take control of his inevitable demise. This wasn't his first time he contemplated suicide. He'd bought a gun a few years back without telling his wife and kept it hidden in his closet. Once, when she was out of town with the girls, he pulled it out and went so far as to put the barrel to his temple. But the second he felt the cold metal touch his skin, he knew that he wouldn't have the guts to go through with something so . . . final. It was the same story that had played out throughout his life: braver than some, just not brave enough to get where he wanted to go.

That had been an extreme low point, enough for him to seek out a therapist. The initial conversations had been helpful—it felt nice to have someone to talk to about day-to-day stresses, but he never felt comfortable sharing anything deeper. Those sessions quickly began to feel transactional, and he couldn't shake the feeling that this doctor spent more time regurgitating talking points from their previous meetings than trying to develop any strategies conducive to a breakthrough. He felt himself growing increasingly withdrawn and irritable during their conversations and eventually decided to stop showing up altogether.

This frustrating experience further solidified his cynical view of psychology writ large, while simultaneously making him feel like a failure. As much as he knew that it wasn't his fault, the aftermath caused him to sink deeper into the darkness that was beginning to swallow him whole. *Maybe today's the day*, he thought, then waited for that other voice in his head to speak up.

But today that voice wasn't there. Inside his head there was only silence.

Normally when that happened, he'd become uncomfortable and create noise by throwing himself into a new project or starting an argument with Lisa about something inconsequential. Today was different. Today, for some inexplicable reason, Vincent felt calm. Resolute.

Maybe it's finally time to take control. Time to end all this pain. On my terms, he thought before turning the shower knob and grabbing a towel.

He took a deep breath, opened the door, and gently woke Lisa from her slumber with a kiss on her forehead, hoping that when she looked back on this day, she would remember this tiny expression of love.

He continued to drift through the rest of his morning routine in a haze, systematically dressing for work like he did on any other day. He was finishing tightening his tie—all the way under his collar and completely straight per usual—when he looked up and made eye contact with his reflection in the bedroom vanity. Who was this weary person staring back at him? In his mind, he remained a vibrant twenty-five-year-old kid full of energy—in appearance, at least—and he always found it jarring to occasionally catch a glimpse of his middle-aged reflection in a storefront window.

That's not to say that he wasn't aging well. He'd always kept himself in good shape, fearing that once he let himself go, it'd be ten times harder to get back to where he started. He still had a full head of hair, an increasingly rare trait among his peers, and the gray patches that had developed around his temples complemented his salt-and-pepper beard.

In fact, just the other day, when she found him staring self-critically in the mirror, Lisa had told him, "You're looking better than ever as you head into those Clooney years." But all he saw in his reflection were imperfections. He couldn't help but fixate on things like the deep wrinkles settling across his forehead, or the burgeoning love handles folding over the sides of his pants. Even his shoulders had started to roll forward ever-so-slightly—cruel evidence that his body was losing its long, slow battle with gravity.

But what bothered him the most was his eyes. For years now he hadn't recognized the eyes that stared back at him in the mirror. They were tired. Drained from years of self-doubt, regret, and an overall feeling that the life he was meant to live had passed him by.

None of these thoughts were new, but unlike most days, Vincent didn't feel the unwelcome knot of anxiety growing within his chest. He felt calm, as if none of this mattered anymore. *Maybe today is the day,* he thought once again. *Why else would I feel so disconnected from the thoughts that torture me every other day?*

Suddenly Vincent heard Lisa yelling from downstairs, jarring him from his daze. "Viiiiince," she hollered, "where did you put the new bag of coffee? I can't find it in the pantry anywhere."

"It's the cabinet above the coffee pot!" he yelled back, louder than he intended.

"Ah, found it! Thank you!" Lisa replied, apparently unfazed by his excessively loud reply.

Taking one last look at the stranger in the mirror, Vincent sighed and walked over to his bureau to grab his gym bag. Duffel in hand, he started heading toward the kitchen before turning around, then digging through the back of his closet until his hand grasped the rough, stippled polymer covering the pistol's handle.

———

He was greeted on his way down to the kitchen by the sounds of the typical morning chaos. Lisa moved about like a woman possessed, cooking breakfast for everyone all at once while simultaneously packing up school lunches—a feat made significantly more complicated since their fifteen-year-old daughter, Violet, had decided she was a vegan. Lisa was positive this was a phase, but despite Violet developing into an almost identical copy of Lisa physically, Vincent knew she was more like him in personality than Lisa would willingly acknowledge. Even if Violet did change her mind, the embarrassment of admitting she was wrong would be enough to keep her stubbornly eating rabbit food for years, maybe decades.

"Mom, when's breakfast going to be ready?" his youngest daughter, Charlotte, shrieked from the living room. "If we don't eat soon, we're going to be late for school, and you know today is the day I get to present my science project at the school fair!"

If Violet was Vincent's progeny, then little Charlie was Lisa's through and through. At twelve, she was whip-smart and had already started actively pushing boundaries to find the limits of her power. Her most recent scheme involved getting her classmates to distract their teacher while Charlie commandeered Mrs. Key's phone, ordered five extra-large Domino's pizzas—she had apparently memorized Lisa's credit card information the night before—and returned the phone before her teacher had realized it was missing. An hour later, the delivery guy arrived at the school with their order, and Mrs. Key, confused but not wanting to offend the delivery person, took the pizzas and threw an impromptu pizza party for the class.

If Mrs. Key hadn't happened to notice an outgoing call to an unrecognized number later that evening, Charlie probably would've gotten away with it—a fact she wasn't shy about highlighting as her parents dealt with the fallout.

Fortunately, Vincent could count on Lisa to step in and lay the hammer down when Charlie got too bold. Vincent could never say no to his baby girl, and Charlie knew it.

"It's going to be finished soon, honey! Two minutes! And we're going to get you to school with plenty of time to spare, don't worry. As long as we're on the road by seven, we're golden," Lisa hollered back. Vincent snuck a quick look at the clock; it was already 6:40. He doubted Lisa could deliver on this promise but was thankful he wouldn't be the one facing down Charlie's wrath. Continuing to take stock of the scene in front of him, Vincent realized that Violet wasn't occupying her typical space on a high-top chair at the far end of the kitchen island.

"Where's Violet this morning?" he asked, setting his duffel down with a louder than usual thud.

"Whoa, whatcha got in there? A dead body?" Lisa joked. "Violet's still up in her room, something about her hair. You know how teenagers can get. I'm sure she'll be down for breakfast."

"Hmmm, alrighty. Need any help?"

"Nah, I'm almost done. Just grab a seat and relax," Lisa said, turning her attention back to the stove.

Vincent plopped down and began to scroll through the News app on his phone. This act, which had begun as a pretentious and self-inflicted attempt to be an "informed" member of the public, had over time become one of the most pleasant parts of his day. It was one of the only times he felt like he actually learned new things as an adult, and it was fun to play the "What would I do if I was in charge?" game in his head. But for some reason, today, he couldn't seem to concentrate. It took him three tries to read the first paragraph of an article that was typically right up his alley; he just couldn't stop thinking, *Who fucking cares what these idiots are doing? None of this matters in the grand scheme of things anyway.*

He forced himself to finish the article before switching to social media and mindlessly scrolling through updates. He didn't really care who'd birthed a pair of twins or who'd tried out the new bar down the road; it was just something to pass the time before he had to switch his mind into work mode.

The clink of his breakfast plate being set down in front of him jolted Vincent from his phone-induced trance. He looked up to say thank you and was surprised to see Lisa trying to suppress a smile. Before he could get a word out, Lisa dropped down and grabbed a gift bag she had been hiding.

"You didn't think I forgot your birthday, did you?" she said, placing the bag on the island next to his breakfast.

Vincent sat there staring at this unexpected development, unsure of how to react. Neither of them were big gift-givers, and as they got older, it was more common for Lisa to talk about what she *would have* gotten him rather than actually buying him presents on his birthday. Which, instead of bothering Vincent, became a running inside joke between them.

"Well, hurry up and open it! Quick, before the kids come and ruin the moment!" Lisa whispered eagerly.

Reaching into the oversized bag, Vincent dug through the crinkly gifting paper until his hands wrapped around the edge of what felt like a vinyl record sleeve. Taking a deep breath, he pulled the record out and was astonished to see a mint-condition, unopened copy of Tool's 1996 masterpiece, *Ænima.*

"How did you find this?" he gasped.

"A thank you to start off would've been nice," Lisa teased, "but I knew you'd been looking for this for a while, so I did some digging and found a guy selling his copy on eBay. Good timing, I guess." Lisa shrugged her shoulders—Vincent could see her start to deflate. Too often her first instinct, whether it was gift-giving, cooking a new recipe, or choosing the paint color for the living room, was always to assume she had messed up, and he quickly moved to compensate.

"Wow, thank you," he stammered. "This is one of the most thought-ful gifts anyone has ever gotten me."

Lisa lit up.

"It's a bummer I never really use the record player anymore," Vincent continued, absentmindedly examining the album artwork.

The brightness in her expression dimmed, and Lisa followed up with a quiet, "There's a card in there for you too."

He hadn't meant to embarrass her. Suddenly aware of his hurtful little throwaway comment, he tried to put some visible enthusiasm into digging for the small card lying flat against the bottom of the gift bag. He pulled it out, opened the envelope, and read the handwritten note on the blank parchment card. Before he could register what he was feeling, his eyes welled up with tears, dutifully held back by tear ducts well trained in the subtle art of keeping his true emotions at bay. Blinking back the tears, Vincent looked up as Lisa walked around the corner of the island to give him a hug. "Happy birthday, baby. I love you," she whispered.

At that very moment, both girls burst into the kitchen and began frantically grabbing food off the kitchen table while continuing to argue with each other about one of the many pop stars Vincent no longer had the energy to feign interest in.

"Girls," Lisa said with her usual firmness when signaling something important, "is there anything you'd like to say to your dad?"

After a brief pause, Violet broke the silence. "Oh! Happy birthday, Dad!"

"Yeah! Happy birthday, Daddy!" Charlie echoed.

They both shuffled over to give him a hug, not knowing how much this simple action meant to him. Perhaps enough to make him reconsider the drastic plans that had been floating around his mind all morning? He wasn't sure, but his family's unconditional love had tickled awake long-dormant emotions within Vincent, at least temporarily.

"How old are you now? Fifty?" Charlie asked mischievously.

"You're killin' me, kid," Vincent fired back, doing his best to seem playful. "I'm only forty-five!"

"Whatever, age is just a number anyway, right?" Violet offered, in what he perceived to be a valiant—and very sweet—attempt to save his ego.

"That's right, V," Vincent said, forcing a smile.

He brought them both in for one more hug before they disengaged, and the girls resumed their original argument.

A few years ago, this gesture would have filled his heart, but today he barely felt anything at all. While not exactly painful, the absence of connection with his daughters was somehow worse.

They deserve better, he thought, getting up to put his dishes away.

"Are you sure you have to go to work today?" Lisa asked as Vincent finished stashing his silverware in the dishwasher. "You always used to take your birthday off, remember? Like a fun little 'fuck you' to the man. It's not too late, you know—I'm free after I drop the kids off. We could go get massages, or see a movie, or just get a little buzzed up at brunch somewhere. C'mon, let's do it!"

Vincent loved this quality in Lisa. The ability to throw caution to the wind and make the fun decision instead of the "right" decision. Unfortunately, due to an impending company merger, on this birthday his presence in the office was required. In fact, it was very likely he would be spending an extra few hours at the office as he did the dirty work of scoping out the reorganization logistics.

"I wish I could, but they're saying it's mandatory that everyone my level or above has to work through the rest of the month so we have everything set up for the official merger date."

"Oh, boo! They can't make it one day without you? Nobody will die because you wanted to have some fun on your birthday," Lisa countered.

"I know, I know. But it's just one of those things where the grief I'll get outweighs the fun I'd have. Tell you what, we can pick a day in February to play hooky and celebrate. Deal?" Vincent offered.

"Deal!" Lisa replied and stuck out her hand to make it official.

Vincent gave her hand a quick shake before she pulled him in for a surprise kiss. He was so caught off guard by her spontaneous advance that all he could muster in response was an awkward peck on the cheek—which seemed to be enough for Lisa, who responded by giving him a loving pat on his butt and saying, "Go get 'em, tiger."

Vincent took one more look at his wife and turned to walk out the door. "Bye, girls," he yelled over his shoulder. "Hope you have a great day—I love you!"

Maybe today wasn't the day after all.

On his drive to work, Vincent allowed himself to drift off, trying to recall a dream from the night before. Over the radio, Elliott Montgomery was launching into a crass diatribe about his old pre-date routine of "walking the dog," but Vincent was barely listening.

These days it was rare for him to remember the scattered remnants of the dreams that did manage to sneak in. But for some reason this dream felt different, more . . . vibrant. He remembered being outside near a body of water. Maybe a pond or a lake. There were trees all around, so it had to be freshwater of some sort. And there was someone else there too, but not someone he recognized. An old guy. Searching for anything that might jog his memory, Vincent grasped at the whisper of the old man's words, "Nothing lasts . . ."

"What a bunch of bullshit," Vincent muttered to himself, thinking the dream could just be him regurgitating shit from therapy that had never worked—self-help nonsense meant to help people feel better about their miserable lives. Nothing *good* lasted—that was for sure. But every bad decision seemed to stick forever, compounding and getting worse and worse over time.

Letting his muscle memory take over as he drove, Vincent allowed the usual cycle of negativity envelop him. Allowing his dark thoughts to run free offered a perverse relief, almost like scratching an itchy mosquito bite. He knew he should refrain but just couldn't help himself. Each passing mile that he drove further from his family seemed to pull him deeper into the darkest recesses of his mind. He'd spent so much time in this space lately that he could almost script how his thoughts would play out.

He would kick off the show by ticking off a mental list of everything he hated about his job. The sterile office environment, meaningless busy work, false urgency and imaginary deadlines, and especially the pompous corporate executives—who seemed to get off belittling people like him.

One time, years ago, the COO of the firm had arranged a surprise visit to their offices. As fate would have it, Vincent's team had been going through a bit of a slump. He wasn't particularly worried about it (they'd eventually get their groove back; slumps don't last forever), but apparently others were. So, in a grand demonstration of corporate leadership, this COO called Vincent up to the front of the big conference room and, with all relevant staff in attendance, began running through every single one of his team's negative revenue statistics and asking Vincent to explain his poor performance.

Thinking about it today caused Vincent's cheeks to burn with embarrassment, and in the moment, he had felt like bursting into tears. There he was, a grown man getting humiliated in front of dozens of coworkers and friends, and there wasn't anything he could do to stop it. He had felt completely powerless.

After making Vincent personally apologize for not meeting company expectations and pledge to work harder, the COO asked someone to play the song "Better Days" by Citizen King over the office speakers. To throw salt in the wound, Vincent was forced to stand in front of his coworkers while the COO encouraged everyone in the audience to sing the chorus with him. To describe this as a waking nightmare would be an understatement.

None of his friends had ever had to deal with that type of derision. They'd all somehow figured out how to carve out respectable careers and constantly seemed to be moving up in the world. Even his old college teammate Daryl, who had the intelligence of a Dalmatian, was now the CEO of an uber-successful home renovation business. Hearing Daryl describe the new beach house he was building at an alumni event—his sixth house—made Vincent feel sick with envy. And small.

It was no wonder he'd lost touch with so many of them—he brought nothing to the table. He didn't blame his friends, though. Why would they want to be associated with a loser like Vincent Palmer?

Hell, *he* didn't want to be associated with a loser like Vincent Palmer any longer.

Not to mention the fact that he couldn't even seem to muster up the decency to show his wife the gratitude that she deserved earlier that morning. Per usual, she did an excellent job covering her true feelings, but Vincent noticed the excitement in her eyes dim as soon as he opened his stupid mouth.

It's too bad I don't use the record player anymore. Seriously? *That* was the type of reaction he thought was appropriate after receiving such a thoughtful gift?

His chest started tightening, and what little energy he'd had leaked out of his body. It was almost as if he could *feel* the heavy dark circles forming under his eyes—no amount of caffeine could help shake this lethargy. Once again, he'd been defeated before the day had even begun.

What's the point? he thought. *Every day is exactly the same. Nothing changes. Nothing will ever change.*

There is one way to change things, a voice in the back of his head responded, causing him to glance down at the duffel bag sitting in the passenger seat.

The sound of someone laying on their horn forced Vincent back into reality, and it didn't take long for him to realize the horn was directed at him. Taking a moment to recalibrate, he realized he was stopped in front of a "Road Closed" sign and had apparently gotten so lost in his own thoughts that he just sat there idling in place. There was another sign with an arrow instructing him to take a detour toward the Broadlands, a notoriously dangerous area just outside of the business district. Vincent had no clue how long he had been immobile, but he quickly reoriented and followed the signs he hoped would get him back on track.

It always surprised him how much poverty existed right outside of the city limits. Drive a few blocks one way and you'll find yourself traveling through a canyon of pristine, towering skyscrapers as far as the eye can see, but take a wrong turn and in that same distance you could find yourself in what felt like a war zone. What he saw in the short time spent navigating the Broadlands' crumbling streets startled him. Dilapidated buildings leaned precariously, their windows covered with grime or boarded up with rotting wood. Faded graffiti adorned walls, and rats moved freely from yard to yard in broad daylight.

Finally, Vincent came to the last turn on the detour, and as he began to head back toward the city, he noticed a group of men huddling around a firepit in the front yard of a house that looked one bad storm away from collapse. *Those don't look like people you should mess with*, he thought and continued onward.

CHAPTER TWO

Walking into the garage elevator beneath his offices, Vincent braced for the typical dread-inspired anxiety he experienced before every working day. Instead, he was once again met with the feeling of detached calm, unbothered by what was bound to be a particularly miserable day at the office. Unable to reconcile his thoughts and his feelings, he let out a deep exhale, pressed the button to take him up to the fourteenth floor, and instantly felt the responsive lurch of the elevator beginning its slow ascent.

Vincent looked down at his watch to see its hands at eight and three—the detour had thrown him further off schedule than he initially registered. Fuck. There was no way he was getting up to fourteen without running into someone.

Perfectly comfortable keeping to himself and existing in silence, he hated small talk. Why did everyone else feel the need to speak simply because they happened to be in the same place at the same time?

He consciously engineered his commute around when the fewest number of people tended to arrive and depart the office. If he could manage to get into the garage before 8:00 a.m., that normally saved him from the morning rush and allowed for a few extra moments of peace before the bullshit began.

The elevator dinged and began to slow down. "Ground floor," a woman's pre-recorded voice purred over the intercom as the doors opened to reveal the only person in the office that Vincent actually liked.

Amanda Knotts had been the top performing salesperson at his company over the last decade, and she made sure everyone knew it. She was a tenacious salesperson with a sharp wit, an endearingly sarcastic sense of humor, and an impressive ability to manipulate situations to her advantage using all of the tools at her disposal—including her supermodel-esque good looks and height.

Vincent took a stealthy look at Amanda's figure while she tapped away at her phone, still unaware that the elevator she requested had arrived. A former collegiate volleyball player, she stood at 5'10" but always seemed taller at work due to the variety of multi-inch Louboutin heels she wore religiously. However, standing at 6'3" himself, Vincent was one of the few coworkers she couldn't physically intimidate. Letting his eyes drift up from her shoe selection, Vincent's gaze lingered on her perfectly toned and surprisingly bare lower legs poking out from beneath her camel-hair overcoat. A few years back, this sight would've caused a primal excitement to stir, but those days were long gone.

Not even frigid temperatures will stop her from making a good first impression, was the only thought he could conjure.

"Good morning, Vince," Amanda said, her tone subtly implying that she'd caught him checking her out. "Happy Birthday!" she added, lifting her voice back to its normal register. "What in the world are you doing here? You never work on your birthday!"

"I know, I know," Vincent replied with a sheepish smile, "but we've got the guys from Erickson coming in for the first time today, and Toby basically told me that if I'm not here, I can kiss my job goodbye once the merger's finalized."

"Oh, fuck Toby! That bald douchebag is all talk," Amanda shot back. "They can't fire you—you're the only person who actually knows how to keep the lights on around here. If they let you go, I'd be right behind you—there's no way I'm gonna stick around to break in a new manager."

"Well, hopefully it doesn't come to that . . ." Vincent mumbled.

In between small talk about their weekend plans, Vincent discreetly took in the rest of Amanda's look for the day. She was sporting a brand-new, extremely flattering tan Louis Vuitton overcoat that he was sure covered up a low-cut blouse. Her shoulder-length dark-brown hair was perfectly coiffed, and she was wearing more makeup than normal, enough that it distracted from her crystal-clear blue eyes. Amanda's hands and nails were perfectly manicured, and she sported multiple rings that Vincent was sure cost at least five figures each. But, as had been the case for the past five years, her left ring finger remained naked.

It was clear that she was pulling out all the stops to impress their new corporate overlords. Vincent looked down at the cheap suit-and-tie combination he'd selected for the day and realized he might be under-dressed for the occasion. Ordinarily this type of revelation would've set off alarm bells inside his mind, but he just didn't have the energy to care about such trivial things today.

Before he knew it, the elevator jerked to a halt, revealing the humble lobby of Forrest Dunlop Consulting. As Vincent expected, it was an absolute madhouse of bodies rushing through the hallways as everyone prepared for the arrival of Erickson's upper management.

"Here we go," Vincent said, groaning.

"Oh, come on! You'll be fine," Amanda replied, giving him an affectionate smack on the arm and turning the corner to the bullpen.

Allowing his gaze to follow her first few steps toward the door, Vincent turned in the opposite direction to greet Miss Nadia, their receptionist, and peeked into the main conference room to see if Gil, their regional director, had settled in yet. Sure enough, Gil was sitting at the head of their twenty-five-foot conference table, peering over half-rimmed glasses at his brand-new laptop.

Vincent tried to sneak by unnoticed, but just when he thought he'd gotten away, he heard a muffled, "Palmer! Is that you? Get in here."

"Fuck," Vincent whispered under his breath as he turned on his heel, prepared his best kiss-ass smile, and headed into the conference room. "Hey there, boss, you ready for the ball busters today?" Vincent said, forcing a friendly tone.

"I don't want to hear any of that. We need to treat these folks like family. There's no reason to start things off on the wrong foot," Gil replied sternly. He looked up at the clock at the front of the conference room. "Eight-twenty is cutting it a little close, no? Didn't think today was important enough to show some initiative and be here early enough to make sure all your ducks are in a row?"

"I would've been here earlier, but I hit some roadwork on the way that set me back half an hour. Don't worry—I'm all set for my part of the presentation," Vincent sputtered, hoping his weak explanation would be enough to end the conversation.

"Well . . . that's good. Just make sure you don't screw this up for the rest of us. If we play this right, we'll all stand to make a lot of money once this deal is finalized."

Gil dropped his gaze back to his laptop, and Vincent took that as his cue to leave. On any other day, this exchange would have caused Vincent to spin out into a silent rage. He hated when people talked down to him simply because they had a fancier title printed on their business cards. But today he couldn't find the energy to get worked up.

It didn't matter. None of it mattered anymore.

Vincent could hear the buzz on the other side of the door as he swiped his key card and stepped into the bullpen, a football-field-sized room filled with cubicles as far as the eye could see. The nervous energy in the office was palpable as roughly two hundred Forrest Dunlop employ-ees—all dressed in their Sunday best—frantically milled about trying to ensure everything looked perfect for when the Erickson VIPs arrived.

Without breaking stride, Vincent began his typical fifty-foot walk to his corner cubicle. Ten years ago, when he was promoted into his current branch manager role, Forrest Dunlop's leadership had offered him one of the coveted offices on the far side of the bullpen. But in a misguided attempt to show solidarity with his colleagues, Vincent had turned their offer down and elected to inhabit a cubicle like everyone else. Initially, this humble act resulted in an overflow of goodwill and instant respect among his former peers and subordinates.

Over the next few years, it seemed like he could do no wrong. Everyone followed his lead and attacked new initiatives with double the intensity he expected. But the good times didn't last. He soon began losing his top performers to competing consulting firms offering money and elevated titles Vincent would never be able to match.

As his best employees and friends started fleeing for greener pastures, Vincent's district director Toby began pressuring him to put butts in the seats. Before he knew it, Vincent found himself surrounded by strangers closer in age to his daughter with whom he had no hope of forging any meaningful connections. Somehow he'd managed to perform well enough to keep Toby and Gil off his back, but the last five years had been a struggle as he was consistently passed over for promotions and trapped in corporate purgatory. It had left Vincent feeling like a fraction of the man he had once been within the company. Hardly a day went by without him regretting his decision to pass up the cozy confines of his own office. At least then he would have some way to hide away from the embarrassment.

Arriving at his corner cubicle, Vincent dropped the duffel bag under his desk with an audible thud, took out his laptop, and started powering up his workstation. Before he could start typing in his username and password, he heard a voice from behind him.

"Where the fuck have you been?" the voice demanded.

Vincent froze.

"I thought we established last night that all managers needed to be here early. How the fuck are you late today of all days?" The voice continued through gritted teeth. Vincent spun around in his chair to come face to face with Toby Schiff, his direct supervisor.

Unconcerned with getting answers to his questions, Toby leaned in closer—too close—and continued, "This is the day that will set the tone for how you're perceived by new management. Don't you want to make a good first impression and maybe get a chance to move up for once?"

Toby had been at Forrest Dunlop for a decade longer than Vincent and was known to be a ruthlessly effective salesman, willing to do anything to close a deal—even if it meant ruffling a few feathers along the way. This uncompromising attitude, which clearly stemmed from feelings of inadequacy, allowed him to rise quickly, but he eventually hit a ceiling as his Machiavellian reputation became more well known.

Vincent wasn't surprised to see that Toby had adorned his stocky frame with the perfectly tailored, double-breasted dark gray Brioni pinstripe suit that he broke out for "important occasions." Toby always did go out of his way to make a flashy first impression.

While Vincent quietly admired his fit for the day, Toby leaned in enough that Vincent could smell the cigarettes and stale coffee on his breath. "Seriously, man, you gotta get it together. I'd hate to see this throw you off your game in there later." Before Vincent could attempt to brush him off, Toby gave his shoulder a squeeze, said, "I know you'll find a way to bounce back, bud," and stalked back toward his corner office in his trademark, overly aggressive gait.

"Jesus fucking Christ," Vincent said out loud to no one in particular. "How was I supposed to know there would be an emergency detour today? And I'm not even fucking late!" He paused, took a deep breath, and started laughing. "Whatever, who gives a fuck? All I have to do today is stay awake and say a handful of scripted words."

Shaking his head, Vincent spun back around, logged in, and went about his daily routine of mindlessly scrubbing through emails and kill-ing time before his next meeting.

———

When he stepped into the conference room an hour later, it was already full of his immediate superiors and counterparts. The back wall boasted an ornate breakfast spread, no doubt meant to impress the Erickson VIPs. Professionally made name tags were placed in front of each seat, ensuring that there would be no jockeying for position among the underlings.

After taking an entire lap around the conference room, he finally found his name on the opposite side of the table directly in front of the projector screen. *Great,* he thought, *not only will I be craning my neck the whole time, but I'll have to pretend I'm not totally overwhelmed by the scent of every speaker's cologne or perfume.* As he set his laptop down, he glanced over to see who he would be sitting next to for the next six to eight hours, and his stomach dropped.

Not one second later, he felt a firm hand grasp the back of his neck, confirming that he would be stuck next to Toby for the entire day. Judging by the strong stench of cigarettes and overpowering musk of cologne, Vincent surmised that Toby must've snuck out for one last smoke break before the meeting.

"Looks like we're hunkered down together today, huh?" Toby said as he plopped down.

"Lucky me," Vincent replied, doing his best to pretend this was a pleasant surprise.

"You're damn right, bud," Toby shot back. "I'll be making you look good all day, baby. It's game time!"

Vincent took his seat and began setting up his space, not bother-ing to register the many interactions taking place all around him. Not that he needed to be paying attention; he knew how these types of things always went: Everyone meandering about looking for someone they could corner into a conversation so they could brag about whatever fancy new purchase they made or what celebrity they saw out at dinner—posturing made almost comical by the fact that everyone in the room knew one another's performance metrics and corresponding compensation. Vincent had stopped caring about that shit years ago, if he had ever cared at all.

Suddenly Vincent felt a sharp jab in his left ribs and noticed Toby elbowing him but not looking in his direction. "Toby, what the fuck," Vincent muttered. "Stop."

"Dude—look up," Toby whispered, barely moving his lips and keeping his gaze firmly locked on his own laptop. Before he could register that he was supposed to be slick, Vincent looked across the table and found himself confronted by a pair of perfectly shaped breasts barely contained by a low-cut blouse. Feeling himself blush, he quickly looked away.

"Now how the hell did I end up with the worst seat in the house?" Amanda announced to nobody in particular. Unaware of how long he had been staring, Vincent threw up his hands and said, "Don't look at me! I told them to put you at the head of the table when they asked about seating assignments."

"Oh, I know you wouldn't do this to me, Vince," she fired back with a wink. "Must've been your sidekick Toby over here," she finished, turning and walking toward the back room to pour a cup of coffee.

"You see that?" Toby said, turning to Vincent and assaulting him with breath so bad it should be illegal.

"See what?" Vincent replied, not knowing what Toby was getting at.

"She was totally flirting with me! God, the sexual tension between the two of us has been off the charts lately. If I wasn't a district director, we definitely would've fucked by now—I just don't feel like dealing with HR. But, damn, if she keeps walking around like that, I might just have to give in."

Vincent gave Toby a slight nod, assuming this would be a satisfactory response, and went back to pretending to review his slide deck. Amanda wouldn't be caught dead in a sexual situation with Toby—she and Vincent had always bonded over their mutual disdain over every little thing Toby did on a day-to-day basis, from his pompous "pump up" speeches in the mornings, to the slimy sales tactics he taught newbies, to the way he walked around with his chest popped out like he was an Olympic weightlifter. The chances of those two hooking up were about as good as Vincent waking up a rockstar tomorrow.

The reality of the situation was that Amanda was flirting with Vincent and had been for some time now. It all started at Forrest Dunlop's annual holiday party a few years back when, in a remarkable lapse of judgment, Vincent had found himself alone in a back booth with her.

They'd always been great work friends but rarely found themselves talking outside of the office. But that night they had been nearly inseparable. Fueled by more than a few Rumplemintz shots and cheap beers, he'd let his guard down and gave into the types of temptations he normally wouldn't have let get past his imagination. Before he could stop himself, his lips were on hers and he felt a momentary passion that was a relic of his past life.

Vincent quickly disengaged, apologized, and rushed out, knowing that one more second would have meant the end of his marriage. In fact, the shame from that passing indiscretion still weighed heavily. He couldn't imagine turning Lisa's life upside down for something so stupid and meaningless. So, despite the intense guilt he carried in the days that followed, Vincent decided that this particular encounter was something she was better off not knowing about.

Out of an abundance of caution, he'd made it a personal rule to avoid any interactions with Amanda outside of the office or absent the presence of coworkers moving forward. Oddly, instead of offending her, his strategy seemed to ensure her continued interest all these years later. Did she think he was playing hard to get? Or maybe he was just the type of asshole to send mixed signals and string her along?

Before Vincent could think further on it, Gil walked into the room, eliciting a hush from the crowd.

"They're here," he deadpanned and walked toward his seat at the head of the table in the back of the room. Everyone hurriedly took their seats and nervously pretended to work on their laptops. A minute later, the five Erickson VPs appeared in the lobby and were escorted into the conference room accompanied by Forrest Dunlop's COO—the same COO who had publicly embarrassed Vincent earlier in his career.

Would've been nice to know that this piece of shit was coming, Vincent thought. *Thanks for the heads up, Gil.*

Everyone stood and engaged in the compulsory polite handshake greetings with all the strangers who were there to identify redundancies. This kind of thing always struck Vincent as odd. Why pretend to be friendly when they were all clearly not on the same team? What was the point of the charade? Was everyone else not painfully aware of how insulting this dog-and-pony show was to the people in this room?

But, despite his gut telling him this was completely fucked, Vincent played his part, gave a fake smile while shaking hands, and immediately forgot the names of these people he hopefully would never see again.

After they finished their rounds, each VIP grabbed a cold Diet Coke—Vincent would never understand why business executives all seemed to slam Diet Cokes like water—and took their seats around Gil in the back of the room.

"All right," Gil announced with an uncharacteristic enthusiasm, "let's get started, shall we?"

And the soul-crushingly boring marathon meeting began.

CHAPTER THREE

After an entire workday of back-to-back presentations, Gil mercifully announced that they were wrapping up for the day. All at once, everyone seemed to relax, and the sounds of excited small talk about where the group should head for happy hour instantly filled the room. Gil quickly popped back up and announced, "For those of you interested, we'll be heading over to the W hotel bar for some celebratory libations." This news caused nearly everyone in the room to cheer.

The noise hurt Vincent's ears. To him, they appeared as a pack of jackals snarling and snapping as they prepared to run roughshod over the smaller animals at the watering hole.

Gil cleared his throat loudly as the cheers subsided. "However," he added, "I'd like all of my Forrest Dunlop folks to hang back for a quick recap before we punch out for the day."

Once the bigwigs had filed out, Gil asked everyone to quiet down.

"All right, there's no use sugarcoating this—that was embarrassing for a lot of you.

Jason, Andrew, Mike, Jeff, Amanda, and Anthony . . . you were the only ones who didn't look like complete dogshit—we'd love to have you join us for drinks down the street at the W. Go ahead and grab your stuff and catch up with the rest of the group."

Vincent's stomach dropped. He'd known it was going to be a rough day, but he didn't think it had gone *that* badly.

"The rest of you," Gil continued, "including you, Toby, aren't going anywhere. Not until you've put together a comprehensive plan for how you'll be driving growth within your branches over the next six to twelve months. Toby, you're the one that gets to decide when they're done—and if those plans aren't airtight, it's your fucking ass."

Without another word Gil packed up his briefcase and walked out of the conference room, purposefully avoiding eye contact with any of the dozen people left sitting in stunned silence. Vincent snuck a sideways glance to his left and saw a vein in the side of Toby's head that looked ready to explode. As soon as Toby heard the elevator doors close behind Gil in the lobby, he slammed his hands on the table. "What the fuck?" he yelled.

Vincent felt himself instinctively flinch.

Nobody said a word.

"None of you have anything to say for yourselves, huh? Not one fucking word out of any of you?"

Everyone continued to sit as still as possible, staring down at the table.

"I should fire all of you, right fucking now! I work my motherfucking ass off every fucking day. And this is what I get in return? You better buckle up, because you're going to be here all fucking night if you have to. I *will not* be embarrassed like this again."

Toby surveyed the room one final time and calmly said, "Does anyone have anything they'd like to add?"

Not one person dared to look up.

"That's what I thought," he said. "Get to fucking work!"

Apparently having said all he needed to say, Toby spun on his heel and stormed out of the conference room toward the elevators.

Everyone remained completely still for what felt like forever. Finally, convinced that Toby was well out of earshot, Vincent decided he should probably say something to the group. He was the most tenured of them all and probably the only one who truly understood why they were the ones left behind.

With a deep breath, he stood up and calmly said, "All right, everyone, that was pretty out of bounds. If you're feeling like you'd like to report this to HR or whoever, you have absolutely every right to tell your story. Just know that."

He could feel the room let out a collective sigh of relief.

"As for tonight, we've got a few options. We can do as we've been told like good little children and work through the night to produce 'coherent' bullshit projections about a future we can't possibly predict. Or we can pack it up, head home, and worry about this shit tomorrow. As far as I know, we're not involved in any of tomorrow's follow-up meetings—that's just going to be district directors and above. Seems like Toby and Gil are scared for their jobs and have decided it's our responsibility to save their asses. Does anyone else see any options that I'm missing?"

Everyone started looking around to see who would be the first to speak up. Vincent always hated this part of public speaking in a corporate setting—the military-like hierarchical structure implied a danger in speaking one's mind, so most people opted to keep their mouths shut.

After about a minute of silence Vincent decided to take matters into his own hands, "Well, I'm going to get out of here. It's my birthday, and after that outburst, I'd honestly prefer to be fired so I never have to be within three hundred feet of Toby or Gil ever again."

Finally, someone in the back spoke up and said, "I think I'm gonna stay put; I can't afford to lose my job right now." The others shook their heads and mumbled in agreement, doing their best to avoid eye contact.

"Fair enough," Vincent replied, packing up his stuff. "Good luck tonight, everyone."

———

Standing in the elevator on his way down to the parking garage, he couldn't quite process what had just happened. Not only had both of his bosses acted like entitled assholes within five minutes of each other but he, Vincent Palmer, was the renegade defying direct orders. His entire life, he'd been the ideal soldier, never questioning his superiors, never stepping out of line, and always doing the "right" thing. But today he just couldn't seem to care less about what those pathetic men thought of him. He couldn't really seem to care about anything. None of this would matter tomorrow.

The mysterious steadiness he'd been experiencing intermittently throughout the day returned, and he was hyperaware of the extra weight in his duffel bag pulling his right shoulder toward the ground as the elevator arrived at its destination.

Pulling out of the garage, Vincent couldn't decide if he wanted to head home or stop by the nearby pub to decompress after one of the stranger days he'd had in the last twenty years. Before he could make a decision, he was forced to a stop in the alleyway behind the garage and found himself staring directly at Toby. Apparently, Toby had decided to handle his irrational rage by pacing in the alleyway and chain-smoking. Vincent just sat there watching him. After a solid ten seconds, Toby spiked his lit cigarette on the asphalt and finally looked up. Vincent watched as it took a moment for everything to register before Toby rushed to Vincent's driver's side door and knocked so hard on the window that Vincent thought it might shatter.

Taking a deep breath Vincent rolled down the window. "Hey, Toby," he said. "Fancy seeing you here."

His overly calm response confused Toby, leaving him momentarily speechless.

"What can I do for you this beautiful evening?" Vincent continued.

"What can you *do* for me? More like, where the fuck do you think you're going?" Toby sputtered.

"Just going out to grab some food for the team. Figured if we're going to be pulling an all-nighter, we need some sort of fuel, right? If we're all starving while putting together these reports, there's no way they're going to be any good."

Vincent was astounded at how naturally the lie came to him. He could see the gears turning inside Toby's head—he wanted to get mad, but Vincent's explanation made sense.

Toby's expression relaxed. "Well, all right, yeah that makes sense. Make sure you grab a few Red Bulls too. Can't have these fuckers complaining about being tired."

Vincent took a second to watch Toby walk back toward the parking garage before letting out a deep exhale. *Holy shit, did he need a fucking drink.*

Having made up his mind, Vincent turned right out of the alleyway toward what used to be his favorite local watering hole until it became yet another thing associated with his shitty job. It didn't matter, though—any place serving alcohol would do. And he still kind of liked the place.

Walking through the door, he was immediately greeted by its signature sour stench. The walls were covered with thousands of stickers left by patrons over the four decades the bar had been in operation, and the staff could be generously described as unpleasant. If you weren't a regular, you'd be lucky to get more than a passing glance from the majority of the patrons.

He'd started coming here a few times a week after work following his mom's passing, but it was only in the last two years that he'd finally been initiated into the crew. Most everyone who frequented The Post Pub was in some blue-collar line of work, so it took a lot for them to warm up to anyone who wore a suit. But Vincent had worn them down by keeping to himself, ordering bottom-shelf whisky and Bud heavies, and never sticking his nose where it didn't belong. He knew his strategy worked when he sauntered in one Tuesday afternoon and Mick, the bartender, poured him a drink before Vincent even had a chance to ask. He didn't know why, but this seemed like more of an accomplishment than anything he'd ever done at Forrest Dunlop.

"The usual?" Mick asked as Vincent took his regular seat at the end of the bar.

"Just Jack today, Mick. Make it a double," Vincent said, avoiding eye contact and making clear he wasn't interested in any conversation this evening.

"Will do, boss." Mick poured Vincent's drink, tapped his knuckles on the bar, and said with genuine concern, "You let me know if you need anything else, okay?"

Vincent appreciated the fact that he'd been able to develop good relationships within this old dive bar. Nobody that he worked with would look twice at the folks that frequented The Post, but Vincent knew that the worst person in this bar was better than all the money-hungry maniacs that had dominated his world for more than twenty years put together.

He quickly found himself lost in thought, trying to figure out why he felt so empty.

Had he ever been whole?

Maybe, he thought, but every time he felt like he was on solid footing, there was something lurking around the corner, waiting to pull the rug out from under him.

Vincent raised the glass to his lips, and the sting of cheap whiskey on his nostrils sent his mind racing back in time, back to the last conversation he'd had with his cousin Eric.

Growing up, Eric was the closest thing he'd had to a younger brother. Their personalities complemented each other perfectly—Eric, the wicked-smart, ne'er-do-well who never met a boundary he was afraid to push, and Vincent, the quiet, overly cautious voice of reason. Eric was also the only person in his life who understood how it felt to have a father walk out the door, leaving the rest of the family to pick up the pieces.

Vincent had been at a concert when they had last spoken. He and Lisa had only recently become parents and—taking full advantage of a night away from Violet—were throwing back drinks and dancing like they did in their early twenties. Midway into the show, Vincent decided to take a break from dancing and noticed that he had missed five separate calls from Eric. Fearing the worst, he immediately walked outside and called back, something he would instantly regret.

It was clear when Eric answered the phone that he was very drunk and looking for a fight. Apparently, he had taken a trip with his girlfriend (who Vincent quietly disliked) and found out that she'd been cheating on him with one of his friends. Vincent had been consistently vocal about his disapproval of this particular relationship, and his initial reaction to hearing this news was akin to an "I told you so," which didn't go over well. Looking back on it now, Vincent realized that Eric was hurting and dealing with that agony by lashing out at anyone and anything that he could—especially those he loved the most—and Vincent should have handled the outburst with more grace. Instead, he decided to swing back.

What followed was an escalated airing of grievances and personal attacks that neither truly meant, but that stung nonetheless. Eventually, Vincent decided to go for the jugular and insinuated that Eric's excessive drinking was the root cause of his problems, causing the exchange that would haunt Vincent for the rest of his life.

"Oh yeah, you're so concerned about my drinking all of a sudden, huh?" Eric had retorted. "Never was an issue before you had a kid when we'd go out barhopping or sit at your house getting drunk for no reason at all. But now my drinking is such a *huge* problem. Fuck you, dude— you're the fucking hypocrite."

"I'm a hypocrite? The difference between my drinking habits and yours is the fact that you do that every fucking night, whether I'm around or not. This is the first time I've had more than two drinks since Violet was born, and you spend all your time at fucking PJ Shuckers getting hammered and driving yourself home. It's a miracle you haven't been in a single car wreck with the way you carry on."

"Like you'd care if I wound up dead in a ditch! You've always looked down on me—you've just been waiting for bad things to happen to me so you can gloat about how much better than me you are!"

"Sure, bud, whatever you gotta tell yourself to sleep at night."

"Whatever. I knew you weren't really on my side. I'm done with this. Have a nice life."

Eric hung up the phone before Vincent could answer, leaving him fuming. That fleeting anger quickly gave way to sadness. They had never had a blowout quite like that, and despite his harsh words, Vincent was genuinely worried. His cousin was in a tough place, and Vincent hadn't been the reliable, supportive presence he needed.

Deciding that a call back would only do more damage, Vincent tried his best to compartmentalize his feelings and put on a happy face for Lisa's sake. He assumed that cooler heads would prevail, and they would talk at some point in the next few days to clear the air.

He'd never been more wrong.

The next morning, he woke up sick to his stomach about how things had unfolded the night before. Not wanting to let their conversation fester, he rolled over to grab his phone to text Eric and apologize. But as he opened his phone, he noticed a text from his aunt that simply said, *Call me as soon as you see this.*

He dialed Eric's mom, who answered the phone crying. It took her a few tries but in between sobs, she finally managed to get out, "Eric died last night. An accident. No seat belt. No one else was with him."

Vincent felt himself slip to the hotel room floor. The deep, heaving sobs that followed felt like they would rip his heart from his chest. They kept coming, and there was nothing he could do to stop them.

It was all his fault, and he'd never been able to forgive himself for that night.

It had been a long time since he'd thought about that call, but as he contemplated the end of his own life, he couldn't help but dwell on his biggest regrets.

Lisa and the kids were only real bright spots in the gray, milquetoast life he'd engineered through his lifetime of safe decisions. But he hadn't been the husband and father they deserved lately. More and more he found himself frequenting The Post after work, skipping the girls' sporting events and after-school activities, and prioritizing a job he despised over the people he loved. But if he spent too much time with the girls, they might see through the veneer he presented. Or, even worse, think that they were somehow the cause of his self-loathing and internalize feelings that could lead them into a similar spiral.

As much as his issues had affected his relationship with his girls, Lisa had really borne the brunt of his struggles. She'd weathered countless ups and downs throughout their relationship. Even in the toughest times, she seemed to be the only person who could see through his bullshit and bring him back to being the better version of himself. Sure, she would get frustrated when he would get in his moods, but who wouldn't? After over a decade of managing his tendencies, she'd begun prioritizing herself and rightfully so. She would go to yoga, or happy hour, or a movie and leave him to his own devices. After all this time, it was only fair that she started putting herself first. Vincent didn't mind and, in a way, it bothered him that he didn't.

Before he knew it, Mick was pouring Vincent his fourth drink, and Vincent realized he was properly drunk. This was unusual. He never had more than two drinks here when he planned to drive home. Tonight he didn't really care—getting into a fatal drunk driving accident would almost be a welcome development. It would make everything so much easier. He thought of the duffel bag sitting in the passenger seat of his parked car and suddenly knew that he wouldn't be able to turn the gun on himself—it would be far too difficult for Lisa and the kids to reckon with something like that. He would prefer them to remember him with some level of fondness.

But what if there was another way? It would be risky, which admittedly wasn't his forte, but he might just be able to pull it off.

He slugged back the shot of whisky in front of him, turned to the other side of the bar to make eye contact with Mick, lifted two fingers to signal he was ready for another one, and closed his eyes. *One more drink*, he thought. *Let's see if this still seems like a good idea after that.*

CHAPTER FOUR

Now, this was weird. How was it that he couldn't really enjoy anything anymore in his life, yet drunkenly whipping around the city in his ten-year-old BMW roadster was exhilarating? He'd always felt a bit carsick sitting in the back of cabs after a few drinks, but being behind the wheel made him feel like he was inside a video game. Now he finally understood why so many people drove drunk— it was seriously *fun*. He would never admit that to anyone, especially not his daughters. But after tonight he didn't expect that this revelation would matter much.

As he sped through the evening traffic, Vincent found himself hoping that the detour he'd slogged through that morning would still be up through the night. The semi-euphoria he had felt a moment ago was suddenly replaced with an intense concentration—for his plan to work he needed those signs to lead him back through the shady outskirts of town. In what felt like the blink of an eye, Vincent found himself pulling onto the parkway.

The moment of truth was near.

One mile out from his exit, there wasn't a detour sign in sight. If one didn't show up soon, the determination he'd built up over the last hour would be gone. Maybe that was for the best. If the detour had been cleared up, that could be a sign that this wasn't what he was supposed to be doing. Then, as if something—or someone—out in the universe had heard his thoughts, he saw a bright orange sign posted right in front of his usual exit. He took a deep breath and followed the arrows toward his destiny.

It didn't take long for Vincent to discover a potential flaw in his half-cocked plan: These neighborhoods looked completely different in the dark. There were barely any functioning streetlights to guide his way, quite unlike his middle-class suburban neighborhood, and it made navigation much more difficult in his inebriated state.

Uncertain that he would be able to find the house he was looking for, Vincent began to slow down and recalibrate. Maybe this wasn't a good idea after all—maybe this had just been a weird day and he should head home.

His focus shifted back to the road, and he slammed on the brakes, narrowly avoiding a collision with a gigantic black dog that had wandered out into the street. It looked exactly like his mom's dog, Rex, whom Vincent had taken in following her passing and had only lasted a few years before succumbing to old age, severing Vincent's last remaining earthly connection to his mother.

Instead of acting startled, the giant labrador held its ground and fixed Vincent with a soul-piercing stare that he was completely unable to break. Vincent sat paralyzed, a cold sweat breaking out across the back of his neck, waiting for the dog to make its next move. Suddenly, the dog let out a deep, baritone bark that sent Vincent's heart into overdrive. Seemingly satisfied with their interaction, the dog slowly moseyed over to the other side of the road, leaving Vincent frantically trying to get his heart rate and breathing under control.

As the car began rolling forward, Vincent happened to glance to his left and realized the house the dog was trotting toward looked familiar.

Coasting a few more feet forward, Vincent could make out the light of a fire around the side of the decaying house and knew that somehow he had ended up right where he intended to be.

After a quick lap around the block, Vincent parked around the corner with a clear view through to the side of the building and the crew huddled around the makeshift firepit. He decided it was best to take a few minutes, gather himself, and game out his next move. Sitting there silently in the darkened car, Vincent felt the eerie calmness return and was overcome with a sense of clarity and determination. He didn't believe in cosmic connections, but something was telling him that the dog was some sort of a sign he was doing the right thing. His mother and Rex had both drifted peacefully to the other side; maybe this was an invitation to join them.

Vincent bowed his head, pressing it into the leather of the steering wheel, and strained to figure out how to move his plan forward. Then, out of nowhere, another car's headlights flooded the cab of his sedan as it pulled up from behind him, hung a left turn, and stopped right in front of the house Vincent was surveilling.

From his vantage point, he could make out three men standing in the side yard around the fire; one of whom looked to be twice the size of a normal person. On cue, the large man began walking toward the beat-up sedan that had just pulled up in front of the house. They were too far away for Vincent to make out much, but as the man approached and leaned over the passenger side of the sedan, a few things became clear: The man was gigantic, pushing seven feet tall and weighing at least three hundred pounds, and they were in the middle of some sort of transaction. Within thirty seconds the interaction was over, and the sedan continued on into the night while the giant lumbered back toward the fire.

Vincent looked down at the duffel bag in the passenger seat, back up at the men by the fire, and suddenly realized that there was a hulk-sized hole in his plan: He was idling in the middle of the road and had no idea how to properly grab the men's attention. Apart from tonight, he'd only ever seen drug deals initiated in the movies, and those all seemed to happen effortlessly. Well, most of them were effortless—the rest were violent and deadly.

Feeling his cheeks flush with embarrassment, he glanced to his left to see if the men had noticed his car sitting in the middle of the street. They were engaged in a heated conversation and had yet to register that he was parked nearby. Sensing his momentum starting to fade but unwilling to give up without some sort of effort, Vincent rolled his window down and nervously shouted, "Hey! Any of you holding?"

The men fell silent and glared his way. He guessed this wasn't typically how things were done, but there was no turning back now. After a quick conference, they appeared to agree that the big guy should be the one to handle the interloper. Vincent felt a slight tinge of regret as he watched the man menacingly saunter toward the car. Wearing a thick black winter coat over a hoodie, black jeans, and Tims, the man looked even larger up close. You could tell by his body language that he knew how intimidating he could be and regularly used that to his advantage.

"You lost?" Big Man asked in a comically deep register, leaning over the driver's side window.

"No," Vincent stammered. "I think I'm exactly where I want to be," he added after a moment, feeling his confidence return.

"Listen, man, this ain't no place for someone like you to be hanging around after dark. I'm gonna give you one chance to get out of here before things get bad for you. You got me, bro?" Big Man replied.

Vincent knew this would be his last chance to drive off and write tonight off as a strange anomaly. But he'd spent his whole life surrendering to fear in one way or another and couldn't stand the thought of slinking off in defeat—again. He'd made it this far; why not push it a little further? He had nothing to be threatened by, and nothing telling him he couldn't see this plan through. *Fuck it*, he thought. *It's time.*

"I got you," Vincent said softly, "but I really need some help, man, and I'm not talking about drugs or anything like that."

"Well I ain't no fucking therapist, so why don't you go ahead and get the fuck on outta here before I make things a lot worse for you," Big Man replied, leaning further into the window frame to show Vincent he was serious.

At that moment something strange happened. Any lingering vestiges of fear Vincent had been feeling evaporated. His heart rate slowed, the calmness overtook him, and he began what he hoped would be the sales pitch of a lifetime.

"Listen, buddy, I'm gonna be straight with you—I'm in a real bad spot. It may look like I've got my shit together with this monkey suit and BMW, but the truth is I'm a degenerate gambler. Was somehow able to keep things under control for a while, but I hit some really fucking bad luck recently. I was fuckin' chasing it and lost pretty much everything on what I thought was a sure thing."

Vincent took a breath and glanced at the man to see if he was buying it, but he remained stone-faced.

"I've been able to keep the sharks at bay with a payment plan while also keeping my family in the dark about all of it. But I got fucking fired today and only have enough to make my next payment, and pretty soon this is all going to come crashing down. These people are going to make my life hell, my wife's going to fucking leave me as soon as she finds out, and I'll probably never see my daughters again. And that's my best case scenario!" Vincent continued, ratcheting up the emotion and holding back alligator tears. "I need some fucking help, man, you understand?" Vincent stole another glance at the giant. He could tell that the Big Man was close to taking the bait.

"So what the fuck do you want me to do about all this? I ain't no bank, motherfucker," Big Man replied.

"I don't need you to be a bank—I need you to be an executioner." Vincent let those words hang in the air for a moment and watched the man process what he was suggesting. He couldn't seem to form any words, but he wasn't making a move to leave. Vincent got the feeling that he might have him on the hook. "Look, I've still got life insurance. This is the only way that I can make things right for my family."

"Motherfucker, who do you think I am? You think I just go around killing people because I live in the hood? Man, get the fuck outta here with this bullshit," Big Man spat back and started walking back toward the firepit.

Vincent was prepared for this; he knew this type of request would be met with some form of resistance. It was an insane ask, made all the more ludicrous by the fact that this person was a complete stranger. "What if there was something in it for you?" he asked.

The giant stopped in his tracks. "Like what?" he replied, without turning back around.

"Cash. A lot of it. In your pocket. Tonight." Vincent said, his tone ice-cold.

That seemed to get his attention. After taking a second to gather himself, the giant turned around and said, "So let me get this straight— you'll pay me in cash to kill you?"

"That's exactly what I'm offering," Vincent responded.

"Prove you're good for it then. Show me the cash," Big Man shot back, making it clear that he was someone who had been stiffed on big promises before.

Vincent reached down and pulled a stack of cash out of his duffel bag. He'd made a quick pit stop at a nearby ATM after he left the bar, knowing he'd have to prove he was good for the money if his plan were to have any chance of success. Lisa would probably be pissed to see that he'd raided their savings account, but Vincent was fairly confident the substantial life insurance payout he'd set up a few years ago would lessen the blow.

"Five K," he said, holding the bundle up for the man to see.

"All right, let me get that up front then," Big Man said, taking a step toward the car with his hand out.

"Ah-ah-ah," Vincent chided in a sing-song voice, putting the money down on the passenger seat. "This cash stays right here, in plain view, until the job is done. Then you can grab it and high tail it out of here."

Vincent could see the wheels turning in his head as the man considered his next move. He didn't seem to have any immediate qualms with the act itself but was signaling skepticism. Vincent sat quietly while the giant thought things through. After an entire career spent in sales, Vincent knew when to give a prospect enough space to think, and he wanted Big Man to take his time envisioning what he'd be able to do with the cash.

"Okay, let's say I do agree to this crazy shit. How do you wanna do it?" Big Man finally responded.

"Quick and dirty," Vincent said, knowing he was now in the home stretch. "We just make this look like a carjacking gone wrong. You bust in the driver's side window, reach in, and . . ." Vincent pressed two fingers to his temple and used his thumb to mimic a trigger being pulled.

"And you just assume I'm packing?"

"Well, yeah, but that doesn't really matter. I've got a gun you can use. You can keep it afterward, if you want." Vincent paused to see if he could sense any objections from Big Man but was met with an interested silence. He decided to push forward with the closing pitch. "Listen, you'll be doing me a favor. Trust me, if I had a better way out of this mess, I'd gladly take it, but my back is completely up against the wall. What I'm proposing is merciful compared to what will happen to me and my family if I start missing payments."

Big Man continued to sit silent, ruminating on what Vincent had just laid out for him. At this point the ball was entirely in Big Man's court, and they both knew it; he just had to decide if he trusted what Vincent was telling him.

"Listen, man, this plan is all well and good, but I can't be doing this shit right in front of my fucking house."

Vincent knew this was the final stress test. As long as he could overcome this objection, the sale would be made.

"Already thought of that. Up around the corner is a secluded road that would be a perfect spot. It'll look like I got turned around heading home through this detour."

Big Man nodded his head in affirmation but didn't say a word.

———

A few minutes later, Vincent found himself sitting alone in his dark car, anxiously waiting for the Big Man to stroll around the corner. Well, anxiously wasn't quite accurate. His heart rate had slowed, and the sense of calm he'd experienced throughout the day reappeared the second the deal was closed. He couldn't wait for the sweet release of death. For the first time in years—maybe ever—he was in control of his own destiny, and he was determined to see things through. The prospect of a long nap seemed divine.

After what seemed like forever, he finally saw the Big Man round the corner with his crew in tow. He hadn't planned for any unexpected guests and could only assume this was not something that would work to his benefit. Warning bells started going off in his head, and he rolled down his window and hollered, "They can keep a lookout by the corner. Just you and me, Big Man, otherwise I'll go find someone else who wants to make some easy money tonight."

The three men stopped in their tracks, and after a quick exchange, the two interlopers nodded and started back toward the street corner. Vincent let out a deep breath as Big Man came toward the car.

With Big Man roughly fifty feet from the car, Vincent's awareness of his surroundings dialed up to eleven. All at once, his senses shifted into overdrive. He heard the faint chirp of crickets as if they were lodged directly in his ear, felt his vision focus so sharply that he could see every individual dried leaf scattered on the street despite the near pitch-black conditions, and felt his skin cells come alive, as if an electric current ran through him.

Vincent's heart was thumping in his chest like an unmuffled bass drum as Big Man took his final steps and placed a gloved hand on the top of the window frame.

"You ready?" he said, leaning in close enough for Vincent to get a clear look at his face for the first time. A long scar ran vertically down the left side of his face, highlighting a milky, blind left eye. He sported an unkempt goatee, and when he spoke, Vincent could see the glint of silver caps on each of his canine teeth. He seemed to radiate a power realized through a lifetime of violence. Vincent knew for certain that he had selected the right partner in crime, but he was no longer so sure that was a good thing.

"Hey!" Big Man said, clapping gloved hands in front of Vincent's face, "I said are you ready to do this, boy?"

"Yes," Vincent stammered. "Yes, I am."

"Okay, so hand me that gat and let's get this shit over with already," Big Man replied, holding his hand out expectantly.

"Wait, first we need to make this look legit and think through all the angles," Vincent said, regaining confidence and feeling the neurons and synapses in his brain firing to full capacity. "Here's what we'll do: I'll hand you this gun and roll up the window. From there you'll smash the window in with the butt of the pistol so the glass falls inward. Then, well, then you pull the trigger. After it's done, you need to empty the glove box and center console. Leave the driver's side door open. I want this to look like a real carjacking so my family doesn't have any questions. You got me?"

Vincent paused and looked up at Big Man to make sure he was following and wouldn't fuck this up at the finish line.

"Yeah, man, I break the window, snuff you, snatch your shit, and get the fuck outta Dodge."

It really was that simple.

Vincent took a deep breath and reached over to grab the gun in the passenger seat. "One more thing," he said, looking Big Man directly in his eyes.

"What's that, boy?"

"Make sure it's in the head. I don't want to leave anything up to chance."

Big Man grinned. "You got some nuts, man. I ain't ever met anyone this crazy before."

"I need to know you're going to hold up your end."

"Like I said, I got you. Now give me that fucking Glock and let's get this over with already. It's fucking cold out here."

Vincent handed the gun over to Big Man, the electric sensation surging through his body. He rolled up the window, and Big Man immediately smashed it in with the butt of the pistol. "You got any last words?" he said solemnly.

Vincent looked up and felt every hair on his body stand up. This was it—this was his last chance to bail, to go home to Lisa, and pretend this was all a fucked up dream. But he couldn't turn back now—everything was working out perfectly according to plan. He'd felt like a passenger all of his life, and he'd come too far to quit.

Vincent took a deep breath. "Just make sure it's in the temple. Clean and simple. Lights out."

Big Man nodded and pointed the gun at Vincent's head. "You want to watch it happen?" he said.

"Better if I don't."

"I got you," Big Man said and pulled the hammer back with his thumb until it clicked into position. "Last chance," he said.

"Just fucking do it already," Vincent replied through gritted teeth.

"All right, your funeral."

Time slowed to a near stop and Vincent recalled an article he'd read a few years earlier about people committing suicide by jumping off the Golden Gate Bridge. Many were successful, but to a man, the handful who survived the fall said the first thought they had after stepping off the bridge was that they didn't want to die.

Out of the corner of his eye, Vincent could see Big Man's index finger applying pressure to the trigger, and, suddenly, every fiber of his body was screaming for him to do something, *anything*, to stop this from happening. He tried to get the right words to communicate that desire from his brain to his mouth, but everything was moving too slowly. Finally, he managed to get his vocal cords to activate and utter a faint, "Stop." In the same moment that the word escaped his lips, the blast of the gun rang out, his field of vision closed in, and everything began to go dark.

CHAPTER FIVE

Vincent was floating. He tried opening his eyes, but the darkness remained, making it impossible for him to know if his eyes were open or closed. In fact, he wasn't sure that he had eyes at all. No matter— he would accept this new environment without further question.

He wasn't sure how long he'd been in this impossibly tranquil space. It could've been a second; it could've been a year; it could've been a decade. He didn't really care. He'd never felt so secure, so removed from all his earthly torments. He was at peace. He quit trying to connect with the senses that were omnipresent in his past life and let his mind truly relax. He still felt conscious, but without ego. Vincent Palmer was no one and nothing.

After some indeterminate amount of time, he heard a faint pulse in the distance. Surprised to learn that his ears worked, Vincent stretched to figure out where the sound had come from. Another pulse rang out, sounding closer but still hiding its source. It sounded like something you'd hear deep in the depths of a Tibetan monastery, but it felt intimate. Perhaps it was a song or melody he'd known in a different lifetime.

"So familiar, soft and steady, like a long-forgotten embrace," a voice cooed in the distance, startling Vincent. "This body, this life, holding you close . . ." the mysterious voice continued, accompanied by a low vibration, almost like sound waves traveling underwater.

What was happening? Could it be that his time in this newfound haven was running out? He wasn't ready to move on from this. Not yet. He needed to figure out how to hang on, but as he struggled to do that, the sounds marched on.

"We drift away from the memories, landing softly and choosing . . . choosing to be here, right now."

What were they talking about?

The instantly recognizable feeling of anxiety began digging its claws in as a hot flush came over him. For the first time since he'd entered this realm, he could feel his heart, and it was beating furiously.

"Hold on; stay inside," the voice chanted all around him.

That's exactly what I'm trying to do! Vincent thought as he mustered all his agency to try and figure out what was happening.

"This vessel cradles me, reminding me that I belong . . ."

Vincent tried thrashing, thinking this must be some sort of dream. To his surprise his right foot kicked out and hit a wall. No, too squishy to be a wall, but he now knew he had a foot, and that was progress.

"This being is eternal . . ."

Something was changing around him, and the mysterious voice seemed to be wrapping up its prayer. Time was running out.

"All the pain is an illusion . . ."

The voice finished and Vincent was suddenly bombarded by piercing sounds of electrical feedback, a blinding light, and a sensation similar to being pulled beneath a wave. Powerless to stop what was happening and more terrified than he had ever felt, Vincent braced for the worst.

"Why isn't he crying?" Vincent heard a woman ask. "Somebody help him! Please! He should be crying! What is happening to my baby?"

His eyes were still adjusting to the light, but Vincent could feel the pressure of giant hands all over his body, and all around him he heard a cacophony of frantic conversation and the continued cries of the woman. "Please tell me what's happening!" she pleaded. He recognized the woman's voice as one he'd heard millions of times before. She was sobbing.

"What's wrong with him?" a strained but familiar male voice asked.

"He's not responding to the CPR, doctor, and we can't seem to get his lungs to activate," someone said nearby.

"Keep trying. How are his other vitals?" another man responded.

"Why is he so blue?" the familiar voice asked.

Vincent was finding himself overwhelmed and overcome with exhaustion. He desperately wanted to return to wherever he was before all of this madness. Maybe if he closed his eyes and let go, he'd be welcomed back.

"He's flatlining . . ." Vincent heard faintly in the background as his eyelids drifted shut. He felt that peaceful feeling begin to embrace him, as comfortable as a warm blanket on a crisp winter evening. But before he could fully disengage, Vincent felt his eyes flutter open one final time and he heard one of the men saying, "I'm so very sorry, Mr. and Mrs. Palmer—there's nothing else we can do."

CHAPTER SIX

"Vincent! It's time to wake up; we're running late!" a woman's voice shouted from another room. The voice was incredibly familiar, but Vincent couldn't figure out where he'd heard it before. Despite his curiosity being piqued, Vincent kept his eyes closed and decided to fade back into a comfortable slumber. Right before he fully crossed over into the dream realm, he heard a door handle jiggle, something push the door open, and he was jolted awake by a large shaggy dog fervently licking his face.

"That'll get you moving," the woman said from the hallway, laughing as she walked back to wherever it was that she came from.

Now that his eyes were open, Vincent took a second to gather his bearings and figure out where he was. After a few seconds spent shaking the cobwebs out of his brain and wiping the slobber from his face, he noticed an Arizona Wildcats poster on the wall, just like the one he had in his room throughout his early childhood. Opposite the poster was an old rocking chair sitting next to a trunk Vincent knew was full of toys without even needing to open it. He looked down and locked eyes with Luna, the energetic labradoodle that had been his chaotic partner in crime early in life.

What the fuck was going on? The last thing he remembered was . . . a hospital? Was that it? He wasn't totally sure, but he clearly remembered the peaceful dark place he was yanked from. And the events leading up to what he had expected to be the last moments of Vincent Palmer's life.

"Hear that, honey?" the woman said playfully from another room. "It's your song, so you better get your little butt out here before it's over!"

Sure enough, Vincent could hear the opening chords of Garth Brooks's "Standing Outside the Fire" playing on a radio outside of his room. It was then that something clicked and he jumped out of the bed, sprinted out of the room, took a left down the hallway, and came to a dead stop in the open kitchen/dining room he'd spent so much time in during his youth. His movements were automatic, and though he felt them, it was almost as if someone was moving his body parts for him. Speechless, he stared as his mother packed his bag lunch and danced to their favorite song—she was exactly how he remembered her.

"Mommy?" Vincent squeaked, trying to confirm what he was seeing was real. He hadn't called his mother that in decades, but somehow it slipped out that way.

His mother looked up and smiled, "Good morning, handsome. How are you feeling today?"

Everything about her exuded warmth, from the loving twinkle shining through her turquoise green eyes to the little crinkles on the bridge of her nose that only appeared when she was genuinely happy to see someone. She looked so vibrant and full of life. Gone were the wrinkles and wisps of white hair, replaced by smooth, glowing skin and thick red hair that no hair dye would ever be able to replicate. This was the version of his mother who appeared in his mind's eye when he would drift back to a time when life didn't feel so difficult.

He'd missed that joyful smile more than words could adequately express, but when he tried to tell her this, nothing came out. His fists balled up in frustration, and he couldn't get his throat to loosen up enough to allow his vocal cords to activate.

"Oh, honey, what's the matter?" she cooed, running over to wrap Vincent in a big bear hug. "Come on, there's no reason to cry! Listen, it's your favorite part," she said as Garth launched into the chorus and Vincent found himself dancing with his mom, his worries completely forgotten.

After the song ended, Vincent plopped down at the kitchen table and dove into a bowl of Cocoa Puffs. He knew something strange was happening, and his mind was kicking into overdrive, attempting to make sense of the impossible. He was himself, but he was also this kid version of himself at the same time. However, a gentle hand running through his hair was all it took for him to ignore the impulse to dissect the situation and simply appreciate the gift he had been given. His mother's death had left him completely gutted, but today, sitting and watching her put the finishing touches on his bag lunch, he felt whole again. He didn't care if this was a dream or hallucination; he planned to soak up every moment.

As Vincent finished slurping up the last of the now chocolate milk in his cereal bowl, his mom popped over, wrapped him in another hug, kissed him on the cheek, and playfully whispered, "Vincent Bryan, we have T-minus five minutes until the shuttle departs to take you to school. Can you complete the mission of getting dressed and brushing your teeth before it takes off?"

Vincent remembered these little games his mom used to play with him growing up. She always figured out how to make the most mundane things fun. She embodied love. He felt happy tears begin welling up behind his eyes again but jumped out of his chair before his mom could see and started running down the hall back to his room. "I'll be ready, Mommy!" he shouted.

Before crossing the threshold into his room, he stole a quick glance backward and caught a glimpse of his mom's authentic smile. He had forgotten how good it felt to love and be loved by someone so uncondi-tionally, unburdened by anything else happening in the world.

———

It wasn't until they were in the car that Vincent allowed his brain to start analyzing the circumstances he found himself operating within. He wasn't totally certain how old he was right now, but his mind still seemed like his own. The memories of his "real" life remained, and his ability to process information was much greater than his childlike form suggested. But for some reason anything he said was translated into kid-speak—if he could manage to get words out at all. It was almost like there was some sort of filter between his brain and mouth recalibrating his thoughts into words that were more suited to some-one of his age.

"Hey, Mom," Vincent said sheepishly from the back seat of their old, beat-up Subaru Leone, "where are we going today?"

"We're going to school, silly—it's Tuesday," his mom replied.

"Yeah, but which school?" Vincent pried, trying to get any sense of how old he was supposed to be.

"Sewell Elementary, sweetie. Are you feeling okay?" She turned quickly to give him a concerned glance. "Why are you asking such strange questions?"

He wanted to tell her that he didn't know why—that his last adult memory was of a large man he had hired to kill him—but those words wouldn't come; they were caught in the mysterious, invisible filter lodged in his throat. Instead, all he could manage was, "I'm fine, Mom. I just had a strange dream last night and want to make sure it's not true. Am I still in Mrs. Brown's class?"

"Oh, honey, you're messing with me. Mrs. Brown was last year. You're not a kindergartener anymore—you're a big first grader! Woo!" his mom exclaimed, trying to lift the mood.

"So . . . Miss Quintana is my teacher?" Vincent said, feeling like he was beginning to find his footing.

"Yep! And we like Miss Q, don't we?" his mom said, flashing him a smile in the rearview mirror.

"Yeah, we do like Miss Q!" Vincent said, throwing his hands in the air for some inexplicable reason.

He paused for a moment, looking out the window and taking in the passing surroundings. In the distance, Mount Lemmon looked down on the city of Tucson, framed by the breathtaking tapestry of pink, orange, and gold characteristic of a classic Arizona sunrise. Tan ranch-style homes lined each side of the street, many with front yards peppered with cacti and mesquite trees.

"Hey, Mom?"

"Yes, Vincent?" his mom replied, pretending to put on an air of formality.

"What month is it?"

"It's March, sweetie. March eleventh, to be exact."

"Oh," Vincent said, trying to figure out if the date had any significance.

If he was in the middle of first grade, that meant it had been about a year since his dad walked out on them. Which meant that in only a few short months, he'd be whisked to the other side of the country, a victim of his mother's ill-fated engagement to Devon—easily Vincent's least favorite replacement father-figure.

He hadn't thought about this period of his life in decades; he'd been more than happy to bury the unpleasant memories in the darkest depths of his psyche. But it was impossible to keep those past experiences contained while he quite literally took a drive down memory lane.

Fractured scenes whipped through his mind as if they were slides on an old-school carousel projector. He was sitting on the back porch, basking in the bright blue glow of a bug zapper while a storm raged inside, the slam of their front door indicating the worst was over. As was his relationship with his father.

Now he was seated at a metal table in a sterile room across from a woman pretending to be his friend. The walls were cinder blocks painted white; someone had scratched words Vincent didn't recognize into the table. It was freezing, and all he wanted to do was go back to class.

"Just admit that you stole those cards from Paul, and this will all be over," the woman said.

"But I didn't," Vincent replied. "Why would I lie?"

The woman shook her head. "Vince, we all know what you did. Just come clean or we'll have to call your parents."

He wanted to fight back, but he just couldn't do that to his mom. She had enough on her plate.

"Fine, I stole the cards."

He was leaning on the fence surrounding the soccer field, watching one of his classmates practicing soccer with his dad from afar. Vincent wanted what that kid had so badly it made his stomach hurt.

Why isn't my dad here to teach me? What did I do that was so bad?

An errant kick sent the soccer ball rolling toward Vincent, and the father called for Vincent to join them.

I don't deserve it, he thought, turning and sprinting away as tears streamed down his face.

"It's a pretty nice day, huh?" his mom asked, yanking Vincent back to the present. "Should I drop you off by the soccer field while you wait for the first bell?"

"Sure," he replied, catching a glimpse of the beige stucco school façade up ahead.

Not missing a beat, his mom hung a quick left, looping them around the backside of the school building and coming to a stop in the same spot Vincent had been driven to tears all those years ago.

"Have a good day today, sweetie!" his mom called out as he hopped out of the back seat.

"Thanks, Mommy," he replied, ready to join the gaggle of elementary school children causing a ruckus nearby. But before he could push the door closed, something stopped him in his tracks.

Who knows if I will ever get to see her again?

"Hey, Mom?" Vincent squeaked.

"Yes, honey," she said, turning back with a slight look of concern.

"I love you a lot, and I'm so glad you're mine," he continued, doing his best to keep tears from welling up in his eyes.

She placed a hand on her heart and gave him a look that was somehow a combination of relief, guilt, pride, sadness, and most of all, love. Pure, unequivocal love. Vincent knew that look well; he'd worn it more times than he could count dropping the girls off at school in the early days.

"I love you too, sweetie," she said, quickly gathering herself and following up with, "Now go get out there and have some fun before the bell rings."

He smiled ear to ear and blew her a kiss before shutting the door and heading off.

———

It was a uniquely crisp Arizona morning, cool enough for there still to be some frost on the grass but sure to heat up within the hour, and it seemed like more people than usual wanted to hang out before classes started. Unperturbed by the crowd, Vincent marched on toward the field, fully prepared to join in the fray.

Typically, the morning soccer games were dominated by the fourth and fifth graders whose parents dropped them off early for school. Occasionally, a ballsy third grader would nudge their way in and summarily get their ass kicked badly enough to keep them from stepping foot on the field for at least another year. It was completely unheard of for anyone younger to join the game, and for good reason. This wasn't a sanctioned event with referees; it was streetball. And if you weren't careful, you'd be starting your day in the nurse's office or, in rare cases, carted off to the emergency room. Vincent had spent years on the sidelines, too timid to ever attempt to join the morning games. But today would be different. Today, he was going to show them what he was really made of.

He could hear the frantic yells on the field and feel the intensity ratcheting up on the sidelines as he confidently strode up to the field. All this commotion had to mean that the current game was coming to an end, meaning that he'd only have one shot to get on the field before the first bell caused the crowd to disperse.

But then, as he meticulously planned out his next move, and without any warning, another boy shoved Vincent from behind, nearly knocking him to the ground.

Vincent spun around, ready to rip someone's head off when he realized that the kid who had pushed him was his childhood best friend, David Simmons. David always loved pushing his buttons and doubled over laughing when he realized how upset this surprise attack had made Vincent.

"Geez, Vinnie," David managed to get out through fits of laughter, "what's got your undies in a bunch?"

Knowing that getting mad would play right into David's hands, Vincent quickly cooled his temper, brushed off his shoulders, and said, "Oh I'm not bothered at all—just getting ready to jump in the next game."

David's jaw dropped. "You're . . . you're gonna try to play?" he stammered.

"That's right," Vincent replied. "Gonna show them that I'm just as good as they are."

David started laughing again. "But, Vinnie, they're all fourth and fifth graders. Even if you do make it on the field, they're gonna crush you."

"We'll see," Vincent said, smiling.

Just then the crowd cheered, and Vincent looked up to see one of the teams celebrating on the field followed by pandemonium on the sidelines while everyone jockeyed for the chance to challenge the reigning schoolyard champs.

"Time to go," Vincent managed to get out as he turned to run toward the fray. He quickly realized he could exploit his height—or lack thereof—to join the next game. Being shorter meant he could dart in and out of the crowd unnoticed and plant himself firmly in the middle of the team that was heading out to the field. He was pretty sure nobody would notice him until the game had already started. And if anyone tried to kick him out, he'd just stand his ground. Who at that age knew how to handle a first grader walking around with the mentality of a forty-five-year-old adult? He'd had to deal with the likes of Gil and Toby for years—these kids, even the meanest, couldn't hold a candle to that kind of seasoned bullying.

After about a minute of frantic shuffling, Vincent was able to slide into the middle of the group that seemed to have secured the next game. At the last minute, he stripped off his jacket, feeling the cool morning air start to give way to the stifling Arizona heat. This also meant they probably had less than ten minutes before the bell rang, just enough time for him to make his mark.

As he trotted onto the field, still somehow invisible to his teammates and opponents, he glanced over to the sidelines and saw David in the front row, sporting a look somewhere between admiration, disbelief, and fear. Vincent flashed a wily grin and turned to survey the field and get his bearings. It'd been years since he'd played soccer, but he was fairly certain that his adult brain would allow him to take advantage of anyone on that field. Well, as long as his tiny new body could keep up.

The other team started on the offensive and began their march down the field. Vincent hung back and tried to get a feel for their game plan. Overall—and unsurprisingly—these kids were completely disorganized and seemed to know absolutely nothing about soccer. After a few quick passes, Vincent realized that they were all telegraphing where the ball would be going. If he watched their eyes, he should be able to intercept the pass and start a break downfield, but he needed to wait for the right moment to strike. While he was solidifying his plan, an errant pass landed out of bounds on the left sideline, and Vincent knew this was his shot.

One of the opposing players ran over to grab the ball and quickly toss it back inbounds, and as soon as the ball left his opponent's fingertips, Vincent sprang into action in order to jump the route and have a clear path to the goal at the far end of the pitch. He met the ball perfectly in the halfway point between the sideline and intended target, leaped in the air, stopped the ball with his chest, swiftly gathered it underneath his feet, and took off.

At first, he could hear the crowd erupt, but after a few steps, there was only the wind rushing past his ears, the steady beating of his feet, and his heart thumping in his chest as the adrenaline coursed through his veins. He was moving as fast as he could get his little body to go, but he could feel the opposing team gaining on him quickly. Twenty yards out from the goal, he knew that if he didn't take a shot soon one of the bigger kids was going to take him out. Hard. He let instinct take over and started angling as if he would be shooting toward the right side of the goal. As he moved, so moved the goalie, giving him exactly the opening he needed.

Suddenly, Vincent took a stutter step as if he was about to shoot, and he saw the goalie flinch toward the right. Without a second to spare before a pissed-off fifth grader got close enough to slide tackle him, Vincent seized the moment and kicked the ball toward the left corner of the goal. Having allowed his center of gravity to shift the opposite direction, the goalie could do nothing more than helplessly flail as the ball sailed past him into the back netting. Vincent couldn't remember the last time he'd felt so euphoric.

The crowd erupted in cheers while Vincent stood frozen in front of the goal in a state of joyous disbelief. He'd spent hours daydreaming about this exact scenario when he was little, and he wanted to treasure this moment for as long as possible. But before he could soak everything in, he found himself on the receiving end of a second blindside shove, except this time he ended up on the ground with a face full of dirt.

"How do you like that, twerp?" Vincent heard a voice sneer from above him.

The surprise attack had left him face down, temporarily paralyzed and scrambling to figure out how he got there.

"I said, how do you like that?" the voice chided, lording over Vincent.

"Uhhhh . . ." Vincent groaned pitifully as the pain started to set in.

"Yeah, I bet that hurt, you little prick! That's what you get for thinking you can step foot on this field," the voice continued.

Mustering his strength, Vincent managed to flip himself over and get a look at his tormentor. Towering over him was the biggest, baddest fifth-grade bully he'd ever seen in real life. This was not good. Vincent began thinking through his options while his tiny child body took its sweet time shaking off the temporary paralysis. Then, in the distance, he heard the warning bell ring, signaling to the students that they only had five minutes left to get to class.

"Now, that's what you call divine intervention," Vincent sputtered.

The bully leaned over, lowering his face inches from Vincent's. "Looks like you just got saved by the bell," he snarled.

"My thoughts exactly," Vincent said, but the bully didn't get that either.

"Your luck's gonna run out," the oversized boy said, spitting on the ground right next to Vincent. "I'll see you after school, punk."

With that, the bully stood up, kicked Vincent in the ribs for good measure, and headed toward the school building. As he watched the bully disappear into the crowd, Vincent hoped that would be the last time he'd ever see that face, but his gut told him this wasn't over. He continued laying in the fetal position for a few more seconds before David came over to check on him.

"Hey, are you okay?" David said, sounding shaken.

"Yeah, I'll be alright. Just a little dirty, that's all. How about that goal?" Vincent replied, grinning.

"Vinnie, that was incredible! You scored a goal in the morning game . . . against the fifth graders!"

"Yeah, that was pretty cool. Told you I could hang with them," Vincent said, grabbing David's outstretched hand to pull himself off the ground. "We gotta get to class; don't want Mrs. Q getting mad at us for being late." He brushed the rest of the dirt off his shoulders and headed inside toward his first-grade classroom with his best friend in tow, excited to see what the rest of this day had in store for them.

CHAPTER SEVEN

Vincent never really loved school growing up, but he was pleasantly surprised to learn that being a first grader was much more fun than he remembered.

The day kicked off with handwriting practice, which quickly devolved into chaos since first graders, it seemed, had attention spans akin to those of goldfish. He was getting a kick out of the general sense of lawlessness that permeated throughout the classroom. The kids didn't seem very interested in following directions, and Mrs. Q was more than happy to go with the flow, surely due to lessons learned after years spent corralling herds of tiny nonsense people.

After about an hour of handwriting "practice," Mrs. Q announced naptime, and Vincent planned to take full advantage of this mid-morning reprieve. As an adult he'd always wished naptime had remained part of his daily routine and briefly considered moving to Spain—only partially because of his desire to participate in their practice of prioritizing daily siestas—but never quite had the guts to pull the trigger and uproot his life. With that in mind, he grabbed a blanket, settled in next to David, and closed his eyes.

He wanted to sleep along with everyone else, but this momentary respite shifted his adult brain into high gear and sent him down a rabbit hole instead. What was happening to him? Was this the afterlife? And if it was, why did it feel nearly identical to his past life? Could it be that all of this was just a bad dream?

These questions continued to swirl around inside his head until his brow finally relaxed and, unable to resist sleep any longer, he conked out.

———

Not long after naptime, the class broke for lunch and recess and Vincent started to think that everyone's preconceived notions of heaven might have been wrong. In reality, heaven was being a first grader, and he was loving every second of it. How was it that he only remembered this time as sad and distressing? Was it possible that his father's departure had cast a shadow over this entire period of his life? If that were the case, he was even more glad of this chance to appreciate the brightness of childhood that, somehow, he had forgotten.

The cafeteria was a raucous, chaotic mess of tiny bodies zipping around and vying for seats at the long rectangular tables positioned in neat rows in the center of the room. As he entered, Vincent noticed a steady stream of students already filing through the double doors that led to the playground outside and was reminded that the goal for lunch was to eat as quickly as possible to maximize the amount of time available for recess.

David managed to find them a seat at a nearby table, and Vincent settled in, curious and excited to see what his mom had packed for him earlier that morning. He was not disappointed. Digging through the brown paper bag, he pulled out a turkey sandwich on white bread, cut in triangles, with a separate plastic bag filled with pickles so they wouldn't make the bread soggy, a small bag of pretzel sticks, a Capri Sun pouch—Pacific Cooler, his favorite flavor—and the *pièce de résistance*, three freshly baked homemade chocolate chip cookies. It was exactly what he hoped it would be.

Unable to help himself, Vincent started with the cookies, savoring the melt-in-your-mouth texture and perfect chocolate chip–to–cookie ratio before ripping into the rest of his lunch.

Delightfully stuffed, he was ready to join the rest of the kids outside.

Beneath the rays of a relentless desert sun, Vincent bounded around the playground, not knowing if this would be the last time he'd ever get to climb the monkey bars or fly down the slide. By the time he heard the teachers call a five-minute warning, he had a stitch in his side from so much running around, but he still jumped into a game of freeze tag.

He would make the most of every minute of freedom afforded to him.

The afternoon proved to be even more eventful. As his noisy group filed back into the classroom, they were greeted by Mrs. Quintana's teenage daughter, Maria.

Vincent had completely forgotten about Maria. He stood frozen, staring at the young lady who had been his very first crush.

His forty-five-year-old brain couldn't help being amused—Maria was at least twice his size.

He remembered how every week she used to visit his first-grade class as part of a high school work-study program that allowed students to earn class credits as teaching assistants. Maria always found unique ways to connect with the students, and she had immediately sniffed out Vincent's love for the Arizona Wildcats basketball team and consistently came prepared to discuss how his favorite players had fared in their latest game.

On top of that, she had curly, shoulder-length brown hair, bright green eyes, and an infectious smile. With her bubbly personality, Maria was an instant favorite, especially with the boys. Vincent was no exception. With butterflies floating around his tiny stomach, he headed back to his seat and marveled at the fact that he was getting to experience so many things that had faded from his memory.

———

Vincent spent the rest of the afternoon doing everything he could to garner Maria's attention.

Despite his communication abilities being filtered—for the most part—through the mouth of a seven-year-old, Vincent found that his math skills remained fully intact. Mrs. Q and Maria seemed pleasantly surprised with how well he was handling the more complex questions and showered him with praise after every correct answer.

It had been so long since Toby or Gil had given Vincent anything that resembled positive feedback that he'd almost forgotten how nice it felt to receive any recognition for his abilities. He'd spent so much time fixating and internalizing outside criticisms that he'd allowed himself to forget he was someone who had talents and was worthy of praise. How could he have let those two assholes convince him otherwise?

Whatever, he thought, *they're gone now. No need to worry about what they think about me any longer.*

By the time they had wrapped up arithmetic, the class was giddy with excitement about arts and crafts. Mrs. Q pulled out all the stops and announced that she'd be letting the class paint for the last hour of the day. With Maria's help she deftly organized the desks into four different stations, covered them with plastic, and rolled out a cart of various painting materials.

Looking around, Vincent swore he could see some of his classmates frothing at the mouth while watching Mrs. Q get everything set up. Nobody got this excited about art as an adult. Well, that wasn't exactly true. There were plenty of people who maintained creative pursuits into adulthood; they just weren't very common in the corporate world in which he'd spent so much of his time.

When Mrs. Q finally announced that the kids could come up to the front of the class and grab their materials, it was like waving the checkered flag at the Daytona 500. Within seconds, every kid in the class was sprinting to the supply cart, frantically grabbing everything they could get their hands on. Never one to enjoy pushing through crowds of people, Vincent hung back and only walked up after most of the kids had grabbed their loot and headed to one of the four stations. There wasn't much left on the cart, but Vincent managed to grab a paintbrush and a few shades of paint and walked over to paint with David.

It was amazing how drastically the energy could shift in a room full of first graders. Moments earlier Vincent had felt as if the class would engage in a full-on mutiny if Mrs. Q didn't acquiesce to their demands, but now that everyone was painting, all had become right with the world. His classmates wore nearly identical expressions of focused intensity as they carefully smeared paint across their paper canvases and did their best to bring their imaginations to life. To his left, Vincent noticed a little girl painting what could generously be described as a family portrait and felt the sharp sting of guilt—it looked exactly like one of Charlie's early paintings that still hung on their fridge all these years later.

A shiver ran down his spine, and he felt his whole body shake off the negative thoughts beginning to take hold. He could deal with those later, but right now he was going to enjoy the simple pleasures associated with being a kid again. He felt a smile creep across his lips as he grabbed a paintbrush and got to work creating what he hoped would be a masterpiece.

He'd always enjoyed the arts growing up but had eschewed that passion as his athletic pursuits had become more serious. For some reason it hadn't seemed possible to pursue multiple passions simultaneously during his adolescence, so he'd decided to prioritize sports. It was a shortsighted decision that he regretted well into adulthood—one of many *what-ifs* he tended to fixate on in his darker moments.

In no time, Mrs. Q was announcing that the class had only ten minutes of painting left before the final bell rang. It was just enough time for Vincent to put the final touches on what had turned into a sloppy picture of a soccer game at sunset. Turned out that Vincent still couldn't paint worth a shit, but he sure had a blast doing it again.

"All right, class, eyes and ears up front for a second," Mrs. Q announced from the front of the room. Everyone stopped what they were doing and shifted their attention to the front of the class.

"I'm going to announce the names of everyone who is registered for Aftercare. If I call your name, that means you should stay seated when the first bell rings, and we'll all walk to the playground together on the second bell. Everyone who understands please put your hands on your head."

Astonishingly, every student, including Vincent, put their hands on their heads to acknowledge they understood the direction. Mrs. Q knew how to run a room full of little kids, that was for sure.

"Perfect! So, our Aftercare list for today includes Annabelle, Braden, David, Heather, Jessica, Johnny, Tommy, and Vincent," she continued. "Does anyone have any questions?"

Everyone shook their heads.

"Excellent, feel free to talk among yourselves while we wait for the bell. Great day today, everyone!" she said and began cleaning up the art supplies scattered throughout the room.

After the first bell rang and three-quarters of the class had departed, Vincent decided to have one last bit of fun. He grabbed his painting, quickly scribbled on the front, "Miss Maria, will you be my Valentine?" and confidently strode up to the front of the class.

"Um, Miss Maria," Vincent said in his shy, child voice that he wished sounded just a tiny bit more grown up, "I wanted to give this to you." Holding out his hand, Vincent was suddenly overcome with embarrassment and felt his face heat up.

"Aw, thank you, Vince!" Maria responded, gently taking the paper from him. She studied the painting, and he saw a grin appear on her lips. "Oh, sweetie, I'm so honored that you'd ask, but Valentine's Day already happened this year. Tell you what, I'll give you first dibs next year, okay?"

"Um, okay, Miss Maria, that sounds good. I'm gonna make sure to ask again next year though!" Vincent replied, feeling his confidence return.

"That sounds like a plan to me," she responded with a wink.

Before Vincent could head back to his seat, the second bell rang, and Mrs. Q led the group out to the playground, where they would spend the next few hours waiting for their parents to get off work and pick them up for the day.

CHAPTER EIGHT

Aftercare at Sewell Elementary School was a complete crapshoot. Depending on which chaperone was on duty, the environment could range from absolute pandemonium to military-esque, orderly boredom. As he approached the playground, Vincent spotted Miss Spencer—with her classic ear-to-ear smile and frizzy hair, wearing one of her trademark lavender dresses with Birkenstock sandals—and smiled. The rest of the day would be a free-for-all.

When he was a kid, he was never really bothered by the fact that he was an Aftercare regular. He realized pretty early on that everyone who stayed late either had two parents who worked or was being raised by a single parent, like he was. Instead of being ashamed, he always took pride in the fact that his mom worked a full-time job to provide for their family. Plus, spending an extra hour or two out on the playground with the other kids felt like more of a reward than a punishment.

While Miss Spencer was busy organizing a double-Dutch jump rope line for the girls, Vincent and David made their way straight for the swing sets. One of their favorite things to do was pretend that swing jumping was an Olympic sport and launch themselves as far as they could while the Aftercare teacher wasn't looking. David always seemed to win, but Vincent felt like today might be his day. Before he could find out for sure, they heard a voice call out from the nearby basketball courts:

"Hey, punk, where do you think you're going?"

Vincent froze, terrified to turn and face the fifth-grade bully who had assaulted him on the soccer field earlier.

"That's right, I'm talking to you, little kid," the bully continued. "I told you I'd be seeing you after school. No bell to save you now."

"Come on, Vinnie—just ignore him. He's not going to do anything with Miss Spencer watching us," David said, trying to console Vincent.

"You're right," Vincent said quietly. "Let's head over to the softball field. We'll stay away from the older kids, and they'll probably just forget about us."

"Sounds like a great plan to me—I'll race you over there!" David said, taking off before Vincent had a chance to reply. He glanced over his shoulder at the basketball courts to see the group of fifth graders huddled together. What were those vultures plotting?

For a moment, an image of the group of Erickson VIPs flashed before his eyes, all wearing dark suits and huddled over a desk, looking at something . . . but what was it? Vincent felt his mind stepping in and finishing the daydream, willing him to get close enough to see what they were up to. He could see Gil at the head of the table, surrounded by the bigwigs and sketching something with the egregiously expensive Montblanc pen he only used to sign important agreements. But this looked like a picture, not a contract. Vincent took a step closer, and realized Gil was drawing a coffin.

But whose coffin was it?

"Come on, Vinnie! Catch up already!" David hollered, snapping Vincent out of his daze. With a jolt he took off and did his best to catch David before he stepped foot on the dirt infield.

———

From their vantage point behind the backstop of the softball field, Vincent and David were able to keep Miss Spencer and the main playground in full view. They were far enough away that it might take some effort to grab her attention, but if anything were to happen, she would easily be able to identify the trouble. The flipside of their positioning was that their view of the basketball courts was partially obscured by the standalone trailers that housed the kindergarten classes due to the school's overcrowding. This made Vincent slightly uncomfortable, but he figured they could just keep a regular reconnaissance cadence to track the movements of their enemies.

David seemed completely unbothered by the fact that a bully four years their elder was interested in beating the shit out of Vincent. Instead, he was convinced they were out of danger and safe in their semi-secluded hideout. "It's fine, Vinnie," he kept saying when Vincent would look over at the bully. "Nothing's gonna happen."

After noticing that the fifth graders had resumed their basketball game, Vincent started to let his guard down and joined David in grabbing some rocks and drawing the map of an imaginary city that they would one day govern as co-presidents.

As the Arizona sun began its slow descent, coloring his surroundings in a hazy, golden glow, Vincent found himself blissfully unaware of how much time had passed since class ended or what was going on around him. It was so easy to enjoy the present moment as a kid with no responsibilities that he wasn't even concerned he could no longer hear the giggling and cheering of the jump-roping girls across the park. Nor could he hear the sound of a bouncing ball followed by the occasionally *rung* of a shot hitting the steel rim. Instead, he remained intensely focused on drawing the most realistic building facade he could, until he heard the snap of a breaking twig behind him and felt the hair on the back of his neck stand up.

"Well, well, well," he heard a threatening voice hiss from behind the softball field, "Look what we have here. It's the little twerp that thinks he's hot shit because he cheated in a pick-up soccer game. Oh, and his wimpy boyfriend."

Vincent looked up and realized that Miss Spencer and the girls had disappeared behind the main school building. This was not going to end well.

"What's the matter, you little pussy? Can't turn around and face your beating like a man?" The fifth-grader continued, "If you don't stand up, then this is going to be ten times worse for you."

The bully's motley crew of followers began taunting Vincent in the background, and he knew there was no escaping. His only option was to figure out how to win this fight. He wouldn't be able to out-muscle this behemoth, but since he was operating with advanced software inside of rudimentary hardware, he might be able to outma-neuver him.

"You've got three seconds, kid, or I'm going to start kicking the living shit out of you: one, two . . ."

Vincent pressed his hands firmly into the ground and grabbed a fistful of sandy dirt, pushed up, and rose to his feet. He had a plan, but he wanted to give diplomacy a try before resulting to violence.

Turning to face the bully, he said, "I don't want any trouble. I'm sorry I jumped in the game. I've just always wanted to play with everyone in the mornings and didn't think I'd even touch the ball. If I promise not to play in the morning games anymore, will you leave me alone?"

The bully seemed caught off guard by this negotiation technique, and his expression temporarily softened. His eyes began blinking rapidly as he tried to figure out how best to respond. Before he could say anything, one of the nearby goons chimed in: "Screw this kid, Andy—kick his fucking ass!"

Vincent's fate was sealed. And his nemesis now had a name.

Andy's face hardened into a fresh scowl. "You should've thought about that before you embarrassed us, kid," he said. "You're gonna take these lumps like a man. It's the only way you'll learn your lesson."

"Okay," Vincent sighed, "if you're sure . . ."

Before Andy could make a move, Vincent whipped a handful of dirt directly in his eyes and charged into a flawlessly executed double-leg takedown. While Andy howled in agony and frantically tried to get sand out of his eyes, Vincent quickly moved into a mounted position and began raining down punches and elbows. Mixed martial arts wasn't a part of the mainstream collective consciousness back when he was a kid, but as an adult Vincent watched every UFC pay-per-view religiously. He'd even had the chance to chat with some fighters at a prefight event in Vegas and knew that they hated getting hit with elbows more than anything else.

Unfortunately for Andy, this afternoon he had chosen to put himself on the receiving end of a ground-and-pound clinic, and Vincent had no plans to stop until victory was assured.

Sweat was pouring off his forehead as Vincent used all his strength to maintain his mounted position while Andy writhed underneath him, arms valiantly covering his face from the barrage of elbows and fists raining down from above. Vincent knew he needed to empty the tank and hit Andy with everything he possibly could. His seven-year-old body would only allow him to hit so hard, but he was confident if he could throw enough volume, Andy would soon tap out.

Just as Vincent was starting to feel his energy start to plummet, he noticed that Andy was no longer actively trying to buck him off of top position. He was breaking, and it was now or never if Vincent wanted to have any chance of winning this fight. He took a deep breath and unloaded with every ounce of strength he could muster.

After what felt like ten minutes—but was probably closer to ten seconds—Andy threw his hand up and gasped, "Uncle."

Exhausted, Vincent rolled off Andy and stared up at the cloudless sky feeling his chest swell with pride.

The closest he'd ever come to getting into a fight in his past life was in third grade, but he'd chickened out, cementing his reputation as a coward for rest of his elementary school days. He'd always wondered what it would feel like to stand his ground, and now he finally knew.

The feeling didn't disappoint. He felt powerful, but it was more than that. He finally felt at peace with what had happened all those years ago when he'd been so ashamed and humiliated.

Was all this a part of why he didn't trust people? Why he was always looking over his shoulder? He could finally let that go and move on . . . except now it was too late. He was already dead and gone.

Andy's crew rushed over to help their leader while Vincent lay on the ground catching his breath and basking in the glory of his victory. Within a few seconds, David rushed over and yanked him up in a congratulatory hug.

"Vinnie!" he shouted, "You did it! I can't believe it! You actually did it!"

"Yeah, I guess I did," Vincent mumbled, still in a haze.

Aware that openly gloating or hanging around too long might invite a rematch, Vincent slung his arm around David and started walking toward the gym building, where the few remaining Aftercare kids typically congregated.

Vincent could hear faint giggles as they turned the corner to rejoin the rest of the Aftercare group. David was rambling a mile a minute, recapping what Vincent had just done and still in disbelief over what he had witnessed. Vincent wasn't registering a word that David was saying and could tell that he was experiencing the full aftereffects of an adrenaline dump. His mind was in a fog, his hands were shaking, and all he wanted to do was grab a seat and recover on one of the picnic tables scattered around the asphalt outside of the gymnasium.

Actually, what he really wanted, more than anything, was to see his mother coming to pick him up from school.

Vincent was desperate to sit down on one of the benches ten feet ahead of him, but with every step forward, he felt like time was slowing down. It was strangely similar to the feelings he had sitting in his car for the last time in his previous life. He glanced over his right shoulder and could see David's mouth moving, slowly, but the only sound he heard was a high-pitched ringing. Turning to his left he saw Miss Spencer using chalk to draw on the ground, but her movements were lethargic and unnatural. The ringing in his ears continued and an uneasiness settled in.

Suddenly, the ringing stopped and he heard a voice behind him hiss, "Hey, kid, we're not done with you yet."

Before Vincent could turn around, he felt two hands collide with the middle of his back and thrust the top half of his body forward. The shove was so perfectly timed that he didn't have time to brace his fall, and the instant his head hit the pavement his entire world went black.

———

A guttural shriek filled the air and snapped Vincent back into consciousness. He was completely dazed, drifting in and out and still unable to see, but he could hear the continued screams. There was something familiar about them.

Slowly his other senses began to return, and he could feel a pair of fingers on his neck.

"He's breathing and still has a pulse," Miss Spencer's voice announced from directly above him.

At this point Vincent realized he was lying flat on the ground and tried to roll onto his side to stand up. But try as he might, he couldn't seem to get his body to respond. Next he tried to get his eyes open, but he couldn't even manage to make that happen. He opened his mouth to speak and let Miss Spencer know that he was all right, but the only sound he could muster was a faint groan.

This isn't good, Vincent thought to himself and once again felt darkness closing in all around him.

———

It was impossible to know how much time had passed before a voice cut through the darkness. "It's going to be all right, baby, I promise. We're going to get you to the hospital, and they're going to fix this."

His mother.

Emerging from the in-between realm, Vincent was greeted by her voice, which was shaking, and her soft, warm hand grasping his. He attempted to return the squeeze but was still unable to get his body to do his mind's bidding. His vision remained totally black, but it felt as if he was moving, and the random chimes, beeps, and radio chatter in the background made him assume he was in the back of an ambulance. If he wasn't so completely devoid of energy, he would have been terrified. But right now all he wanted to do was rest.

"Fuck, he's flatlining! Get the EKG fired up—I don't know if we're going to make it to the hospital!" He heard someone sobbing in the distance and, realizing this may be his last chance, he mustered up the strength to give his mom's hand one last squeeze before succumbing to the pull of the darkness once again.

CHAPTER NINE

"Wake up! We're gonna be late for morning workouts!" a frantic voice hollered, immediately followed by a hand gripping Vincent's shoulder and jolting him awake with a forceful shake.

"Fuck! Mac is going to run us to death if we're not in the gym in ten minutes. Wake the fuck up, Palmer! We need to get moving!"

Vincent had no idea what was going on or who the young man was who was yelling at him. "Where am I? What's going on?" he muttered, trying to gather his thoughts.

"The fuck?" the man (or was it a kid?) replied. "You're in your fucking room, bro. Goddamn, get your ass in gear. Coach McGarrity is going to kill us if we're late."

"Coach McGarrity?" Vincent said groggily.

"Yes! Palmer, I swear to God, if you don't put your team gear on right now, I'm leaving and will not hesitate to throw you right under the bus when he asks why I'm late."

Vincent sat up, wiped his eyes, and looked around the room. To his left there was a wall covered in old movie posters and a small closet. To his right, a pair of windows covered by sloppily hung sheets. Clothes blanketed the floor, and he was sitting on one of the two twin beds pointed toward a tiny TV sitting atop an old desk covered in Hot Pockets wrappers and loose papers.

Holy shit. This was his college dorm room. And that was Tony—his college *roommate*—yelling at him. What the fuck was happening?

Before he could think too deeply about this discovery, he was hit in the face by a pair of gym shorts.

"Put your fucking shorts on, dude, we're leaving. What is with you this morning?" Tony whisper-screamed in exasperation.

Knowing he would have to figure things out on the run, Vincent hurriedly pulled the shorts over his boxers, grabbed a shirt off the ground, and followed Tony out the door.

It wasn't until Vincent stepped outside of the dorm building and was greeted by the crisp, chilly late-autumn air that his mind started to kick into gear. Hours ago—or was it minutes?—he was a first grader. But today he was suddenly fourteen years older and walking across a college campus toward his most hated activity: 6:00 a.m. off-season workouts.

But what happened to little Vincent?

The last thing he could remember was floating in and out of consciousness in an ambulance. That certainly wasn't a scene he remembered from his previous life, and it sure felt more real than any dream he'd ever had. Did his presence here, in western New York, as a college student mean that little Vincent had survived? Were he and little Vincent even the same person? Not to mention that other guy who had decided to cut his life short?

Thinking of that version of himself made Vincent shudder.

"Whoa, watch out!" Tony yelled, throwing his arm up to prevent Vincent from walking straight into a bright-purple, souped-up Dodge Charger as it whipped into the Drewyer Center parking lot.

He remembered that car! It was all coming back now.

"Fucking Trevor," Tony muttered under his breath. "Why can't that guy just chill for one day? Fuck sakes."

Almost everyone hated Trevor, including Vincent, who was a regular target of his unpredictable bouts of aggressive confrontation. Looking back at his college years, he almost felt bad for Trevor—his overcompensation and consistent punching down were clear indicators of some deeper insecurity. But back in those days, Vincent just did his level best to avoid Trevor's wrath by steering clear of him whenever possible. He'd used that strategy often over the years that followed, yielding increasingly disappointing results.

Unshaken by this predawn, near-death experience, Vincent followed Tony in his hurried march toward the "Athletes Only" entrance around the back of the building. Ten yards away from the door, Vincent could feel a pit in his stomach start to develop. These early morning workouts were bad enough when he was mentally prepared for them; he could only imagine how terrible the next two hours were about to be given his current state of mind.

"Nice of you two to join us," McGarrity announced as Vincent walked through the weight room doors.

"Sorry, coach," Tony mumbled, avoiding eye contact as they shuffled past and joined the rest of the team in pre-workout stretches.

After their first set of high-knees, Vincent felt the pit in his stomach start to dissipate. He didn't dare glance McGarrity's way for fear of inadvertently setting off one of Coach Mac's famous temper tantrums, but he felt like they'd avoided the worst-case scenario. After a few more dynamic stretches, Vincent shook off the last of his grogginess and was shocked by how good he felt. His muscles felt dense and explosive, without any hint of the nagging tightness and joint pain he'd become accustomed to in middle age.

But there was a tightness in his head that wasn't so welcome—a bothersome feeling that someone was watching his every move, waiting to call him out for even the slightest misstep. The feeling was vaguely familiar, a relic from a past life when he was desperate to gain the approval of coaches, stepfathers, or bosses and devastated when they inevitably found him wanting. It was a strange sensation considering how indifferent he had been toward his superiors in the years leading up to the night he decided to blow up his entire life. Yet here he was again, worried about living up to another man's expectations.

Was this feeling some sort of clue hinting at why he had been sent back to this specific moment in time? Or had he just gotten so used to being numb that all his emotions felt more intense?

It was hard to tell just yet, but he was certainly going to keep an eye out for any other signs that might point toward some answers.

Stretching continued for another ten minutes, and as they were wrapping up, Vincent found himself pleasantly surprised by the amount of energy filling the room this early in the morning. He remembered these sessions being much more subdued affairs, with everyone irritably going through the motions until they were finally excused. Had they been, or was that just how he'd perceived it because he had taken this time in his life for granted? On this morning his teammates appeared almost giddy to start their day in the weight room.

"Why is everyone so pumped up today?" Vincent whispered to Tony.

"Did you forget?" Tony asked. "It's the last morning lift of the year, dude. And the seniors are throwing a huge party at the Baseball House tonight. I wouldn't be surprised if some of them start drinking as soon as we get out of here."

"You know," McGarrity yelled loud enough to suck the air out of the entire room, "I was gonna let Raggiano and Palmer's tardiness slide this morning. I really was . . ." he trailed off and began pacing around the room. "You all know how much I hate when people are late—"

"We weren't late."

Everyone turned in Vincent's direction, in complete disbelief that he would dare to challenge McGarrity. Vincent himself couldn't believe he was the one who actually said it! He wasn't even confident that they weren't late, but seeing his teammates' look of astonishment flip to fear and rage, Vincent knew that he was going to have to dig himself out of this hole. Quickly.

"Is that right, Palmer?" McGarrity said, making a beeline toward Vincent. "What time do these workouts start?"

"Six o'clock, sir, always have," Vincent replied with what he hoped sounded like confidence.

"That's right. Do you know what time you and your little sidekick walked in that door?"

"Couldn't have been any later than five fifty-eight," Vincent said, hoping that Coach Mac wouldn't call his bluff. Either way, he wasn't going to back down—he'd spent enough of his life letting people walk over him and wasn't going to spend another second getting pushed around.

"I don't think so. My watch had you here at six on the dot. And, like I always say, if you're early, then you're on time, and if you're on time, then you're late. Do you know what that makes you, Palmer?"

"It makes me five minutes early."

"What?" McGarrity said, clearly expecting a different response.

"Coach, your watch is always five minutes fast. So, if your watch had us in here at six, then we were really here at five fifty-five."

McGarrity's eyes narrowed. Vincent could tell he was not going to like what was coming next, but he kept his eyes locked on Mac's. If decades spent dealing with various emotionally stunted assholes had taught Vincent anything, it was that these kinds of people counted on their prey folding under pressure. Unfortunately for McGarrity, this version of Vincent was no longer the folding type.

"Palmer, I don't know what has gotten into you today but I've got half a mind to run the rest of these guys into the dirt while you sit on your ass and watch. Let them sort this all out for me later today."

The team let out an audible groan, knowing their worst fears had just been confirmed.

"But I'm feeling generous this morning, so I'll give you a chance to get everyone out of what I'm sure will be a highly intense cardiovascular workout."

Vincent's stomach dropped. How could he have forgotten about McGarrity's nonsensical mind games. There was almost zero chance he was going to be given a challenge he could accomplish. He silently braced for the worst but kept eye contact with McGarrity. This fucker wasn't going to get the satisfaction of thinking he could rattle Vincent Palmer.

"Here's the deal—if you can do twenty-five pull-ups in one set, nobody runs. If you can do thirty, I'll make this a free lift, and everyone can stay for as long or as little as they'd like. You can use whatever grip you want, but no straps and no kipping, and you need to be fully extended when you're hanging down, with your chin past the bar on the way up. Trevor is in charge of counting full reps—and, Trevor," McGarrity turned to face the overly intense senior, "if you miscount one of these reps, you'll stay after and run extra. Sound good?"

"Sounds good."

Vincent stepped up to the pull-up bar with the team's fate hanging in the balance. His heart was beating so hard he felt like it was about to jump out of his chest, and he wanted nothing more than to turn and bolt right out of the gym. But he knew he had to push through.

He'd never done twenty pull-ups before, let alone thirty. As the team circled around the pull-up bar, he could feel their energy begin to flow into him. That was the key—he had to do this for them, not for himself. If he was ever going to break a personal record, it was going to be today, and it was going to be for something bigger than his own ego. *That* was why their energy felt different today than it had all those years ago. They hadn't changed—they'd had the same energy back then. He'd been the one going through the motions, not them. He'd been too caught up in his own feelings, his own competitiveness, to truly think of them as teammates—even though his relationship with them was the only thing that made all of these trials and tribulations worth it in the end.

As he stepped up to begin his set, Vincent felt McGarrity's hand clamp down on his shoulder and heard him growl, "You know, nobody's ever done thirty pull-ups in a row in this weight room before. Do you really think *you* can set a school record?"

"Watch me," Vincent fired back, breaking McGarrity's grip on his shoulder and springing up to grab the bar.

His arms felt like pistons driving his body up and down with more force than he'd ever experienced. In a snap, he had fired through ten and began feeling like thirty wasn't completely unattainable. With every rep he could hear the tone of his teammates shift from hopeful to determined. Their support kept him pulling in rhythm, and by the time he reached his nineteenth rep, Vincent knew victory was within reach.

His twentieth rep was where things began to shift. After easily pulling his chin over the bar, he felt sweat start to slip between the cracks of his right hand. Vincent knew that he only had two, maybe three reps, before this became a major problem.

By the time he was descending from rep twenty-four, the moisture had gotten so bad that he was hanging on by the tips of his fingers. Vincent guessed that trying for another pull would likely end in him being thrown off axis with enough force to loosen his left hand. He knew what he had to do . . . give up the right hand on his own terms so he could attempt to switch to a supinated grip.

The instant his arms locked out he tightened his left hand's grip and allowed his right hand to fall to his side. His teammates let out an audible gasp, and a hush fell over the room as they waited with bated breath to see how he'd maneuver through this adversity.

Staying calm, Vincent reached up with his right hand and grasped the bar, this time with his palm facing toward him, and in one swift motion swung his weight to the left and flipped his left hand before his momentum swung him back to center.

The room erupted as Vincent eased his chin over the bar for his twenty-fifth pull-up. In unison, his teammates began chanting: "Vince! Vince! Vince! Vince!" as he continued in his quest for thirty.

Twenty-seven and twenty-eight went as smoothly as his early reps, and he began to believe he was going to accomplish what seemed impossible mere minutes ago. While he allowed his mind to wander slightly into the future, his twenty-ninth rep was threatening to derail his grand ambitions. His momentum nearly came to a complete stop, and his entire body began to shake as he struggled to get past this plateau.

Despite being one of the worst leaders Vincent had met, McGarrity did occasionally stumble into moments of proper motivation. As if he knew exactly the wrong thing to say at the right moment, McGarrity gloated, "Looks like he can't handle the pressure after all."

But it wasn't McGarrity's voice Vincent heard; it was his father's.

Biting down, Vincent willed himself past the sticking point and easily over the bar.

While his teammates hooted and hollered with excitement, he descended one final time, allowing himself a pause once his arms hit full extension. Looking directly in McGarrity's eyes, he said, "Looks like we're all going home," and threw his entire being into the goal of getting his chin above that bar. Vincent felt like his eardrums would pop from the sound of cheers as he inched over the bar, and by the time he hit the ground he was buried in a dogpile of exuberant teammates.

CHAPTER TEN

"Dude, I can't believe you just did thirty fucking pull-ups!" Tony yelled as he placed both hands on his shoulders and used Vincent to exuberantly catapult himself in the air. In truth, Vincent couldn't really believe it either.

"There was no way I was gonna let everybody down, man. If Mac's gonna wake up and be a prick, then I'm gonna put him back in his place," Vincent said.

"Bro, that was a School. Record." Tony continued. "Like holy shit! What was your PR before today?"

Vincent glanced at the ground. "I dunno, somewhere around seventeen or eighteen, I think."

"Eighteen? Yo, we just witnessed a fuckin' miracle, man! *You* performed a fuckin' miracle!"

"Never underestimate the power of spite, my friend." As soon as he'd said it, Vincent knew that wasn't what he really meant. It was that speech filter thing again. Which was starting to make sense—the people he had known wouldn't recognize him if he was totally different than the Vincent he had been. He hadn't done thirty pull-ups out of spite— he just didn't want to let his teammates down.

Which begged the question: Was he the Vincent of twenty-something years ago or the person he was in the weeks and months leading up to his death? Or was he someone different altogether?

"Come on," he heard Tony saying, "let's head over to the cafe and grab some breakfast."

Vincent nodded in agreement as they took a right and headed west toward the dining hall at the bottom of campus.

———

There was a palpable buzz reverberating throughout the dining hall as he and Tony scanned their student ID cards and began perusing the breakfast spread. Vincent had forgotten how much excitement pervaded college campuses heading into the weekends. He could sense that every student in the cafeteria was daydreaming about the fun they would have later that night. The world was full of possibilities.

Had he felt that way? Or had something been weighing him down already, this early on, and he just hadn't put his finger on it?

Given the chaotic start to his morning, he hadn't been able to focus on anything that wasn't right in front of him. But being back in his college dining hall gave him a sense of security that allowed his thoughts to drift.

Browsing the morning spread, he felt a twinge of regret creep up in the back of his mind. Everyone in the dining hall seemed to be having a blast, yet he didn't remember his college days being all that fun. Instead of taking advantage of his youth, he'd forsaken the more joyful aspects of these years for a single-minded quest to achieve goals that seemed trivial in hindsight. How many formative experiences and memories had he passed up trying to prove his dedication to a sport he didn't even watch on TV as an adult?

It wasn't all bad, a voice in the back of his head reminded him.

That was true; there were always a few days a year when he would allow himself to let loose and act like every other kid on campus. One of those rare occasions was the end of the fall baseball season, which just so happened to be today.

Once he had loaded his plate up with an unreasonable amount of breakfast foods (he intended to take full advantage of his overly active twenty-one-year-old metabolism), his focus shifted to finding a place to sit. Before he could finish scanning the full room, he heard a friendly voice pierce through the crowd.

"I'll be goddamned if I'm not getting shit-faced tonight after the miracle we witnessed this morning," Eddie Marx announced to the table of baseball players posted up in the back corner of the room, breaking into his signature boisterous laugh. "I mean, if there was ever a day to celebrate, it's today, right? I thought McGarrity was going to literally puke when Palmer was going for that last pull-up. Fuck, boys, we're going to get proper sloshed tonight in the name of Vincent the Conqueror!"

Eddie had always been one of Vincent's favorite teammates, but he couldn't ever remember a time when he felt that affection was recip-rocated. It was kind of nice hearing someone wanting to celebrate his achievements. Not that he hadn't accomplished some notable things when he was in school the first time (or whatever he should call his past experience), but he was always quick to dampen any praise he received. Dealing with a rotating cast of wannabe father-figures had taught him early on that most compliments disguised ulterior motives. Whether those were earning brownie points with his mother or being passed up for a promotion because he was just "too valuable" in his current role, Vincent learned time and again that flattery wasn't to be trusted.

Plus, the way he saw it, if he could accomplish something, it was almost definitionally unworthy of acknowledgment. At least that's what he told himself. So, when Eddie, or anyone else, said something kind or inspiring, Vincent would shut them down. Before long, the praise came less and less, and eventually it dried up altogether. This time around, he didn't plan to brush off the compliments.

He was going to lean in and let himself connect with these guys.

"So, what's on the docket for tonight, fellas?" Vincent asked, striding up to the table of teammates who immediately went wild and broke into another "Vince! Vince! Vince!" chant. He gave a slight bow in acknowledgment, motioned for everyone to calm down, and took a seat. "But seriously, guys, when are we going to start celebrating?"

"The drinking commences for Daryl as soon as we get back to the house," one of the seniors announced from the end of the table.

"Yeah, we're gonna get a head start while we set up for a banger at the Baseball House," Big Tim, their senior first baseman, interjected. "And it sounds like the women's soccer and hockey teams will be making an appearance. You gonna actually participate tonight, Palmer?"

"Hell yeah, dude, baseball's over for the semester, and it would be a sin not to celebrate dunking on McGarrity like that!" Vincent replied, getting the boys riled up once again.

"That's what I like to hear," Tim said. "Make sure you bring your party pants because this is going to be a night we'll never forget."

"Did you hear what they said about the girls' soccer team coming?" Tony asked as they headed back across campus to their dorm.

"Yeah, sounds like it'll be a pretty good time. You got your eye on one of the soccer players?" Vincent replied.

"Me?" Tony shot back. "I was talking about *you*! It's not exactly a secret that you've had a crush on Kaitlin since the day you stepped on campus."

"Kaitlin? Kaitlin who?"

"Come on, dude—we live together, and I've seen the way you look at her. Kaitlin Darcy!"

Vincent hadn't heard from, or thought about, Kaitlin Darcy in decades. Back when he was in college, he'd spent years wishing he could muster up the courage to ask her out. She was his year and they shared the same major, so they always had at least one class together each semester. But it wasn't just the familiarity that drove college-age Vincent's infatuation; Kaitlin was also a stone-cold knockout, and funny enough to land a gig on *SNL*. More importantly, she was about as down-to-earth as one could get, which made her exponentially more attractive than the high-maintenance girls who seemed to make up the majority of the female population on campus.

Maybe, just maybe, this whole alternate reality he was living through would provide him with the opportunity he'd missed out on all those years ago.

"Isn't she dating someone right now?" Vincent asked Tony, bracing for the inevitable bad news. "She was with that one guy for a while, wasn't she?"

"Yeah. Clarinet player, studying forensic entomology or something odd like that. Weird guy. Cool, but weird. But dude," Tony stopped walking and placed a dramatic hand on Vincent's chest. "I heard they broke up. You know I've been trying to talk to Jessica Anders, and she said she saw Kaitlin crying in the bathroom after practice yesterday. She wasn't positive what it was about, but she heard Ramona Everett giving Kaitlin a pep talk about other fish in the sea. This may be your shot, my man!"

Holy shit, Vincent thought. *This is too good to be true.*

Or it would be, if he weren't already married.

For the first time since he was thrust into this surreal odyssey, Vincent's thoughts shifted to Lisa. He felt a sharp pain in the center of his chest, thinking about how callously he'd deserted the love of his life. Before he had any chance of stopping it, a flood of questions rushed through his mind.

Had she found out what had happened yet? Did the girls know? Who would be there to take care of them while they dealt with their grief? Were they grieving? Did they hate him?

Vincent took a deep breath to steady himself. It was natural to feel regret now, he reasoned, but there was no real way for him to atone for his mistakes. Even if he could get in touch with Lisa, what would he say?

"Hi, um, my name is Vincent, and you don't know me yet, but you will in a few years. We're going to get married and have two beautiful daughters, and then I'm going to . . ."

He couldn't even imagine telling her what he had done.

Regardless, there was nothing he could do in this moment to make things right with her. Maybe he'd get that chance in the future—or some version of the past—but the only thing he could control was how he reacted to his current reality. It was best to surrender, to enjoy what he could while reliving a time in his life that he'd long ago written off as wasted.

———

Sitting on his dorm room bed, Vincent felt like he finally had a chance to breathe after what had been a whirlwind few days. Well, at least it felt like it had been a few days. He wasn't sure how much time had passed since the night he died. It seemed like he had been able to retain his memories but they were . . . foggy.

Was this some sort of fucked-up second chance? It didn't necessarily feel like that—he couldn't remember McGarrity allowing someone to compete their way out of a punishment. That was a completely new development.

Was he just reliving his life over again while his real brain slowly shut off? He recalled reading somewhere that brain activity could continue for something like seven minutes after someone's heart stopped. Some scientists theorized that during this time people would relive their entire life over again without knowing that their physical body was completely lifeless. But he wasn't reliving his life. These experiences had all been significantly different than his past ones. It also felt like he had agency in these realities—to some extent, anyway. Plus, he could remember his past and was very aware that something inexplicable was happening.

Maybe this was some sort of alternate reality where everything seemed the same but there was a tiny variation that made this world different. In his thirties, he'd discovered simulation theory and, while not certain it was true, always had trouble disproving the theory completely. Perhaps these new realities he kept waking up in were slightly altered simulations for him to navigate. It was possible, but it wouldn't really explain the random time jumps and residual memories.

"You okay, dude?" Tony said from across the room. "You've been staring into space for like ten minutes straight. Want me to grab you a Gatorade from the machine down the hall?"

"Sorry," Vincent replied hastily, shaking himself out of his trance. "I'm good—just got lost in a daydream."

Vincent hesitated for a second and then decided that now was as good a time as any to start pushing some boundaries. Perhaps he just needed to ask the right questions to get the answers he was searching for.

"Hey, Tony," he said. "What do you think happens to you after you die?"

Tony didn't hesitate. "Time is a flat circle, my friend. Everything we've ever done or will do, we're gonna do over and over and over again. Forever."

Vincent was floored. All he could do was stare at Tony, astounded that he was able to deliver such a coherent answer with the utmost confidence. It was as if he'd been waiting for Vincent to ask that exact question.

"Do you really believe that?" Vincent finally replied, unsure that he really wanted to know the answer.

Tony took a beat, looked down at the floor of their dorm room, and looked up with a smirk. "Nah, I'm just messing with you, dude," he said with a chuckle. "We learned about Nietzsche and his theory of eternal recurrence in my intro philosophy class last week. Guess it stuck."

Vincent remained motionless, trying to process the significance of this interaction within the context of his surreal and fantastical recent experiences.

"Snap out of it, man," Tony said, giving Vincent's shoulder a firm smack. "We've gotta get down to Franklin Center in fifteen minutes, or Dr. Angel is going to knock five points off our final exam scores."

"Yeah, I don't think I'm going to go to class today," Vincent said absentmindedly.

"What are you talking about? You never miss class. What is going on with you?" Tony replied, looking concerned.

"Look, it's Friday, we don't have finals for another two weeks, and you know Dr. Angel's threats are all empty. Let's go hit instead. I bet nobody's in the cage this time of day."

"I don't know, man . . . what if she's serious about docking points on the final? You know I need all the help I can get in that class."

"Whatever. In twenty years you're not even going to remember the name of this class. Plus, if time is a flat circle, wouldn't you rather spend it crushing baseballs over and over and over again?" There was that filter again. What Vincent was really trying to say was, "I might not be here for long, and what little time I do have, I'd like to spend with you."

Tony took a deep breath and again dropped his gaze toward the ground in serious thought. Suddenly, his head jerked up, revealing a mischievous grin.

"Fuck it; let's go hit!"

CHAPTER ELEVEN

One of Vincent's favorite places in the world was the indoor batting cage underneath the baseball stadium's press box and grandstands. Having never believed he had any natural talent, Vincent had spent hours upon hours in that windowless room trying to perfect his swing, foregoing many of the more fun activities his teammates regularly prioritized. Hitting in the cages was a compulsion borne of insecurity. He understood that now, but that didn't make him any less excited to grab a bat and start hacking away with one of his best friends. Today was about enjoying his time, for however long he had it.

After ten minutes of Tony struggling to get the team's beat-up old boombox working, the opening chords of Thin Lizzy's "The Boys Are Back in Town" filled the cage, and they launched into the regular rhythm of their practice routine.

With Tony delivering a steady diet of meatballs down the middle, it only took Vincent a few swings to find his groove. It had been decades since he'd last picked up a bat, but it seemed like he was incapable of doing anything but smashing line drives into the back of the net.

"My God, Palmer, you just can't miss today!" Tony said, barely dodging another screamer back up the middle.

"I feel pretty good," Vincent responded.

"I *feel pretty good*," Tony mimicked in a sing-song voice, tossing a ball behind Vincent. "You're smacking balls so hard the sound's hurting my ears."

"All right, I guess I'm feeling *really* good," Vincent replied with a grin. "Tell you what, I'll bet you I can go ten straight into the back net on a line."

"Oh yeah? What happens when I win?" Tony fired back.

"If you win, I'll text Kaitlin and ask her if I'll see her at the Baseball House later tonight. How about that?"

"All right, bet. What if you win, Mr. Hero?"

"Easy—I win, you buy the booze for tonight."

They shook hands and returned to their places, ready for battle.

———

They were still arguing about who won the bet as Tony screeched into the parking lot of Lewiston Liquors, popping the curb and startling a gaggle of sorority sisters clinging to their recently purchased plastic handles of vodka and rum. Vincent was startled by how much the temperature had dropped as he stepped out of the truck. Heavy clouds were building overhead, and his intuition told him that a snowstorm was headed their way.

"Holy shit, you're almost as bad at driving as you are at keeping count." Vincent said as they burst into the liquor store.

"Don't change the subject, that last one didn't count, and you're not going to change my mind. We bet that you could hit ten in a row into the *back* net, not the top net," Tony shot back.

"If it hits the spot where the top net connects with the back net, then it counts. Everyone knows that. Don't even try to pretend like you have a leg to stand on here."

"Whatever, you just can't handle losing," Tony said as he browsed through the rum aisle. "Tell you what, though—you text Kaitlin right now, and I'll pay for your booze. Not like you can drink more than five beers without passing out anyway."

"Fine, but this is not an admission of defeat, just for the record," Vincent replied, smirking as he pulled a flip phone from his pocket and started searching through his contact list.

"How does this sound: *Hey, Kaitlin, heard you might be out and about tonight. Will I see you at the Baseball House later?*"

"Ew, what are you, like fifty years old? Who texts like that? Give me your phone." Tony chided, snatching the phone out of Vincent's hand.

Without missing a beat Tony typed, *Hey you, we're throwing a rager at the Baseball House tonight. You should come,* and before Vincent could object, hit send. "Now we're all squared up. What kind of beer do you want?"

"Um, I guess Blue Lights will do the trick. Maybe get a twelve pack, just to be safe," Vincent replied.

Despite seeming unfazed by their interaction, Vincent's stomach was doing somersaults—which was odd. His rational adult brain wasn't all that concerned about whether some college girl texted him back, but apparently his early-twenties nervous system cared very much. He hadn't felt this nervous about a girl since he first started dating Lisa all those years ago. Or was it a few years from now?

Either way, it had been decades since he'd experienced these types of butterflies and all his mind could focus on was the fact that he'd just opened himself up for rejection—another thing he hadn't experienced in quite some time. He knew it was foolish to be worried about this—he'd asked plenty of girls on dates throughout his life and experienced the full spectrum of success, always finding a way to shake off the failures along the way. But for some reason, right now he felt the same way he had felt in college on the few occasions when he mustered up the courage to pursue more than just friendship with his female classmates.

Before he could delve too deeply into his past issues with self-confidence, he felt a buzz in his pocket and instinctively grabbed his phone to see who the incoming text was from. To his great relief it was a group text from Big Tim, who lived at the Baseball House:

Fellas, we just got back from Sam's Club and Home Depot with a shit-load of supplies. Anyone who's done with class for the day wanna swing by and help us get set up? We'll make it worth your while ;).

"Well, it looks like we should probably head over to the Baseball House, huh?" Tony sighed, looking at Vincent for permission to bail.

"Yeah, I guess so," he replied. "It's the right thing to do."

"Dammit, Palmer, I need worse friends. You're too fucking responsible sometimes."

———

A light snow had begun falling as they pulled up to the back entrance of the Baseball House, situated on the corner of Fischer and Wilson Avenue. While it was technically a standalone house, there was only about ten feet between every residence on the block. This design gave the impression of a close-knit neighborhood of rowhomes, and for all Vincent knew, that may have been the case . . . before the baseball players moved in two years prior.

From the moment Vincent had stepped foot on campus, it seemed like there had been an ongoing feud between the players renting the house and their next-door neighbors. Back then, he'd never understood why the locals would have so many issues. But, having spent his late twenties dealing with terrible neighbors, he was pretty sure that he would walk out of the party tonight with a bit more compassion.

On cue, Daryl, who was sporting a freshly shaved mohawk, kicked open the back door, walked out onto the deck clad only in his underwear and ski goggles, slammed two beers together over his head, and proceeded to pour both of them in his mouth—or at least his general facial area. Roughly fifteen seconds later, after most of the beer had drained from each can, he spiked them over the railing, screamed, "Daryl rules!", flexed, and walked back inside. Tony turned toward Vincent and said, "What a shitshow," and they both busted out laughing.

Walking up the steps to the back deck, they could hear the sound of classic rock music growing louder and louder. By the time they opened the door, it was almost deafening, and they were greeted by one of the strangest sights Vincent had ever seen: Ten of his teammates, wearing only their underwear and snow boots, were hard at work covering as much of the house in plywood as they possibly could. And by the looks of the overfilled trash can in the middle of the room, they'd been drinking for most of the day.

Before Vincent had a chance to properly digest the scene, he felt Trevor's vice-like grip tighten around his shoulders. He braced for the worst.

"Ladies and gentlemen, allow me to introduce the man of the hour: Viiiinnccceeennnttt Paaaaalllmerrrrr!" he yelled, eliciting a round of cheers from the room.

Vincent felt the tension in his shoulders release, relieved that, for once, Trevor wasn't intending to terrorize him.

"Nice of you to join us, Palmer, but you missed most of the fun stuff. We're about done now," Trevor continued.

"Done with . . . what? What the hell are you all doing here?" Tony chimed in.

"Oh, not just in here, the entire house," Trevor replied.

"Okay, fine—what the fuck are you guys doing to this house?"

"Isn't it obvious?" Trevor said, genuinely dumbstruck by Tony's inability to comprehend the madness they were witnessing.

"Dude, just tell us what is going on," Vincent interjected, finally snapping out of his stupor.

"We're covering the entire house with plywood, duh."

"Okay . . . but why?"

Vincent's question seemed to stump Trevor and after about ten seconds of searching for an answer, he threw his hands up and said, "I dunno, because it's something to do, I guess. It was all Daryl's idea, I think."

Tony nearly choked on the Gatorade he was drinking and began coughing up a lung.

"You okay, lil' buddy?" Trevor said, smacking Tony on the back as if he were choking on a piece of food.

In between gasps, Tony managed to find enough air to say, "Why would anyone listen to one of Daryl's ideas? He's fucking nuts."

"Don't worry, bro, our guy Daryl can be a bit eccentric, but he's on the money with this one. Everyone who's anyone is going to be here tonight and we're going to throw the party of the century. It's gonna be legendary."

"Whatever you say, Trevor. This all just seems very strange and pointless," Vincent said, sparing Tony the need to respond. "But since we're here, anything we can help out with before we head back to the dorms to get cleaned up?"

"Funny you should ask," Trevor said with a wry smile. "I think Daryl's got a bit more in the basement to finish. Head on down and help him out, and we should be good to go after that."

The opening riff of AC/DC's "Hell's Bells" smacked them in the face as they opened the door to the basement, but it wasn't until they'd gotten to the last few steps that they realized Daryl had unintentionally begun the process of finishing the Baseball House basement. What had previously only been concrete floors and support beams now had what appeared to be a main area and a side bedroom. The plywood he had installed, while rudimentary, really impacted the space.

"Whoa," Tony said softly as he took it all in, "Daryl fucking finished their basement."

"Holy shit! Who knew he had this sort of vision? It's like they hired a professional to come in and map everything out," Vincent replied, awestruck by the sheer industriousness of college kids with too much time on their hands. What he wouldn't give to have that kind of time again. Would Violet be the type to participate in these types of hijinks once she got to college? Would Charlie?

Out of nowhere, a feeling of dread washed over him—he would never know what the girls would be like once they went to college. He wouldn't even be making it to their high school graduations.

He was snapped out of his daze by the sound of a bottle exploding somewhere in the newly created bedroom, followed immediately by the excited cheering of the very person whose work they were admiring.

Daryl was still whooping and hollering as Vincent and Tony entered the room. The first thing Vincent noticed was that there were two giant circular targets drawn on the far wall. The second thing he noticed, after stubbing his toes and nearly falling on his face, was that Daryl had built a raised platform that covered the concrete floor.

"What's all this for?" Vincent asked Daryl, trying to ignore the sharp pain he felt in his foot.

"I haven't quite figured that out yet, but I bet someone turns this room into something fun," Daryl responded absentmindedly.

"Okay . . . but why did you build this weird platform thing on the floor?" Tony said.

"Oh, that's for the empties," Daryl responded with a proud smile.

"Empties?" Tony replied, still confused.

"Yeah, man, check this shit out!" Daryl shouted, twisting the top off a bottle of Miller High Life, taking a knee and chugging the beer within thirty seconds. Then, still on one knee, he held up the empty bottle and bowed his head almost as if he was saying a prayer. Tony and Vincent exchanged a quick glance, steadying themselves for whatever might happen next.

After about ten seconds, Daryl's head snapped back up and he let out a loud, extended belch.

"Now check out my pop time!" he shouted before shuffling his feet and firing the empty bottle at one of the targets on the wall where it promptly exploded into a thousand pieces.

"Wooooooooooo!" Daryl screamed, breaking into another victory dance.

"THAT WAS FUCKING RAD!" Tony exclaimed. "Give me a bottle—I gotta try this!"

"Ah-ah-ah," Daryl clucked back, "gotta save room for the party, my man. Can only hold so many empties."

"What do you mean?" Vincent asked. "What can only hold so many empties?"

"The floor, dude. Here, check this out," Daryl said, waving them toward the wall with the targets.

As they got closer, Vincent could see that there was about a three-foot gap between the wall and the edge of the platform, which was open. While he was connecting the dots, Daryl began sweeping the broken glass into the open space underneath the platform.

"You're a mad genius," Vincent said. "Was all of this your idea?"

"Oh yeah, sure," Daryl said nonchalantly, still sweeping up broken glass in his underwear. "Always thought it would be cool to do something like this. Then everyone could really party without worrying about making a mess. Why else would you cover a house in plywood?"

"How'd you know how much plywood to get?" Vincent said, waiting for Tony to snap out of it.

"I didn't, but I tell you what—the good folks at Home Depot can tell you how to do just about anything, man. We walked in there, told them what we wanted to do, and that was that."

"Daryl, you truly are an original, my friend."

"Ha, I know—my mom hates it. But I gotta be me, right? Don't figure I can be anyone else," Daryl said before using his index finger to clean out his exposed belly button.

"How do you stay so carefree?" Vincent replied quietly.

The question seemed to momentarily stump Daryl. Still wearing his ski goggles, he looked up at the ceiling before shifting his gaze to the floor. After what felt like an eternity, he raised his head to make eye contact with Vincent, shrugged, and said, "You know, the way I figure it, we only got so much time in our lives to have fun. So why not try to have as much fun as possible when you get the opportunity, right? Gotta stay present, my dudes, otherwise you'll drive yourself nuts worrying about the past or the future. Enjoy your time. It might end quicker than you think."

They all stood in silence for a few seconds before Daryl ripped another belch, patted them both on the shoulders, and headed upstairs without another word.

"Bro, what the fuck just happened?" Tony said, finally turning to Vincent.

"I think Daryl taught us a life lesson," Vincent replied, putting his arm around Tony's shoulder and guiding him back upstairs.

CHAPTER TWELVE

Pulling up in front of their dorm building, Vincent felt a giddy excitement rising within him. For a moment he let go of the paranoia that had been nagging at him since he woke up in the morning and allowed himself to accept this new reality, however brief it might end up being. Tonight was going to be a good night. He could just feel it.

The temperature had dropped well below freezing, so they decided to leave the beer in the car as they headed toward the dorms, saving them the trouble of trying to sneak two cases into the "Alcohol-Free Residence Building." Opening the door, they were greeted by the high-pitched rabble native to a large group of twenty-something-year-old women, and seconds later they saw the majority of the women's soccer team heading their way, laughing and talking over one another.

They traveled in a noisy pack, reminding him of Violet and her teammates on the JV soccer team after practices. Which made sense since they weren't much older than her. The thought made Vincent slightly uncomfortable.

"Oh shit, dude," Tony whispered, lightly tapping Vincent with the back of his hand. "There's Kaitlin Darcy!"

Sure enough, there was Kaitlin tucked into the back of the pack, her unmistakable light hazel-green eyes perfectly accentuating an olive complexion and dark brown, almost black, shoulder-length hair.

"You gonna say anything?"

"Uh, I mean, I guess I will if it makes sense. She never texted me back, though," Vincent replied.

"So what? That's all part of the game, dummy," Tony said, sounding excited about the potential for drama. "You better think of something soon; they're coming right for us!"

"Just keep walking; I'll figure something out."

Before he could figure out what to say—or if he should say anything at all—it was Kaitlin who made the first move. Positioned at the side of the group, she happened to glance up and make direct eye contact with Vincent. But instead of looking away as he normally would have, Vincent held her gaze. The lively flicker in her eyes reminded him of Lisa, though they couldn't hold a candle to his wife's uniquely bright, emerald greens.

"Vince!" Kaitlin yelled, throwing her hands up in the air. "I haven't seen you in forever! Where have you been hiding?"

"Just keeping a low profile until the cops get off my back," Vincent said. "I could say the same about you. Where are you heading at this hour?"

"Oh, you know, heading to the store to grab some vodka and lemonade."

"Oh yeah? Well, don't pregame too hard. If what we just saw at the Baseball House is any indication, tonight's gonna be one for the record books."

"Let me guess—they decided to buy two kegs instead of one and hang up Christmas lights in the basement? Groundbreaking stuff . . ." Kaitlin shot back, playfully rolling her eyes.

"No, they decided—" Tony attempted to say, before Vincent jammed an elbow into his ribs.

"They . . . swore us to secrecy," Vincent said, holding a finger to his lips. "The only people who get to experience their vision are the ones brave enough to show up blind."

"Ooh, so mysterious. Well, we might just have to make our way over there and see for ourselves. We heard the hockey team's throwing a party too, though, so it depends on what the group wants to do," Kaitlin replied.

"Just let the group know that there's no way those hockey neanderthals could pull off what we've set up for tonight," Vincent said.

"I'll see what I can do," Kaitlin replied, "but I've got to go catch up with the rest of the girls. See you later, maybe?"

"I hope so," Vincent said before turning and walking toward the elevators. It wasn't until they got into the elevator that he realized that Tony was staring at him.

"Why are you staring at me like that?" he said.

"Because when did you pick up that kind of game?" Tony replied.

"What do you mean? I was just messing around trying to get her over to the Baseball House."

"Yeah, but . . . that was like, actually smooth. You've never been smooth like that—always quiet or goofy, or both. But never smooth."

Vincent shrugged, and the elevator opened to the eighth floor. He hadn't been trying to be smooth. He just felt . . . comfortable in his own skin for once. He certainly hadn't been trying to flirt, but he could see why Tony perceived it that way.

"Come on," he said, "let's get ourselves ready for whatever tonight is going to turn into."

———

The snow was really starting to pick up as they pulled into the eerily quiet neighborhood and parked in front of the Baseball House.

"Why do you think it's so quiet?" Tony asked.

"Dunno, maybe the neighbors already called the cops?" Vincent replied, glancing around for any signs of life and coming up empty. "Well," he continued with a shrug, "I guess the only way to find out is to head inside."

Tony nodded in agreement, and they both hopped out of the truck and headed toward the front door.

They entered the house to another outlandish scene playing out in the middle of the living room. Nearly two-thirds of the baseball team were standing around a large oval dining table, intently watching something that Vincent couldn't quite discern. As he moved closer, he noticed that Tim and Trevor were on opposite ends of the table staring daggers at one another, each with a nearly empty gallon of milk in their hands. In between them was an egg timer showing five minutes until it would go off. The room was completely silent.

"What's going on over here?" Vincent whispered to Eddie, who was diligently watching the scene before them.

"We were all hanging out and drinking after finishing up the plywood and apparently Tim called Trevor a pussy or something like that. Things got a bit heated, but then good ole Daryl suggested they settle their differences with a gallon challenge. A 'Wisconsin Duel' is what he called it, I think."

"What's a gallon challenge?" Tony chimed in.

"It's one of those wacky internet challenges that's supposed to be impossible to complete. Basically, you have to drink an entire gallon of milk in sixty minutes. But nobody ever finishes because your body can't process that much lactose at one time. Or something like that," Eddie continued.

"It looks like they're both pretty close though, and there's only five minutes left," Vincent said.

"Why do you think we're all so quiet? Nobody thought they would get this far. It's a battle of wills at this point. I mean, look at them— they're not doing so great."

Eddie was right. Upon closer inspection, Vincent noticed that Tim was actively shivering and extremely pale. Trevor, on the other hand, seemed steady but was beginning to turn green. It wasn't clear who was in worse condition, but they both had what looked like the equivalent of one small glass of milk left in their carton.

Suddenly, Tim slammed his fists on the table and shouted, "All right! Enough of this, Trevor; it's time to find out who the winner of this dual is. On the count of three, we chug the rest of this milk and see who can hold it in for the last three minutes!"

The room broke out in cheers as Tim stood up on his chair, counted to three, and they both chugged the remaining milk. The energy around the table began to build as they headed into their final minute. Tim returned to his chair and began writhing in distress, while Trevor remained stoic and uncharacteristically quiet. Despite being in obvious discomfort, they held firm in their stubborn refusal to yield to each other. Then, with ten seconds remaining, Trevor lurched forward unexpectedly. His hands gripped the side of the table as he tried to hold on for another eight seconds. Finally, with three seconds left, Trevor broke, turned to his left, and projectile vomited a stream of milk into a strategically positioned trash can.

Tim threw his arms up in victory as the egg timer went off and immediately threw up the gallon of milk that had been gestating in his stomach. Once he'd finished, he stood back up on his chair and motioned for quiet.

"Gentlemen, what you just witnessed was a war of wills," he gasped. "I have nothing but respect for Trevor and will absolutely, positively, without a doubt, *never* be doing that again." He paused to let out a belch so deep it caused the floor to shake. "Now that we've finished our Wisconsin Duel, it's time to get this fucking party started. We've got a shitload of beer out on the back deck, so everyone grab a cold one and let's get it going!"

Over the next hour, the party began to take shape with each room of the house developing its own personality. In the living room, the large oval table was being used for a game of twenty-one-cup beer pong, the basement morphed into an impromptu dance floor, and the rooms on the top level provided a quiet haven for casual drug use and ill-advised sex acts. At least that's what Vincent assumed—he rarely found himself on that level of the house.

Gradually, the male-to-female ratio began to even out, but there was still no sign of the women's soccer team—or Kaitlin.

"Where do you think the girls are?" Vincent leaned over and asked Tony under his breath.

"What do you mean, bro? There are girls everywhere, just look around," Tony replied, starting to slur his words.

"Well, yeah, but I mean the soccer girls."

"Psssh, don't worry about them. I bet they don't even show up. Look how many senior girls are here right now! This is the best party I've ever been to!"

Vincent took a second to survey the room and noticed that the crowd seemed to skew older, relatively speaking, of course. He also noticed that everyone seemed to be getting extremely drunk very quickly.

"PALMER!"

Vincent looked toward the beer pong table and saw Trevor motioning him forward. His body was standing up for him before he had even willed it to, and he was hyper aware of the fact that every eye in the room was trained on him as he made the slow walk toward what was surely going to be an unpleasant exchange, like every other interaction he'd ever had with Trevor.

"What's up, Trev?" Vincent heard himself say, trying to mask his unease.

Without a word, Trevor wrapped Vincent up in a hug so tight that he felt like his ribs were on the verge of breaking. After an excruciating ten seconds, Trevor released him, grabbing his right wrist and violently yanking his arm in the air like you would with a prize fighter who'd just won a championship fight.

"Listen up, you motherfuckers!" Trevor announced. "This man right here is a hero of the highest magnitude. Not only can he do more pull-ups than anyone I've ever seen, but he also has balls the size of pineapples. So, raise your fucking beers and join me in a toast to the baddest motherfucker around these parts: Vincent Palmer, The Coachslayer!"

The room exploded with cheers of admiration, devolving into chants of "COACHSLAYER! COACHSLAYER! COACHSLAYER!"

Trevor wrapped Vincent in another hug, kissed his forehead, and said, "You're welcome, Palmer," and then turned his attention back to the game of beer pong.

Before Vincent could figure out what he should be thankful for, he was immediately surrounded by girls, all very interested in learning why he was the hero of the day. For a split second, his mind flashed back to that last breakfast with his family. Then, like now, he was overwhelmed by attention he wasn't completely sure he deserved.

Deciding he wasn't all that interested in hogging the spotlight, Vincent subtly called Tony over and assumed the role of wingman. Helping his friend meant more to him than some random one-night stand, and Tony was all too happy to take advantage of Vincent's generosity.

CHAPTER THIRTEEN

A s novel and amusing as his newfound notoriety as "The Coachslayer" was, Vincent was starting to feel a little tired of all the attention. He eventually ducked downstairs in the hopes that a change of scenery might afford him some desperately needed anonymity. He wouldn't normally be interested in spending time in a club-like atmosphere, but he figured there was no way it could be worse than having to deal with drunk college kids asking him to tell the same story over and over again.

As he neared the bottom of the stairs, Vincent was momentarily stopped in his tracks by the scene in front of him. The entire main floor was packed wall to wall with sweaty bodies gyrating to the beat of obscenely loud house music. Before he could fully process how much the party had evolved, he felt one of the girls in the crowd grab his hand and pull him into the pit.

Time didn't seem to exist in the basement, and every song seemed to stretch on for hours. Vincent decided to lean in and found himself rolling from one dance partner to another, blissfully lost in the moment. He had all but forgotten about Kaitlin until he felt a tap on his shoulder and was greeted by her thousand-watt smile. Before he could register what was happening, Kaitlin threw her arms around his neck and brought him in for a hug.

"You have no idea how happy I am to see you!" she shouted over the music.

"Really?" Vincent replied, feeling hyper aware of how sweaty he'd become.

"Yes! This party is absolute insanity! Have you been upstairs at all?"

"Um, not in a bit, maybe an hour? I dunno, it's hard to tell time down here," Vincent yelled back.

"What?" Kaitlin yelled in his ear, a little too loudly.

"Maybe we should go find somewhere quieter to talk!" he shot back, pointing upstairs.

"Lead the way!" Kaitlin said, locking arms with Vincent and giving him a sly smile.

———

Emerging from the basement was like entering another reality, a feeling that was becoming all too familiar. He couldn't help but notice that some of the walls had been stripped of their protective plywood layers and featured scattered holes throughout the exposed drywall. What the hell had happened up here? And where did all that plywood go?

A big crash followed by a rapid series of smaller bumps shifted his attention to the stairs that led to the top floor of the house, and he turned just in time to see a body come tumbling down into the living room. The entire room went silent, attempting to process what had just happened before the stranger jumped up, yelled "I'm fine!", yanked the stair railing off the wall, and gave everyone drinking in the living room permission to burst into celebration.

"Come on—I know the perfect place for us to talk," Vincent said, leading Kaitlin around the chaos and up the stairs toward the top floor.

The top level of the house was curiously quiet compared to the party unfolding below. Vincent tried to ignore his feelings of uneasiness and escorted Kaitlin to the master bedroom at the end of the hallway. From what he could remember, this was Tim's room, and it was the only room in the Baseball House that was always off limits during parties. Which made it all the more surprising when he opened the door and was greeted with a "Whoa, ocupado, hermano" that seemed to emanate from nowhere.

"Um, Tim? Is that you?" Vincent asked, trying to figure out where the voice came from.

"Who's Tim?" the voice responded.

"Just the guy who lives in this room," Vincent said, flipping on the lights to find a freshman peeing in the far corner of the room.

"Dude! What the fuck are you doing? There's a bathroom right here!" Vincent snapped, pointing to the door immediately to his right.

"Oh shit," the kid replied. "No worries, man, I'm about done. Thanks for looking out, though."

The oblivious kid zipped his pants and turned to walk out the door. "Take care of yourself, big fella," he said, breezing past as if what just happened was completely normal.

Vincent stood frozen, unable to make sense of what he'd witnessed.

"What . . . what just happened?" Kaitlin stammered.

"I honestly don't know. I don't think I've ever seen something like that before. That kid better hope that Tim never finds out about this—he'll kill him."

"Well, I'm not getting involved in any of that, and I'm *absolutely* not hanging out in a room that smells like urine. How about we go to one of the other rooms down the hall?"

"Sure thing, let's get out of—"

"WOOOOEEEEE! LET'S FUCKING GO, BOYS!"

Vincent was stopped mid-sentence by the sound of someone shouting in the hallway. He knew that voice well and was certain that they should avoid whatever it was that was happening out there. "This is going to sound crazy, but I think we should stay here for a minute," he warned.

"You're right, that does sound crazy, but yes, I agree. Do you know who's yelling out there?"

"It's Trevor, and it sounds like he's heading off the rails," Vincent said, grabbing Kaitlin's hand and slowly backing away from the door. "If we're lucky, he'll get distracted by something and head back downstairs."

"Why are you describing him like the T-Rex from Jurassic Park?" Kaitlin replied softly.

"Because that's exactly what it feels like when he goes off on one of his drunken rampages. He is without a doubt the most insane person I've ever met, and alcohol doesn't typically make him any more rational," Vincent replied, focused on the thundering steps marching closer and closer to the door.

The steps stopped and Vincent felt Kaitlin grab his arm, bracing for the worst as tension filled the room. After what felt like a few minutes of silence, Vincent felt his shoulders relax. "Well, maybe he ran out of st—"

Suddenly, the door burst open and Trevor appeared holding two large knives in his hands while Kaitlin screamed in terror.

"Heeeerrrrreeee's Trevor!" he bellowed.

"Jesus fucking Christ, Trevor! What the fuck are you doing?" Vincent shouted, instinctively stepping in front of Kaitlin to shield her.

"Rock climbing!" Trevor replied with a wild glint in his eyes. Without any further context, he turned to his left and jammed both knives through the drywall a few feet over his head as he tried to get his feet on the wall, apparently attempting to scale the wall using kitchen knives. At first it seemed like he might actually be able to pull off this half-baked stunt, but after only a few seconds perched on the wall like Spider-Man, the drywall gave out and Trevor fell backward, taking the knives and a chunk of the wall with him.

Trevor was temporarily stunned by the fall, but Vincent's gut told him something worse was about to follow—he felt himself lunging for the slightly ajar bathroom door positioned between him and Trevor, pulling it open at the exact same moment that Trevor sprung up from the floor and launched both knives in their direction.

Thunk! Thunk!

For a split second, Vincent was numb with shock until Kaitlin's renewed screaming brought him back to reality. He grabbed her arm and bulldozed past Trevor, yanking Kaitlin along into the hallway.

He didn't have time to contemplate the smell of smoke wafting through the air as they sprinted down the hall toward the staircase. It wasn't until they were halfway down the stairs that Vincent realized that where they were headed might end up being more dangerous than what they were fleeing.

The scene they witnessed back down on the main floor stopped them dead in their tracks. The rowdy party they had left behind only a few minutes prior had somehow devolved into something closer to a riot. Nearly every male had stripped down to their underwear, was ripping the plywood off the walls, and throwing the remnants into a makeshift bonfire in the middle of the living room. The flames were touching the ceiling, and everyone in the room was chanting, "Burn it down!" repeatedly, in unison.

It was hard to tell how long he and Kaitlin stood there staring at the insanity unfolding before them, but he was unceremoniously snapped out of his trance after Eddie Marx threw a bathroom mirror into the fire, causing it to shatter into a million pieces.

"We've gotta get out of here," Vincent said, grabbing Kaitlin's hand. She remained still, frozen in place by the unbelievable events taking place all around them.

Suddenly, Tony came running over with one of the girls from earlier in tow. "Bro, we need to get out of here right fucking now!"

"You can say that again! Can you drive?"

"I've got no choice. We don't want to be anywhere near this place when the cops show up!"

The four of them made their way toward the front door and were immediately greeted by a gust of sub-zero wind and a scene pulled straight out of *The Thing*. Apparently, the innocuous snowfall from earlier had transitioned into a full-scale blizzard, and the entire neighborhood was blanketed in thick, white snow. The sound of sirens echoed in the distance.

"Can your truck handle this type of snow?" Vincent yelled over the wind.

"Campus is only a mile away; I think we can make it back," Tony said, before running toward his truck and frantically wiping snow off the windows.

Vincent rushed to his side to help before Tony unlocked the doors, and they all piled in—Tony and the girl in the front and Vincent and Kaitlin in the back seat. It took a few attempts before Tony could get the starter to turn over, but Vincent was elated to hear the engine roar to life on his third try. Tony floored it, sending the truck sliding into the road and causing the bed to fishtail into a parked car on the opposite side of the road.

"Whoops," he said, momentarily letting his foot off the gas in hesitation. "Fuck it, I'll just have to figure that shit out tomorrow." He managed to get the truck back under control and sped toward the main road leading back to campus. Vincent realized he was holding his breath—the four-lane road with no median could be dangerous in the best of conditions. They had to make a left out of the neighborhood, and visibility was almost nonexistent.

Somehow, Tony guided the truck safely across two lanes and was able to get the vehicle stabilized despite the massive amounts of snow and ice covering the asphalt. It seemed like they were going to make it back safely.

"Man, can you believe what just happened?" Tony said, turning around to grab Vincent's attention.

"Look out!" the girl up front screeched, as another car's brake lights came into view a few yards ahead.

Tony yanked the wheel to the left to avoid rear-ending the car in front of them, but the lack of traction on the roadway sent them sliding sideways into oncoming traffic. He struggled to regain control, but there was no friction beneath the wheels, and the truck continued to slide across the opposite lanes.

For a split second, Vincent registered the sound of sirens blaring, and as he looked out of the rear passenger side window, he saw the lights of a fire truck rushing toward him.

CHAPTER FOURTEEN

Vincent's head snapped forward, jolting him awake as the plane's landing gear made contact with the runway, filling the cabin with the roar of outside air resistance.

When did he get on a plane?

And where exactly was he going?

He had a fleeting thought about Kaitlin and Tony, but before he could dig through the events leading up to their demise, a gentle squeeze on his arm startled him out of his stupor. All thoughts of the past dissolved as he locked eyes with the young woman sitting in the seat next to him.

"I was starting to worry you would never wake up," Lisa said, a half-serious look on her face. "You weren't joking when you said you needed a big nap. I'm worried about you, sweetheart—you're working yourself too hard. It's going to catch up to you eventually if you're not careful."

Without waiting for a response, she gave his arm another loving squeeze, flashed a smile, and got up to grab her bag from the overhead bins.

Lisa was a sight for sore eyes after these last few days. She seemed so young and light compared to the last time Vincent had seen her, like the old pictures that served as a harsh reminder of simpler times and the relentlessness of aging. If he had to guess, he'd say they were in their late twenties or early thirties, and he made a mental note to try and grab a newspaper in the airport to confirm.

Ding-Ding.

"Ladies and gentlemen," came the pilot's voice over the intercom, "it's my pleasure to welcome you to Jacksonville International Airport. Whether you're visiting or making your way back home, we hope you enjoy your stay and would like to thank you for flying with us today."

"Why are we in Jacksonville?" Vincent said groggily.

"Um, it's your friend's wedding," Lisa replied, raising an eyebrow at him. "Don't you remember insisting that we make this trip despite receiving what could only have been a last-minute invite?"

"I did? But what about the kids? Who's watching them if we're here?"

"Kids? Honey, we don't have any kids," Lisa said, a worried look on her face. "Are you all right? I'm starting to get freaked out over here, so if you're joking, please stop."

"I'm fine," Vincent mumbled, knowing he had to alleviate her doubts. "I'm just having trouble waking up. Must've been having a dream about kids or something—no idea why I said that. I appreciate you tagging along for David's wedding."

"You're welcome, sweetie—you know I love a good wedding! Just wish we didn't have to fly all the way to Florida for this one," Lisa responded, her concern for his sanity appearing to vanish.

Relieved, he focused on trying to get his bearings in this new reality. Name-dropping David was a risk that paid off, and now he at least had an anchor point for what this trip was all about. He remembered getting invited to this wedding years ago, but he and Lisa had decided against booking the last-minute flight and never made it. He'd come to regret that decision, feeling it was a missed opportunity to reconnect with a friend who had at one time felt like a brother.

Vincent and David had lost touch after elementary school when Vincent's mom had gotten engaged to Devon, a naval officer stationed in the DC area whom she had met through an old-school dating service. Outside of Devon's sole visit to Arizona—when he proposed—their relationship had been exclusively long-distance. So it was a bit surprising when the decision was made that they'd be packing up and moving to the east coast. Vincent wasn't particularly thrilled about leaving his life behind and starting from scratch in an unfamiliar place, understandably.

One of the biggest downsides to the move, outside of having to adjust to his potential stepfather's idiosyncrasies, was that he would never see his friends again. It stung to say goodbye. Especially to David.

As fate would have it, following his college graduation, Vincent found himself back in DC, couch-surfing while he searched for a job and serendipitously ended up reconnecting with David through mutual friends. They were both trying to jump-start their careers and decided to go in on a place in the city. It was the perfect match at the perfect time.

Of course, being two broke kids, they quickly realized that the only way they could afford to live near the bustling downtown nightlife would be to find a third roommate. Taking a chance, they posted an ad online and, after a handful of *interesting* interactions, they found Brandon, whose zany lightheartedness was the perfect addition to their group.

Their house played host to countless pre-games and parties, but it was also where Vincent began to take small steps toward true adulthood. This was the first time in his life that he began thinking and talking about the future, all while keeping one foot solidly grounded in the present.

It also happened to be when Vincent first met Lisa, sending him down the path that would lead him toward the rest of his life. Or whatever his previous existence could be called, given recent developments.

As Lisa joked with the other passengers loitering in the aisle and waiting to deplane, Vincent was transported back to that time. He could never seem to pinpoint exactly why his friendship with David deteriorated, but he knew that the day he moved out was the beginning of the end . . .

"That should do it," David said, shoving the last of Vincent's boxed belongings in the back of the moving truck. Both were struggling, having spent the night before taking one last lap around their favorite neighborhood haunts before Vincent flew the coop.

"Looks like it," Vincent said, covered in sweat and breathing heavily. He felt a sudden sadness come over him as he stared at the columns of cardboard boxes packed into the back of the U-Haul. "I'm really going to miss this place," Vincent continued. "Never imagined a day when I'd want to live anywhere else. Feels like the end of an era."

"Pshh, I always knew you'd be the first one out of here," David replied, his tone unexpectedly standoffish.

"What do you mean?"

"Come on, Vinnie, I've known you since we were little kids. You're always keeping one eye on the exit, ready to bolt the second you feel the slightest bit of fear."

"Oh, the drama," Lisa scoffed, appearing out of nowhere to throw a ratty gray blanket into the back of the truck. "Can you believe I almost forgot my baby blanket?"

"I was kind of counting on it," Vincent joked. "Can't believe that thing hasn't disintegrated in the wash by now."

"Whatever, it's just a girl thing. You boys will never understand," she replied, turning her attention to David. "So, what's Vince so scared of, huh?"

David shifted uncomfortably before locking eyes with Vincent.

"He's scared of ending up alone. That's why you two are moving in together so quickly."

"Ha!" Lisa couldn't help herself. "We've been dating for over a year. In what universe are we moving 'quickly'?"

"She's got a point there, David," Vincent chimed in.

A look of betrayal flashed across David's face, quickly replaced by one of practiced indifference. "I guess you two are just perfect for each other. Can't wait for the wedding," he replied, rolling his eyes.

"Well, you better turn that attitude around before then if you're still planning to be my best man," Vincent said, hoping the olive branch would ease the tension.

Before David could respond, they were distracted by the sound of screeching tires and a loud boom coming from around the corner. They immediately headed toward the noise to see what had happened and make sure nobody was hurt. As they rounded the corner, they instantly recognized the bright red 1998 Pontiac Sunfire that had popped the curb and collided with their neighbor's trash cans.

"Am I too late?" Brandon said, not bothering to acknowledge the absurdity of his entrance. "What else y'all need to get packed up?"

Lisa rolled her eyes but couldn't suppress a smile.

"Your timing is impeccable," David said, "We literally just put the last box in the back of the truck."

"Damn," Brandon muttered, seeming genuinely disappointed. "I'm sorry, guys. I really wanted to help out, but I just got distracted and lost track of time."

"Lost track of time? What were you—" Lisa started to ask before Vincent placed a gentle hand on her arm and took over.

"Since you couldn't help us load up, how about you come with us to the new place and help us unpack the truck? We'll grab some beers on the way and order some pizza. Whaddya say?"

"Free pizza and beer? Hell yeah, brother. Count me in!" Brandon replied.

"Yay!" Lisa cheered.

"Offer is open to you too, David. How about it?"

For a moment, David's expression lifted, before darkening again. "Nah, I think I'll just hang back. I'm exhausted."

"Boo!" Lisa jeered.

"You sure?" Vincent followed up, hoping his friend would snap out of this funk.

David thought for a second but ended up shaking his head. "I'm gonna stay," he mumbled. "Don't feel like heading out of the city."

"Oh, come on!" Lisa said. "It's just over the bridge. Not even a half an hour away! We're still going to see each other all the time."

"Sure," David replied, "but I'm beat. You guys have fun tonight. We'll catch up next weekend or something."

"Your loss," Brandon interjected, slapping David on the back and heading toward the moving truck.

Lisa followed, but Vincent hung back for a second.

"Guess this is it, huh?" David said, avoiding eye contact.

"Get out of here with that!" Vincent shot back. "It's like Lisa said, we're still going to hang out all the time. It's not like this is the end of our friendship or anything."

"Whatever you say," David said and walked glumly back inside.

It wasn't instantaneous, but over the next few years, the weekend hangouts became fewer and far between until eventually they stopped communicating altogether outside of the occasional "Happy Birthday" text. Brandon and Vincent stayed in touch and arguably became closer following the move. But David drifted away.

Then, one day out of the blue, Vincent and Lisa received an invite to David's wedding in St. Augustine, Florida—scheduled to take place two weeks from the date they received the letter. Vincent pushed to make the short-notice trip, feeling guilty over the way his relationship with David had evolved, but Lisa put her foot down. And that ended up being the last either of them had heard from—or about—David.

A nearby burst of laughter pulled Vincent back to the present, and he allowed himself a moment to enjoy the scene playing out in front of him before straining to catch up with yet another new reality.

There was his Lisa—cracking jokes and telling stories to a group of strangers like she'd known them her entire life. Her ability to brighten a room and make anyone her friend was one of the many things that initially attracted him to her, and it was on full display.

It had been so long since it was just the two of them that he had forgotten how breezy and free-flowing their life and relationship used to be. He was still feeling uneasy given how unstable the last few days had been, but he resolved to cherish as much of this time with Lisa as he could.

"Hey, space cadet, let's get going," Lisa said, waving a hand in front of Vincent's face. He guessed he must have once again been stuck in a thousand-yard stare.

"Huh? Oh yeah, lead the way," Vincent replied. "By the way, how long's it going to take to get to the hotel?"

"I think like forty-five minutes? We can look it up when we get to the rental car place."

Vincent looked out the window and felt his stomach drop. He hated driving in the rain, and to make things worse, it looked like it would be getting dark very soon. Oh well—it wasn't the worst thing he'd had to deal with recently.

———

In his previous life, Vincent had avoided Florida like the plague. It seemed like a place that was somehow built for the elderly, the insane, and the ultra-wealthy that were too trashy for New York or Los Angeles. He was surprised to learn that David had ended up near Jacksonville, but given their distance, he had no real way of knowing what inspired the move.

Walking through the airport, Vincent largely found his Florida hypothesis to be correct. He had never seen such a strange mishmash of people milling about as if they had never been outside of their homes before. It seemed like everyone was lost, swerving around aimlessly and apparently unaware there were other people making their way through the terminal. Vincent spotted a few people dragging their duffel bags on the ground and more than a few stumbling around shoeless. The entire building smelled like body odor.

He was close to losing his cool by the time they made it to the exit, having bumped into no less than three people stopping without warning to vacantly stare at an advertisement, but he felt a sense of relief as the line of rental car company kiosks came into view.

"Hey, babe, which company did we use?" Vincent said, picking up his stride.

"I need to double-check; it was through some sort of deal with the hotel. I don't think it was one of the big ones like a Hertz or Enterprise," she replied, scrolling through emails on her phone. "Ah, found it! It says we've booked a car with the . . . Presidential Cab Company?"

They started to slow their pace. "The Presidential Cab Company?" Vincent said, racking his brain for any knowledge of that brand. "I don't . . . I don't think I've ever heard of them. Do you see a sign up anywhere near the other kiosks?"

A quick glance told him that there was no such sign. Before Vincent could get a word out, Lisa had already jumped on her phone and was back on her email.

"It says here that a black sprinter bus outside of Baggage 2 will be available to offer customers a complementary five-minute shuttle to the office location near the long-term parking garage," Lisa said.

"Well, that's unfortunate, but not the end of the world," Vincent said, scanning the exit signs. "Look, there's the exit for Baggage 2. Let's go see if there's a shuttle we can snag."

Lisa gave him a quick nod, and they broke into a brisk march toward the nearby exit doors. Vincent was elated to see a black sprinter van idling right outside the door, and they lifted their pace into a slow trot, not knowing if it was about to take off. When they got to the door, they realized it was locked, and Vincent's heart dropped. Lisa began rapping on the door and yelling for the driver to wait.

"Whoa, whoa, whoa, lil' missy, no need to panic! We ain't goin' anywhere for the next coupla minutes," said a voice nearby, but not immediately within view.

Vincent wasn't sure if he could trust that advice until he saw a man walking around the front of the car holding a handwritten sign saying, "Presidential Cab Company." The man was smoking a Black & Mild cigarillo and looked to be anywhere between forty-five and seventy-five years old. His shoulder-length, bleached blond hair peeked out of a well-worn trucker hat, and he sported a brown Fu Manchu-style goatee, tank top, and jean shorts with no shoes. He was the epitome of the mythical "Florida Man."

"Anyway," the man continued, "I drive this heap twelve hours a day, even though them bastards don't pay me but ten dollars an hour. Here, lemme help you with your bags." He paused, grabbing Lisa's bag and leading them around to the back of the van.

As they finished packing their bags in the trunk, another couple walked up and Vincent was glad to have a buffer between himself and Florida Man once they hit the road. Their seemingly Midwestern bus mates were all too happy to keep their driver busy talking about his various conspiracy theories about world injustices and vaccines. That, or they were just too darn polite to ask him to pay attention to the road while he was driving them to their destination.

Despite the speedy ride, Vincent was not thrilled to arrive at the Presidential Cab Company's dingy, dilapidated, strip-mall-based head-quarters. Even in the best weather conditions, this place would look drab, and there didn't seem to be any rental cars in sight.

"You sure this is the right place?" Vincent leaned over and whispered to Lisa.

"I don't know. We're here for *your* friend's wedding. You think I've ever been to Jacksonville before?" she replied.

Before he could get another word in, Florida Man popped out of his seat, lighting a cigarette faster than Vincent had ever seen a human do before, and announced, "All right, it's officially my break, so y'all feel free to grab yer belongings and git on the road to wherever the hell it is yer goin'!"

He let out an exuberant cackle followed by an extended cough, hopped out of the van and was off, likely never to be seen again.

Lisa and Vincent exchanged a look, grabbed their bags, and hustled over to the rundown storefront. Vincent was eager to get on the road as quickly as possible and didn't feel like getting stuck behind the "nice" Midwestern couple while they wasted time chatting it up with whoever was manning the front desk of the rental car office.

Oddly enough, their experience with the rental company was surprisingly smooth, and within ten minutes, they had loaded their bags into a bright green Honda CR-V and were headed south toward St. Augustine, the coastal town where the wedding was set to take place.

CHAPTER FIFTEEN

It didn't take long for Vincent to learn that the rules of the road were much different in Florida. Despite the rain, it seemed like every car on the highway (including the semitrucks) was going twenty miles per hour over the speed limit and swerving across multiple lanes without warning.

Man, this one might not last too long, he thought to himself, gripping the wheel tightly and frantically checking his mirrors to ensure he wasn't about to get run off the road by one of these maniacs.

Lisa was uncharacteristically quiet in the passenger seat, which made Vincent even more nervous than her typical dramatic gasps did when he was behind the wheel.

"You okay over there, sport?" he said playfully.

"I'm just trying not to lose my shit. This is fucking terrifying!" Lisa replied without taking her eyes off the road.

"Ha! Well, I appreciate you keeping your cool. We should be getting off the highway pretty soon."

"I sure hope so," Lisa muttered, keeping her eyes on the road.

Twenty minutes later, their exit came into view, and Vincent could feel them both collectively exhale as they finally pulled off the highway.

However, it wasn't long until he began to feel anxious again. Their directions led them to a dimly lit two-lane road that felt as if it were in a different country.

"This place is creepy," Lisa said. "I thought St. Augustine was supposed to be nice. This feels like some backwoods, *Deliverance*-type scenery."

"I'm pretty sure we're heading in the right direction," Vincent responded, double-checking that the hotel address in the GPS was correct. "Yeah, it says we're on this road for another ten miles, and then I guess it'll spit us out within a few miles of the hotel."

"That's not too bad. I'm sorry, something about this place is really giving me the heebie-jeebies. I can't believe David lives down here now—I never got that Florida man vibe from him."

"Same here, but sometimes life pulls you in directions you wouldn't expect," he said, not sure if he was making an excuse for David or talking about the absurdity of his current circumstances.

"Very wise, Mr. Confucius. Please tell me more about the mysteries of life," Lisa teased.

"All right, all right, I'll keep my musings to myself, you goober. By the way, do you know if Brandon's coming to this wedding?"

"Um, I'm pretty sure he's flying in tomorrow morning. Are you okay? You're the one who's been texting with him about all the logistics, not me."

"Oh right, totally forgot." He turned to give Lisa a quick apologetic smile. "Sorry, this place is really messing me up. So glad we'll be able to count on him as a buffer during this wedding. I tried getting a feel for the guest list from David, but he never responded. Must've just been busy with wedding stuff or something."

"Among other things," Lisa said. "Oh look, there's our turn! And I think we have time to freshen up and make it to the post-rehearsal dinner reception. I don't know about you, but I need a drink after this weird drive."

"Same here—it's only going to be fun stuff from here on out!" Vincent said, trying to stay as optimistic as possible.

———

They were able to smoothly move through the hotel check-in and get themselves put together with time to spare before they were expected at the nearby welcome party. Vincent managed to shake off the stress of the past few hours, and he and Lisa began the night joking and giggling like a pair of teenagers. He had all but forgotten how loose and silly the two of them used to be together before the responsibilities and stress associated with parenthood. Even still, it felt like there was something missing. Somehow, this version of Lisa and Vincent was still a few years away from the true understanding they'd reached in their relationship.

"So where is this shindig?" Vincent asked, shrugging off the nagging doubts and trying to enjoy *this* Lisa as much as possible while he could.

"It's at the Gin Rickey, which is about a mile and a half away," she replied. "I'm thinking we take a cab."

"For sure. It's still pouring, and I'm not trying to walk around in wet shoes all night."

"My thoughts exactly. Shall we?"

"After you, mi amor," Vincent said with a bow.

Lisa blushed. "Ooh, Mister Palmer, when did you become such a gentleman?"

"I guess weddings bring out the romantic in me," Vincent responded, extending his arm as an invitation to escort her to the elevators. "Let's blow this joint."

By this point in their lives, he and Lisa were veteran wedding guests, having attended dozens of celebrations over the years. But this wedding was a wild card. They hadn't seen David in forever and had never actually met the bride (whom they continually had to remind each other was named Rebecca). The invitations and wedding venue gave the impression that the big day would be an upscale affair, so they assumed the same of the rehearsal reception and dressed accordingly. When Vincent heard the name Gin Rickey, he expected some sort of fancy restaurant with twenty-dollar specialty cocktails and egregiously priced seafood. But as soon as they pulled up, Vincent realized he may have missed the mark—this place looked like a dive bar. Getting out of the car, they exchanged a concerned look.

"Well, I guess this is it," Lisa said, uncertainly. "It doesn't look like what I had expected."

"Me neither, but maybe this is their favorite bar or something?" Vincent said, stepping up to the deteriorating wooden door of the bar and putting a hand on the rusted door pull. "Let's see what the scene is in there before we jump to any conclusions."

"Okay, but if this isn't that fun, let's sneak away and find a nice cocktail bar or something. I didn't get dressed up to sit on sticky barstools and drink Bud Lights all night."

"Oh, you fancy, huh? Well, please allow me to get the door for you, your majesty." Vincent swung the door open and dipped into a bow.

"Oh, you *really* think you're funny today," Lisa said, slapping him in the arm with her clutch as she crossed the threshold into the bar.

Vincent immediately began scanning for any indications that they were in the right place, but all he could see was a long rectangular room with a band setting up on a makeshift stage area toward the back of the bar.

"Are we totally sure this is the right place?" Vincent said. "I don't see anything that even remotely resembles a wedding rehearsal dinner or afterparty."

"Yeah, me neither. . . . Wait! Look over there." Lisa pointed to a doorway situated next to the bar that opened to a narrow hallway. "I bet there's some sort of reserved area back there or something. Let's go check it out!" She grabbed his hand and pulled him along.

The end of the hallway gave way to a set of double doors opening up to a staircase leading to a second floor. Vincent could hear the hum of conversation, clattering of dishes and silverware, and chairs scraping across the floor as patrons moved throughout the upper level. The smell of seafood wafted down.

Lisa gave Vincent a shrug and took a step toward the stairs, but he grabbed her arm to stop her, nodding toward a sign at the bottom of the stairwell: "Reserved for a Private Event until 8:30 p.m."

Vincent glanced down at his watch, "I think we're a little early. I'm guessing they're still wrapping up their rehearsal dinner and will be opening things up for other guests afterward."

Lisa nodded. "That's all right; it'll be nice to grab a drink or two before we have to start mixing it up with strangers," she replied, flashing a smile that he knew meant trouble.

"Come on, Vince, you filthy animal—let's go knock back a few cold ones and get our minds right for this party," she continued, grabbing his hand and heading back toward the bar.

The band was going through their soundcheck as they made their way to the only two open seats at the bar.

"Honestly, I'm kinda glad we have some time to just chill for a bit. I feel like I've been stressed out since the minute we landed," Lisa said.

"Yeah, same here. Plus, I'm starving, so it'll be nice to get some food in us before we start getting into the free drinks. You want to split a chicken strip basket if they have one down here?"

"Now you're speaking my language! And you know we have to wash those down with a couple Miller High Lifes. That feels like the right thing to do when you're in Florida," she replied.

"Well, that and cocaine," Vincent said with a wry smile.

Without missing a beat, Lisa came back with "You holdin'? Cuz I'll rip a few lines in the bathroom right now."

For a second they both sat there and stared at each other, each daring the other person to call their bluff. Finally, after what felt like forever, Vincent broke and they both burst into laughter.

"Man, I completely forgot how much fun we used to have killing time like this at random bars on the weekends," Vincent said.

"What do you mean 'used to have'? We literally did this last weekend, you weirdo!"

"Oh right, must've just slipped into another reality there for a second."

"Oh no, you're not going to be making these simulation theory jokes all night, are you? Nobody gets them, and they're not funny," Lisa said, craning her neck to get a better view of the bar layout. "I'll be right back; I'm going to go find the ladies' room. There better be some chicken strips and an ice-cold beer sitting on this bar when I get back, or you're going to need to find another date for the wedding."

"Ha! You better not take too long or there might not be any chicken *or* beer left for you!"

"You're on, mister," Lisa said and snuck a kiss on Vincent's cheek before darting off in search of the bathroom.

Left alone at the bar, Vincent heard the opening chords to Fleetwood Mac's "Never Going Back Again" and was instantly transported back to the night Lisa had walked into his life all those years ago.

He had organized a happy hour for his team to celebrate the start of summer and, as was common practice back then, had proceeded to bar hop across the city's hot spots. Afternoon faded into evening and what was left of Vincent's crew made their way to the Aviary, a rooftop bar with a near-panoramic downtown view. Despite the perfect weather, there wasn't much of a crowd that night, but there was a musician setting up with an acoustic guitar. Ignoring his colleagues' pleas to head somewhere busier, Vincent decided to settle in and listen to the first few songs of her set. As she serenaded the sparse audience—and Vincent's team departed in search of cheap thrills—he grabbed an open seat at the bar and ordered an old fashioned.

A few songs later, when the singer began playing the opening bars of "Never Going Back Again," Vincent heard a voice directly behind him exclaim, "Oh my God, this is my favorite song!"

Something about the exuberance in her tone tickled Vincent's sense of curiosity and he instinctively turned to see who the voice belonged to. As luck would have it, he turned right as the owner of the voice was about to pass him on her way up to the front of the stage, colliding with Vincent's chest and sending his drink crashing down to the floor, stopping the guitarist mid-chorus.

Her face immediately turned pink, betraying her embarrassment, but the moment they locked eyes, they started cracking up and began sloppily trying to scoop up the larger glass shards scattered across the floor. Vincent was now wearing his old fashioned and figured it was probably time to head home and spare those around him the unpleasantness of his recently applied bourbon cologne. But Lisa wouldn't have it. She insisted on buying him another drink and, after some light haranguing, he agreed, under one condition—that she would meet him for breakfast the next morning.

To this day, he still wasn't sure how he'd gotten the nerve to make that request—Lisa was, and remained, a bombshell. The kind of girl that he never would've had the courage to approach under normal circumstances. But to his great delight, she agreed to see him again, and the rest was history.

Lisa returned from the bathroom, thrilled to see that the kitchen had kicked out a basket of piping-hot chicken tenders and fries for them to dig into. Her excitement over such a small win filled Vincent's heart up in a way that he'd desperately been missing. How stupid he'd been to take this woman for granted! Unsure that he'd get another chance to see her express pure joy over something so trivial, he quietly soaked up the moment.

"What are you looking at me like that for?" she suddenly said, looking up.

"No reason," he said, the throat filter automatically speaking up for him. He wanted to tell her how he felt, how incredibly special he realized she was, and to apologize for not being the man that she deserved—he wanted to be honest and true with her—but nothing came out. Instead, he reached forward and tenderly wiped a spot of ketchup from her lip. It was the best he could do.

As they made their way through their chicken and beer combo, the band got fired up and launched into a collection of oldies that seemed customized to their exact taste. "It's like they tailored this set to play all our favorite songs," said Vincent. "That's a bit odd, don't you think?"

Lisa rolled her eyes. "You're the first person I've ever heard complain about a band playing music they like. Just enjoy it and stop searching for any deeper meaning. Life's more fun that way."

Before Vincent could muster a response, the first notes of "Brandy, You're a Fine Girl" rang out, and Lisa jumped out of her seat and made a beeline for the makeshift dance floor, where she proceeded to sing and dance as if there was nobody in the room but the band and herself. Before long, she was joined by a few other inspired bar patrons, and the entire mood within the bar lifted. Vincent sat in awe of what his future wife had just unwittingly started.

How could he ever have wanted to cut his time with her short?

Before he could fully process that sentiment, the band eased into "Days Like This" by Van Morrison, and Lisa motioned for Vincent to join her. He instantly sprung out of his seat and joined her in a spontaneous slow dance. Lisa seemed to melt into his chest, and Vincent felt himself hold her a little bit tighter than he normally would have. How did the band know this was their song? Throwing his normal aversion to PDA out the window, he leaned in for a deep kiss as the band let the final notes ring out.

"Oh my, Mr. Palmer! That was quite unexpected," said a blushing Lisa.

"Hey, I can be romantic every once in a while," Vincent said with a wink.

"Apparently! I wouldn't mind if you kept that same energy this whole weekend."

"I think that can be arranged," Vincent coyly replied. "But as much as I'd prefer to stay down here dancing the night away, do you think we should head up and make an appearance at David's party?"

"Ugh, I guess so. Let's close out and head upstairs."

———

They stood in the doorway scanning the room for a friendly face. Within seconds of entering the space reserved for private events, it became clear that they knew almost nobody at this party. Lisa was the first one to put all the pieces together. "I mean, we shouldn't be surprised—none of our friends but Brandon were invited. Seems like David found himself a whole new crew down here."

"Yeah, I guess you're right, but . . . I just thought there would be somebody here that I knew. It's not like I never met any of his friends from high school or college," Vincent said under his breath.

"Oh well, I'm sure we'll run into his family at some point. Screw it—let's grab a drink and go make some new Florida friends," she said, grabbing Vincent's hand and marching him toward the bar.

After they each secured a vodka soda, they took a casual lap around the room. The freedom that accompanied relative anonymity had given Vincent a boost—he felt like a lion stalking through the jungle, patiently searching for the right people to engage and not caring if it happened or it didn't.

Suddenly, Lisa made her move and inserted herself into a pack of couples laughing at a joke Vincent didn't hear. Without missing a beat, she jumped in with, "Oh my God, like can you believe these airline companies have the gall to call it 'First Class' on domestic flights? I've been in taxis with comfier seats and better service than the garbage we just dealt with from Delta."

Vincent was dumbfounded. He had no clue why Lisa would say something like that. They'd never flown first class and certainly weren't bougie enough to justify that tone.

Who was this person?

The woman next to Lisa grabbed her arm like she had just found her soulmate and excitedly responded, "Right? My husband and I had the worst experience the last time we flew Delta. Did you know that if you complain they'll give you a refund in points? We do that all the time, even if nothing bad actually happened," she said, nodding to demonstrate that she agreed with her own opinion.

"I've never thought of that! Man, you guys are really smart. Where are you all from?"

"Oh, we're locals—me and my husband grew up ten minutes up the road, and his daddy owns the Mercedes dealership. I'm Tammy, and that over there is my stud-muffin of a husband, Lance. Lance!" Tammy yelled, startling Vincent. "Introduce yourself to these two newbies."

Her husband turned away from his conversation and said, "Oh hey, I'm Lance."

After a quick round of perfunctory handshakes, he asked, "How do y'all know Rebecca?"

"Oh, we've never met Rebecca," Lisa said. "We're on David's side. Vincent was living with him when we first met. What about you all?"

"We met down here a while back," Lance said, the vagueness giving his statement an almost sinister undertone.

"What do you do?" Vincent said.

Lance slowly turned and fixed Vincent with a borderline aggressive stare. "I work for my dad at the dealership. But not like a car salesman or nothing, like operations. Sometimes community outreach if we need to get out there and *build awareness*."

"Oh, nice . . . and that's what David is doing now too? It's been a minute since we caught up."

"You sure do have a lot of questions, don't you, city boy?" Lance snapped, leaning in well beyond Vincent's personal-space comfort zone. Vincent didn't budge.

"Cut it out, Lance," Tammy said, stepping between the two and giving him a hard smack on the arm.

"Yeah, they work together," she said over her shoulder before turning back to Lance. "Would you just be nice for once? Jesus! I'm over here trying to make some new friends, and you gotta be on your bullshit for no reason at all . . ."

Vincent felt a tug on his hand and heard Lisa whisper, "Let's make our escape. I get the feeling they're just getting started."

He waited until they were safely out of earshot before debriefing with Lisa about the bizarre interaction they had just experienced. "What was that guy's problem?" Vincent muttered.

"Oh, who gives a shit! He looks like a wannabe cool guy anyway, probably just trying to impress his stuck-up girlfriend," she loudly replied, glaring over in Lance and Tammy's direction. It was so unlike Lisa to do something like that that Vincent froze for a second before saying, "You're probably right, but maybe let's try not to announce our criticisms of the guest list to the entire room." He kept his tone even, hoping to lower the temperature.

"Oh right," Lisa replied, giving him a nod of understanding. "Gotta keep it cool, stay under the radar."

"Exactly," Vincent replied, scanning the room for somewhere they could anchor themselves and trying to process what he'd just witnessed. The Lisa he knew was never so outwardly confrontational. Although he did have some vague recollections of her being a bit hot under the collar when they first started dating. Maybe this Lisa just hadn't fully mellowed out yet.

"Look, there's an open high-top over in the corner near the bar. Let's go post up there, I'm sure we'll be able to grab David the next time he heads over for a drink."

"Good idea," Lisa agreed. "I could use another myself. Follow my lead, Tex."

"Tex? Since when is that one of my nicknames?"

"I dunno, I just made it up on the spot. Whaddaya think?" Lisa said.

"A little strange. We'll see if it sticks, you goofball. Go grab that table, and I'll get you a refill."

Having been burned by their first attempt at conversing with strangers, Vincent opted to spend the next half hour safely observing from afar. In spite of—or maybe because of—their voluntary isolation, Vincent and Lisa were having a ball people-watching and making up theories about everyone's lives.

"What do you think that guy does?" Vincent said, subtly gesturing toward a man in a tweed jacket with a long gray-and-black ponytail and lightly tinted sunglasses.

"Hmm," Lisa deliberated, "I bet he's either a surfing instructor or . . . the owner of an ice-cream shop."

"What?" Vincent nearly spit out his drink. "The owner of an ice-cream shop? What gives you that impression?"

"I dunno, he just seems like the type," she replied.

"You don't think his hair might get in the ice cream? Wouldn't that be bad for business?"

"I said he was the *owner*, not the one scooping the ice cream," she said matter-of-factly. "What about you? What's your guess?"

"Easy," Vincent said. "He's either a professor or a librarian."

"You think David knows any librarians? You're crazy!" Lisa teased.

"No, I'm not!" Vincent fired back gamely. "Anyone wearing a tweed jacket is either a professor, a librarian, or an author. Everyone knows that."

"Whatever you say." Lisa took a sip of her drink and continued, under her breath, "But I still think he's the ice-cream man."

No matter what the man's occupation was, it was very clear that this was going to be an *eclectic* wedding. There didn't appear to be any consistent throughline to the guests at this welcome party, and the room was organized into voluntary cliques, some of which appeared to be family and some that didn't. Strangely, they couldn't seem to determine which friends were David's and which were Rebecca's.

"Look at that group in the back," Lisa said, rudely pointing in their direction. Again, Vincent had the funny feeling her mannerisms weren't quite lining up with the Lisa he knew.

He looked over, gently pushing her pointing finger down as he did. "Something about them seems off," he agreed.

"Almost *dangerous*," Lisa added, sounding excited by the prospect. The men of the group seemed to be constantly sizing up the rest of the room, mean-mugging anyone who came near and generally giving off the vibe that they didn't want anyone overhearing their conversations. Vincent was trying to avoid jumping to any conclusions, but his gut was telling him that this crew was up to no good.

Lisa snapped him out of his trance before he could go too far down that rabbit hole.

"David!" she shouted, intercepting the groom on his way to the bar and wrapping him in a huge hug. "Oh my God, it's been so long since we've seen you! Congratulations!"

"Oh, um hey, Lisa, thanks," David mumbled. "Glad you guys could make it."

"Hey, congrats, big guy! We're really happy for you," Vincent said, giving David the opening he needed to escape Lisa's overenthusiastic grasp. Vincent couldn't remember Lisa being quite this big a fan.

"Good to see you, Vinnie. It's been too long. Glad you guys could be here."

An odd, slightly uncomfortable silence followed David's greeting—it had been ages since they'd had a proper conversation. Vincent could feel a complicated mix of emotions bubbling up to the surface. He sensed that David was trying to process the same complex feelings. He tried to say something meaningful about this, but the words stuck in his throat in a jumble—that damn filter thing again.

Lisa broke the silence with a friendly, "So how're you feeling about tomorrow? And where's the lucky lady?"

David shrugged. "Oh, she's around here somewhere, probably out front with her friends having a smoke or something."

"Well, we can't wait to meet her. Must be a pretty special girl to have nailed you down! Last I recall, you were quite comfortable living the single life," Vincent said, gently elbowing David in the ribs.

"Yeah, yeah, but everyone has to settle down at some point. Don't worry, I'm sure you'll get the chance to meet her this weekend."

"I certainly hope so!" Lisa chimed in. "It's your wedding, after all!"

"Yeah," David replied flatly. "Guess it is."

"So, how do you like St. Augustine? Never thought I'd see you turn into a Florida man!" Vincent said, trying to lighten the mood.

"It's fine. Same shit, different city, you know?"

Vincent couldn't come up with anything else to say. This felt like the type of conversation he would have at some lame networking event or business conference. Before he could come up with anything, David cleared his throat. "Listen," he said, "it's great to see you guys and I hope you have a good time this weekend. I've gotta grab a drink real quick and keep making the rounds. Drink as much as you want; we've got the bar covered for another hour." David turned abruptly and was gone before either of them could process the fact that he had just blown them off.

"He does *not* look good," Lisa said in a hushed tone, gesturing for Vincent to follow her back to their high-top.

"What do you mean?" Vincent said. "I wasn't really paying attention. I was more focused on how it felt like we just had a conversation with a total stranger."

"Well, yeah, that's kind of my point too," she said with a faraway look. "He looks like a man on the brink of death. Like he's gonna off himself."

Vincent felt a chill run up his spine. *Now was the time*, he thought. The time to tell Lisa the truth. But he couldn't—the thing in his throat that had prevented him from voicing his real thoughts and opinions earlier was causing a full-on blockage. It felt like there was a potato stuck in there.

"His skin looked bad," Lisa went on, "almost gray, and his cheeks were more drawn in than I remember. His teeth didn't look good, and I swear I saw a neck tattoo peeking out over his collar."

She paused, and Vincent was surprised to see tears rolling down her cheeks.

"Plus, his eyes were pretty glassy. It didn't seem like he was functioning at full capacity upstairs. It's so sad."

"I'm not sure . . ." Vincent started, and then it dawned on him. "You think he's on drugs?"

"I mean, I can't say for sure, but that's definitely not the David I remember."

"You're right about that, but there's no way his mom would be letting this all happen if she had any suspicion he was still into any of that shit."

Before Lisa could respond they heard glasses shatter across the room. On cue, David's mom, Susan, raised her hand and slurred, "Sorry, sorry errrybody, isss my fault. I don't typically wear these shoes."

"Holy shit, she's hammered. That is not a good sign," Vincent said in disbelief.

"What do you mean? Who is that?" Lisa replied.

"That's Susan, David's mom. She doesn't drink."

"Certainly doesn't look that way to me," Lisa said.

"Well, something must've changed," Vincent sighed.

"This is going to be a strange wedding, isn't it?"

Vincent locked eyes with Lisa. He wrapped his arm around her and gave a solemn nod. "Probably, but none of this is our problem, so why don't we have a few more cocktails and do our best to enjoy the rest of this evening?"

"Don't threaten me with a good time, Tex. You play your cards right, and you might even get lucky tonight."

"I'll hold you to that," Vincent said with a wink. "I'll go grab us a few martinis. Don't go anywhere."

As was their usual custom at weddings, Vincent and Lisa spent the next half hour discussing what their future wedding might look like. Prior to his proposal, these conversations were like walking a tightrope with Vincent doing his best to stay engaged, but not enough to imply a ring was in her near future. But tonight felt completely different. Not only did Vincent know how their actual wedding would turn out; he also knew how their marriage would end.

Lisa didn't seem to pick up on his reticence to dive into the conversation. Instead she was just tipsy enough to put herself out there and was describing in detail an event that was nearly the complete opposite of their actual wedding. He was torn—it was sweet watching her light up with excitement imagining their future life together, but underpinning that was an intense guilt tying his stomach in knots. Once again, he was overcome with the urge to interrupt and spill his guts, but an obstinate lump in his throat kept his responses relegated to soft conversational grunts of acknowledgment. Lisa, on the other hand, was having so much fun building out her dream wedding that she didn't seem to mind his lack of input.

As Lisa was describing her ideal lineup of bridesmaids and Vincent was doing his best to hide his mortification, he noticed some commotion toward the back corner of the room where David and his groomsmen had congregated. He was far enough away that he couldn't hear what was being said, but he could tell that David was frustrated with whatever was happening. Suddenly, they all put on their raincoats and began heading toward the door.

"And so, I think it would make sense to only have my sister and five of my best girlfriends. More than seven bridesmaids seems like too many, don't you think? Wait," Lisa said, stopping and leaning forward, "where are they all going?"

"I'm not sure, but it doesn't seem like they're too happy about whatever it is they're leaving to go deal with. Uh-oh, here comes Susan," Vincent said, watching her stagger over to intercept David as he made his way toward the door.

Vincent didn't need to hear what was being said to know that Susan was voicing her frustrations while trying not to draw attention to the situation. And while she was talking with David, her second husband Bob decided to insert himself into the conversation. It was immediately clear that Bob had overstepped and made the problem worse.

A few seconds later, David brushed them off and led the rest of the crew out the door without addressing the room or offering any explanation as to why he was ditching his own party.

"This is not going to be good," Vincent whispered to Lisa as they watched Susan and Bob frantically discuss whatever had just happened. After their short conversation, Bob stepped into the middle of the room, and Susan put her face in her hands.

"Uh, excuse me, everyone. Excuse me," he slurred, half-heartedly tapping on his glass like he was about to give a toast. A handful of guests stopped talking and turned their attention toward him.

"Uh, my name is Bob, and I'm David's, uh, stepdad . . . for those of you who don't already know that."

More people stopped talking and focused on Bob, allowing his voice more room to project.

"So, we just want to say thank you all for coming to this rehearsal. We're very grateful to the Bendettis for their hospitality throughout this whole week and wanted to let you all know that we can't wait for Rebecca to officially become a member of the family."

A few people whistled and hollered, apparently unaware that neither Rebecca nor David were in the room.

"So, before you all go, just be sure to grab one of those bags of shit over there on that table." He paused and gestured toward a table near the exit covered in small gift bags, as Vincent tried to process one of the most inappropriate host comments he'd ever witnessed. "We spent way too much time putting those together for all of you," Bob added, "and just want to make sure everyone takes one."

Bob paused again, apparently expecting a reaction from the crowd. Was it laughter? No one was laughing. Vincent stood there frozen in place, eyes wide and mouth agape. He felt deeply uncomfortable but couldn't look away—like he was watching a slow-motion car crash.

After a few seconds of awkward silence, Bob continued, "Well, uh, it's last call at the bar here, so if you want another drink, I'd advise you grab one now. And don't forget to take one of those stupid bags of shit on your way out. Please. See you all tomorrow."

Taking his own advice, Bob headed toward the bar as the room filled with a smattering of uncertain applause and confused murmuring.

"Now that's how you end a party," Lisa said. "What the fuck was that? I've never seen anything like that happen at a rehearsal reception before. I hope David's all right. Something about this all seems very strange."

"You're not wrong," Vincent said. He was genuinely concerned for David's well-being, but he couldn't bring himself to waste an evening with Lisa chasing ghosts. For all he knew his time with her could be nearing its end.

"Let's grab a beer for the road," he said, "and head back to the hotel. I think we'll have a little more fun there anyway."

"You're going to make me blush," Lisa said, giving Vincent a sultry look. "Lead the way, Mr. Palmer; I'm right behind you."

CHAPTER SIXTEEN

When Vincent opened his eyes, he was enveloped in complete darkness. *Here we go again*, he thought, bracing for yet another new reality. But instead he was greeted with a splitting headache.

"Ugh, stop breathing so loud over there, would you?" he heard Lisa say from somewhere nearby.

Startled, he sat up and rubbed his eyes. After a few minutes, they adjusted to the darkness, and he realized that he was back in their hotel room. And Lisa was still here. He hadn't made it through a full day in the same place since his forty-fifth birthday. Did this mean his mystical journey was over? Could *this* be his new reality?

His head was pounding as he scanned the room and tried to gather himself. He dug into his memory to retrace their steps, but things started to get fuzzy after the abrupt ending to the event. *Man, we really got after it last night.*

Behind him Lisa mumbled, "Can you grab me some ibuprofen out of my toiletry bag? My head is killing me."

"Sure thing; I'm in the same boat. We sure had ourselves a night, huh?"

"One for the record books. We're going to have to find a big, greasy brunch to soak up all this alcohol."

"I'm game, as long as you don't mind me having a Bloody Mary. I think I'm going to need a little hair of the dog if I'm going to make it through this whole day."

"Drinking in the morning? That's not like you at all—this is going to be fun!"

"I hope so. Here's your ibuprofen," Vincent said, making his way back from the bathroom and catching a glimpse of the alarm clock on the bedside table. "It's only six forty-five. Let's see if we can get another hour of sleep before we dive into the day."

"That sounds good to me. Get over here and give me some snuggles," Lisa murmured.

"Yes, ma'am," Vincent responded, grateful for every extra second he was getting to spend with her.

———

A few hours later, they were in the lobby anxiously waiting to meet up with Brandon so they could grab some food and start to cure their massive hangovers. Never one to sit still for very long, Lisa was chatting up the receptionist, trying to get an inside line on any hidden brunch gems while Vincent sat quietly and tried to make sense of what had occurred last night.

It dawned on him that he never really found out what happened to David after he moved to Florida. Vincent didn't know what he ended up doing for a career, whom he'd stayed in touch with, or. . . . He hadn't even known if David was still alive. It made him feel like a rotten friend, but given the weirdness of last night, he wasn't sure it was such a terrible thing that he and David lost touch all those years ago.

Before he could get too lost in thought, he heard a nearby *ding* and looked over to see Brandon emerging from the elevator, sporting his signature goofy grin and shaggy haircut.

"Well, well, well! Look what the cat dragged in! How've you been, big fella?" Vincent said, wrapping his former roommate in a bear hug. "Long time no see," he added.

"Ooof, nice to see you too," Brandon replied, trying to wrangle out of Vincent's grasp. "But I saw you guys last week, remember? We grabbed a few beers down at Mister Day's and watched the fights."

"Oh right, totally forgot. Sorry, me and the Mrs. over there had a few too many last night, so I'm a little foggy this morning," Vincent replied, reminding himself to think before leaking anything else that might raise suspicion.

"Brandon!" Lisa yelled from the front desk, flashing a huge smile and waving. "I just got the best recommendation for brunch down by the water. And apparently there are a bunch of cute shops nearby, so we'll have something to do before the ceremony instead of drinking Coors Light and listening to Limp Bizkit in a hotel room."

Brandon and Vincent gave each other a quick guilty glance, silently acknowledging that Lisa had boxed them in.

"That sounds good to me, as long as wherever we're going serves alcohol, because my last twenty-four hours have been a living nightmare," Brandon said, matching Lisa's energy and ripping a "Let's go, girls!"

And with that they headed out into the dreary, overcast strangeness of St. Augustine, Florida.

———

As soon as they were seated at the nearby beachfront brunch spot, Brandon dove into the story of his travel odyssey. Apparently Vincent and Lisa landed in Jacksonville right before a huge storm front had grounded all flights in the southeast, causing Brandon to be rerouted through Atlanta, Raleigh, and finally Miami before he was able to land safely in Jacksonville and make his way down to St. Augustine. As a kicker, his luggage didn't make it on his final flight.

"I'm praying that a courier shows up at the hotel at some point before the wedding. Otherwise, I'm just going to have to buy myself a Hawaiian shirt and stay out of pictures. How was last night? You guys get to see David at all?"

"It was . . . weird," Vincent said, uncertain of how much he should share.

Lisa, on the other hand, took Vincent's hesitation as her cue to jump right into the story. He let her take the lead since she was on a roll and hitting all the key points about their peculiar near confrontation with Lance and Tammy, Susan's drinking, David's aloofness and Irish good-bye, and Bob's sloppy sendoff.

"Damn, that does sound like a strange evening. Even compared to what I've heard about David lately," Brandon said, cryptically trailing off and digging into his tall stack of pancakes.

"Wait, you've been in touch with David?" Vincent chimed in. "I thought he had basically cut everyone out since he left town."

"Nah, we still text every now and then. Mostly about the Orioles, but every once in a while, he'll open up a bit. I never get the full story, just bits and pieces. Shit, I was hanging out with him the night he got arrested down in Virginia Beach."

"He got arrested in Virginia Beach?" Lisa yelled, startling a small family sitting nearby. "Sorry," she mumbled, and gave the family an apologetic wave. "What did he get arrested for? Did you see it happen? Did he go to jail? When was this?"

"Easy there, partner—one question at a time." Brandon took a second to finish chewing his mouthful of pancakes and then contin-ued. "It was about a year or so ago. I was down there visiting my folks and must've posted something online or something. Anyway, I'm hang-ing out at the beach and all of a sudden I get this text from David saying he's in town and asking if I want to grab a few drinks. So I said 'Sure,' figuring it'd be nice to catch up, and I met him downtown later that night. Now, when I say our boy was drunk, I'm talking about Hooter Brown drunk—trouble finishing sentences, stumbling about, real slurry . . . you know. After an hour, I decide it's time to leave since I can barely have a conversation with the guy, and I ask him how he's getting home. He swears up and down that he'll get a cab, and I figure he's a grown-ass man, so I give him a hug and head home. Fast-forward a few hours later, and I get a phone call from some random number. It's about 2:00 a.m. at this point, and I normally wouldn't have picked up, but something told me this could be an emergency. So I answer, and it's David saying that he got popped for a DUI trying to get back to St. Augustine that night and needs someone to bail him out. Being the good friend I am, I call the station, and they tell me I can come grab him the next morning at seven. When I get there, I ask what type of trouble he'll be looking at for the DUI. You know what the cop said?"

"What?" Lisa said, leaning so far over the table it looked like she might lose her balance and fall face-first into Brandon's pancakes.

"He says, 'Well, the DUI is the least of your buddy's problems. It's the stolen car charges that are really going to be a thorn in his side.'"

"Get the fuck out of here!" Lisa shouted, banging her hands on the table and startling the nearby family for a second time.

"Sorry," she said softly, turning her attention back to Brandon. "What did David have to say about all of this?"

"He didn't really get into any details. They brought him out, and he thanked me for helping him and then asked if I could drive him to a friend's house, which I did. It was a quiet car ride; I asked if he was all right, and he said yes but he didn't want to talk about it. So we didn't. And when we got there, he asked me not to tell his mom, gave me a hug, and that was the last I saw or heard of him until I got the wedding invitation."

"Damn, that's pretty intense. I can't believe we're talking about the same person we used to live with," Vincent said.

"You're telling me, brother, you're telling me," Brandon said, sighing.

"Well, we're at his wedding, so hopefully that means he's turned some things around. Right?" Lisa interjected.

"Right," Brandon said.

Vincent nodded, but he wasn't convinced. He tried to tell Brandon that, in his forty-five years on the planet, he knew a downward spiral when he saw one, but his throat jammed when he started to talk, making a choking sound.

"You okay, man?" Brandon asked.

"Yeah, just a tickle," came Vincent's automatic reply.

"Well, clear your throat and finish those pancakes," said Lisa, "so we can go find you a nice Hawaiian shirt and me some new earrings to wear for tonight!"

Brandon told them he'd see them later, and they were off. Lisa's excitement over boutique shops selling garbage to tourists always amazed Vincent. In his past life—his real life?—he used to give her grief over it, even hurrying her along. But now, he was happy to see her enjoying herself while they killed time ahead of the wedding. Even if he wasn't the biggest fan of St. Augustine, he was grateful for these extra moments with her. And so far, nothing and nobody had killed him. Yet.

Oddly enough, he was feeling more protective of his life than he had in years. Maybe decades. Given the last few days, it was hard to know for sure how long he'd stick around in this reality, but he really didn't want to leave. It felt so easy being around Lisa again, and if he could somehow manage to get this to stick, it was possible he'd get another chance to live out those wonderful early years with all three of his girls. He might even be able to stave off the darkness that had landed him here in the first place.

Wishful thinking, a voice in the back of his head hissed.

The voice was right—Vincent knew his actions that night in the Broadlands couldn't be undone. The best he could do was soak up all the time he could with the people who meant the most to him and wait for the other shoe to drop.

He shivered at the thought and tried to distract himself by looking around and focusing on his environment. The town felt like a place out of time. Many of the buildings on the waterfront seemed like they belonged in an old-world country like Spain or Italy, and the ubiquitous palm trees lining the streets appeared to be losing their fight with gravity, some of them leaning so severely that Vincent half expected them to collapse on the traffic flowing beneath them. It wasn't a comforting visual and caused his brain to loop back to other paranoid thoughts. But it was more than just the physical surroundings that made him feel off kilter—there was something in the air.

At least that was how he felt.

Lisa, on the other hand, was having a blast chitchatting with the locals and trying on sundress after sundress, inevitably determining that each one was cute, but not cute enough to buy. However, after some tough deliberations, she did find a pair of hoop earrings she liked, and Vincent was all too happy to foot the bill. After tonight, who knew how many chances he would get to buy her a gift.

"They look great on you," he told her. "Why don't you get the other ones you liked too? Never hurts to have a backup pair."

"Really? They're kind of expensive."

"So what? Small price to pay if they make you happy."

Lisa blushed. "I don't know what's gotten into you, but I could get used to this new sappy, sentimental Vince."

"Well, don't get *too* used to it," Vincent replied, the irony justifiably lost on Lisa.

———

By the time they made their way through every store on the waterfront, it was time to start getting ready for the ceremony, and they headed back to the hotel.

Opening his garment bag, Vincent was pleasantly surprised to find that he had packed a pristinely pressed royal-blue suit, crisp double-cuffed dress shirt, and a pale pink tie for this occasion.

Damn, I used to have some style, he thought, having a little too much fun admiring himself in the mirror.

"You okay in there? I haven't heard any complaining about wrinkles or cuff links, so I just want to make sure you're not passed out," Lisa hollered from the bathroom, competing with one of the loudest hair dryers in existence.

Vincent laughed. "Doing great, baby girl—you're gonna have to watch out tonight, though. Daddy is looking sharp!"

"Oh, you're calling yourself Daddy now? At least there's nobody here for you to embarrass me in front of tonight."

"Very funny," he said dryly. "What're you wearing?" Vincent hoped they hadn't discussed it prior to flying down to Florida.

"I ended up going with the black dress. It's a little revealing, but I figured this is exactly the type of occasion to take a chance." She stepped out of the bathroom and did a little twirl. "So it may be you who has to watch out tonight, mister!"

"Wow, you look stunning!" Vincent managed to get out before she ducked back into the bathroom and resumed her fight with the hair dryer. He grinned and added, "And am I really so whiny about stupid shit like cuff links and wrinkles?"

"Significantly more than any other man I've ever met," she said. "But it's all right; I love you all the more for it."

Before he could say something about how little he cared about that small stuff now, there was a knock on the hotel room door, and Vincent found himself face-to-face with Brandon, who was wearing what had to be the funniest outfit he had ever seen for a wedding. They stared at each other for a few seconds before Brandon said, "I am the Florida Man," and they both started cackling.

Apparently, Brandon's luggage hadn't arrived at the hotel yet, so he was wearing a red, white, and blue Hawaiian shirt, khaki pants with frayed cuffs, flip-flops, and Miami-style sunglasses with rainbow lenses. Carrying a six-pack of Miller High Life, he looked ready for a party, but not a wedding.

Vincent looked Brandon up and down. "Holy shit—I can't believe you're going to wear that tonight."

Brandon just shrugged and said, "You know, at first I thought I might be embarrassed . . . and then I remembered that we're in *Florida*, and I probably won't even be the worst-dressed person at this wedding."

"Yeah, you might be right there," Vincent replied with a chuckle. "I can't wait until Lisa sees this."

"Can't wait until Lisa sees what?" Lisa shouted from behind the bathroom door.

"Oh, nothing, Lis—don't worry about it!" Brandon yelled back, flashing Vincent a devilish grin.

"I know that tone; you two better not be doing anything stu—"

Lisa stood in front of the open bathroom door, slack-jawed and clearly unable to process the glory of Brandon's outfit. After a few seconds, she burst into a fit of hysterical laughter. "What the hell are you wearing?" she managed to gasp.

"I'm just going with the flow, doll. Planning to stand out and snag a future ex-wife at this shindig."

"Stop it! Vince, we absolutely need to get as much photo evidence of this night as possible."

"You don't have to tell me twice—this is pure gold," Vincent agreed.

"You all are just jealous," Brandon said with a dramatic exhale.

"Sure, we are, bud," Vincent replied, giving him a friendly pat on the back.

"Did you read up on this venue at all?" Lisa interjected, changing the subject.

"A little. Isn't it some sort of old casino or something?" Brandon said.

"Kind of. It was one of the first hotels in Florida and had a giant public bathhouse and a casino. People used to come down here and stay at the hotel searching for the fountain of youth."

"That's pretty wild," Vincent said, thinking that he was enjoying a second chance at exactly that: youth. He suddenly had a strong urge for them to know what was happening to him . . . but by now he knew there was no point in trying. He would probably just start choking again.

"And apparently the hotel and casino business went under during the Great Depression," Lisa continued explaining. "A few years later, it reopened and has been running ever since. There are a lot of people online who say that it's run by some Florida faction of the mafia."

"No shit?" Vincent said, now paying full attention. "Do you think that's true?"

"I'm not sure, but I'd keep an eye out for any suspicious-looking characters tonight."

"Hell, I'd be pumped to rub shoulders with a real-life Don Corleone. Maybe he'd be able to point me in the direction of a high-stakes poker game," Brandon said, chuckling.

"Not in that outfit he won't," Vincent shot back, causing them all to break into laughter once again.

"All right, Tweedledee and Tweedledum, the ceremony's in about thirty minutes," Lisa told them. "I think it's time we grab a cab and head back toward the waterfront."

"You're right, you're right," Vincent replied, giving Lisa a quick kiss on the cheek. "Thanks for keeping us on schedule." He pointed at the six-pack. "Brandon, let's take a couple of these for the road."

"Don't threaten me with a good time," Brandon said, stuffing two beers in his pants pockets, "Let's roll—lead the way, Lisa!"

CHAPTER SEVENTEEN

The former Alcazar Hotel was built like a Spanish castle looming over the city of St. Augustine. A pristine courtyard surrounded the fortresslike terra cotta-and-red-brick building featuring two twin towers at its center that immediately drew Vincent's eyes skyward. The rest of the building—or buildings?—was organized in a rectangular layout the size of multiple city blocks. It looked like the type of estate a South American drug lord might own, and it left Vincent momentarily in awe as he exited the taxi.

"Whoa," Brandon murmured as he stepped out of their cab, his mouth falling open as he gazed toward the towers.

"Whoa is right," Lisa agreed as Vincent helped her out of the back seat. "I can't believe David is getting married here."

"I know, right?" Vincent added, looking down at his watch. "Well, we'd better head in and figure out where the ceremony is. It might take us a while to make our way through the compound."

"Good call," Brandon seconded. "Hope they let me in without a suit."

"Don't be silly—David would never kick you out for something like that. Oh look, there's a sign telling guests where to go. Follow me, boys!" Lisa exclaimed, waving them on.

Luckily, they had given themselves a fifteen-minute cushion heading to the venue, and they used every extra minute of that window to navigate the labyrinth of the former hotel and casino. The halls were deserted, making Vincent feel apprehensive. Had they taken a wrong turn? But every time he started to think it would be wise to retrace their steps and was about to say as much, they would see another sign confirming they were on the right path. Brandon and Lisa chatted and joked cheerfully, seemingly not worried at all. Why was he the only one feeling on edge?

Finally, a sign pointed them down a long hallway that eventually opened up into a small chapel.

Relieved to hear the sound of other guests, Vincent picked up his pace, Lisa and Brandon at his heels. However, before they could take their seats, they were abruptly stopped by an obese, overly tan man dressed in all black who referred to himself as an "usher" and motioned them toward a small table in the back corner of the room. Not wanting to rock the boat, they dutifully headed over to the table, where another large man in all black was holding a Polaroid camera.

"Name, please?" the man said in a monotone as they approached.

"Excuse me?" Lisa said.

The man let out a frustrated sigh and pointed to a sign on the table that read, "The bride and groom respectfully request that all guests snap a picture and leave a note for their memories."

"Oh!" Lisa said. "Vince, Brandon—get over here! Now let's pretend we actually like each other and say cheese."

Vince and Brandon did their best to get into position, but the man snapped a picture before any of them had a chance to smile.

"Names, please," the man asked again, apparently unconcerned with the poor quality of their picture.

"Lisa, Vince, and Brandon," Lisa said, doing an admirable job hiding her disappointment with the photo-op.

"Last names?"

"Oh um, Andrews, Palmer, and Jacobs. Why do you need our full names?"

"Thank you; please take a seat," the man responded, scrawling their names on the bottom of the Polaroid picture and placing it inside a photo album.

Lisa didn't budge, and Vincent had a feeling she was about to snap at this odd usher, but before any of them could respond, the organist started playing, signaling the beginning of the ceremony.

"Let's just grab a seat in the back. No need to worry about this bozo," Vincent said, trying to prevent any type of scene.

"Bro, is this the *Jurassic Park* theme song?" Brandon said.

Vincent paused for a second to listen and immediately recognized the song. "Holy shit, you're right. What a strange song to play at a wedding. Do you think David picked this?"

"Who cares?" Lisa interjected. "Both of you need to sit down right now. I'm not about to be standing in the aisle when the processional starts."

"Good call, Lis, good call. Look, there are a few seats we can grab." Brandon pointed to a row toward the back and they headed over to claim their seats.

Shaking off the strangeness of their entrance, Vincent settled in next to Lisa and Brandon and dutifully watched the bridal party make their way down the aisle. David had already positioned himself at the front of the chapel, and as the last pair took their places on either side of the altar, Vincent realized he didn't recognize a single groomsman. He had known David for years and had met plenty of his friends throughout their time living together, but not one of those men looked familiar.

Before he could unpack what that might suggest, the music faded away, and they heard a voice from the back of the room announce the customary "Please rise," signaling that it was time for the bride to make her entrance.

As she always did at weddings, Vincent could hear Lisa struggling to hold back tears as the bride and her father slowly marched down the aisle. Rebecca was wearing an extremely ornate dress with a veil and a long train that required a staff member to trail ten feet behind her to ensure there would be no wardrobe malfunctions. Her father was a massive man with a square jaw and thick head of white hair accentuating his deeply tanned face. Even though he was smiling, he still looked like he wouldn't hesitate to break your legs if you disagreed with him.

Vincent could see David wince as he shook Rebecca's father's hand once they arrived at the altar, all but confirming Vincent's sense that things weren't totally on the level. He felt an undercurrent of tension running through the room and couldn't help but think this wedding was some sort of facade, a glossy veneer covering up something sinister he couldn't quite pinpoint.

It wasn't until they were asked to be seated that he noticed that there was also something odd about the officiant. Standing between the soon-to-be married couple was a man who looked to be in his seventies, wearing thick, wire-framed glasses, a wrinkled charcoal suit, and holding a few loose pages in his right hand.

"Ladies and gentlemen, thank you for joining us," he began, staring directly at the papers he was holding. "As some of you may know, I'm a lawyer by trade, but I've officiated sixteen weddings before this one. This is my seventeenth, and I couldn't be happier for this young couple to be joining their families together. Now, most people don't know this, but I've known Rebecca since she was a little baby, and as she grew up, we became best friends. Which I know is kind of strange for people to hear. But it's true. We were basically inseparable until she turned into a teenager and didn't want to hang out with an old lawyer anymore.

I mean, can you imagine a fifty-year-old man and a ten-year-old girl being best friends? But we have remained close all throughout her life."

"What the fuck?" Vincent heard Brandon whisper.

"Did he just say he was best friends with a ten-year-old girl?" Vincent muttered.

"Shh," Lisa said as the man continued his outlandish monologue.

"And Rebecca's family is just the most wonderful . . . um . . . generous bunch of people you'll ever meet. They're all extremely loyal and, well, competitive. Always trying to one-up each other and be the best they can be. Which is why it was so great when Rebecca brought David into the fold. Like Rebecca and her family, David is also extremely competitive and unwaveringly loyal. They met playing on the same local softball team and were instantly drawn together through their competitiveness. As their relationship grew, we got to see how loyal David was to Rebecca and how his family's values were so aligned with those of the Bendetti family. So, without, further ado, I think it's time to say the vows and make things official. Who has the rings?"

After a few bumbling seconds, the old man grabbed the rings from the best man, but his hand was shaking so badly that he ended up dropping them on the ground as he reached out to hand them to David and Rebecca.

"This is fucking weird, right?" Vincent asked Lisa, under his breath.

"Yeah, but keep it to yourself until this ceremony is over. Florida is weird—get over it already."

"OK, fine. Hopefully this old man doesn't die before they say 'I do.'"

"Will you be quiet? I want to hear the vows," Lisa hissed under her breath.

Vincent turned his attention to the front of the stage as David launched into his vows.

"With this ring, I give you my *heart*, my *promise*, and my *love*, from this day forward," David began, his tone largely flat except for a sarcastic emphasis on the most meaningful words. "You are the best friend—and throwing partner—I could have ever asked for," he continued, his voice now dripping with sarcasm. "And I can't wait to *live*, *laugh*, and *love* you every day until the end of time." David slid the ring onto Rebecca's finger and let out a cartoonishly exaggerated exhale as he readied himself for her vows.

"Did our boy ape these vows from a Hallmark card or something?" Brandon said to Vincent in a hushed tone.

"I mean, maybe?" Vincent replied quietly. "That delivery was certainly . . . something."

"Fucking A, it doesn't sound like homeboy wants to be doing this at all."

"If you two don't shut the fuck up, I'm going to lose my mind. You're being extremely rude right now," Lisa scolded.

"Sorry, Lis," Brandon mumbled, tail between his legs. "I promise we'll be quiet."

She gave them both a glare for good measure and turned back to the altar in time to see the bride and groom exchange "I dos" and their first kiss.

Despite the odd ceremony, Vincent was happy to see the crowd's exuberance during the newlyweds' first kiss. He still had very fond feelings toward David, and while it was clear their lives had diverged, he was glad to celebrate his friend's marriage.

While the bridal party made their way back down the aisle, another large usher sidled up behind Vincent and informed him that the three of them would be the ones leading the guests to the cocktail reception. He didn't look like someone who would welcome any follow-up questions, so Vincent nodded in acknowledgment and on the usher's cue started walking toward a side door that Vincent prayed would lead them in the right direction.

Once again it felt like they were making their way through an underground labyrinth, but this time there were no signs guiding the way. Lisa took it upon herself to lead the charge and proceeded to march forward with confidence despite the general lack of directions. Vincent, on the other hand, was feeling increasingly unsettled. After what felt like ages, the hallway they were traversing opened up into a beautiful high-ceilinged room filled with scattered high-top tables, two bars, and a shelved wall decorated with what looked like at least one hundred glasses of champagne.

"Whoa," Brandon said, stopping to take in their decadent surroundings. "This is super classy, huh? Kinda regretting the Hawaiian shirt right about now."

"Oh, whatever, nobody is going to notice," Lisa said, trying to be supportive. "You just need a few drinks and then you'll loosen up and be able to own this look. What're you having?"

"Well, I might as well start off with something strong. Can you see if they'll make a Manhattan? If not, just grab me a double bourbon on the rocks."

"Aye, aye, captain," Lisa said with a salute before bouncing off toward the nearest bar.

"Can you believe this place?" Brandon said, turning his attention to Vincent.

"Honestly, no. This doesn't seem like David's vibe at all. Back in the day, we practically lived at Showtime, which is like the dirtiest dive bar this side of the Mississippi. I guess he's really grown up over these last few years—never thought I'd see the day."

"Well, that or he's found himself a sugar momma," Brandon mused. "You think?"

"I dunno, dude, maybe. I mean look at all this—you know Bob and Susan aren't footing the bill. And I'd bet my life David doesn't have the funds for this type of extravagance."

"That's a good point," Vincent replied. "Something just feels . . . off, you know?"

"Maybe it was that *Jurassic Park* music," Brandon said.

"Or the shaky lawyer priest," Vincent shot back.

"And all that talk about how competitive they were? What the fuck was that all about? It's not like he's Kobe Bryant or something. Shit, we all used to play darts every weekend at that shithole sports bar downtown, and you and I would beat the brakes off him. David just rolled with it—never even seemed upset. Not exactly the behavior of an extremely competitive person."

"Right, and now he's the most competitive man in the world apparently. And what about this crowd? Do you recognize a single person here?"

"Outside of Suzie and Bob, no. Strange mix of people. Some of these fellas look like they frequent the pharmacies and others look like they make their living shaking down small businesses for protection money."

"Holy shit. Do you think Rebecca's dad is some kind of Florida mob boss or something? It would explain all the huge bodyguard types acting like ushers and why that lawyer spoke so highly of her 'family,'" Vincent said, marking the last word in air quotes.

"Huh," Brandon said. "Never thought of that. You could be on to something, my friend. Guess we'll have to keep an eye out."

"Definitely," Vincent said. "I just can't shake the feeling that David is tied up with a rough crew."

"I'll let you know if I catch any negative vibes," Brandon responded before fishing around in his pockets like a toddler trying to find a piece of candy he put in his pants to "save for later."

"What are you doing, dude? You look ridiculous."

"Hold on, I know they're in here somewhere. Ah!" Brandon pulled his hand out of his pocket and presented Vincent with a fun-size bag of Skittles.

"One of these will make that stress melt right away," he said, sporting an impish smile.

"Skittles?" Vincent said.

"No, dummy! These are edibles disguised as Skittles. Jeez, do you live under a rock or something?"

"I dunno, man—I'm not planning to turn into a zombie at this wedding."

"Relax—each Skittle is five milligrams. All it will do is lift your mood. You'll barely even feel it, trust me."

"All right, fine, give me one. But don't tell Lisa; I don't want to get any shit for this."

"My man!" Brandon said, deftly placing a Skittle in Vincent's right hand.

"Cheers!" Vincent responded, popping the candy in his mouth and glancing around the room to ensure Lisa didn't see their exchange.

"Gonna be a fun night—I can just feel it. And look, here comes Lisa with a little social lubricant. Let's do a little schmoozing and see what these Florida folk are all about."

CHAPTER EIGHTEEN

Oddly, David, Rebecca, and the rest of the wedding party never made an appearance at the cocktail hour. Vincent knew that it was typical to take pictures immediately following the ceremony, but it was also common for the photographer to push to get those knocked out quickly enough for the bride and groom to begin enjoying the party they were throwing.

Before long, the bartenders and catering staff were announcing last call, and the ushers had reappeared and were encouraging guests to make their way toward the reception. Vincent found himself getting swept up in the crowd while Lisa and Brandon continued to chatter away, seemingly detached from what was happening around them.

"Will you guys hurry up?" Vincent called, already making his way toward the exit. "If we don't start moving the party is going to leave us behind!"

Lisa grabbed Brandon's arm and hurried to catch up with Vincent as they entered the labyrinth once again.

After another ten minutes of walking through dimly lit, tunnel-like corridors, they emerged on the second level of the chapel. The altar had been completely removed, revealing twin grand staircases leading down to where they had attended the ceremony only an hour ago. The rows of chairs had been swapped for dinner tables, a dance floor, and a DJ booth, filling the football-field-sized rectangle space one story below them.

Wait, this isn't a chapel? This fucking venue is wild.

"You thought we were in a chapel earlier?" Lisa responded.

"How did you know I was just thinking that?" Vincent shot back.

"You said it. Out loud. Standing right next to me. Are you all right?"

"Oh, I must have just gotten lost in my thoughts. Didn't realize I said that out loud," Vincent said, forcing a chuckle. The edible was really starting to take hold, and the changing surroundings were knocking him off balance.

"You might want to take it easy on the drinks during dinner if you're already having issues separating thoughts from words," Lisa told him. "But this place is gorgeous—look! There are more dinner tables on this indoor/outdoor balcony level overlooking the main floor. Have you seen anything that looks like a seating chart yet?"

Brandon pointed toward the balcony directly across from them, where a group of people were congregating. "That's gotta be it."

"Well, let's go see who David stuck us with for dinner this evening," Vincent said, trying to play it cool as they embarked on the hundred-yard trek to the other side of the giant room.

It took them a few minutes to get close enough to read the large rectangular board containing seating assignments, during which an impatient Brandon headed off to find the bar, but eagle-eyed Lisa stayed the course and eventually found their table.

"Table Fifteen!" she yelled, like someone guessing an answer on *Family Feud.*

"Oh boy, looks like you're gonna be stuck with us!" Vincent heard someone say behind him. He quickly turned around and found himself face-to-face with Tim Robinson, the comedic genius from *I Think You Should Leave Now.*

"Are you . . . are you Tim Robinson?" Vincent asked, feeling starstruck.

"Who, me?" the man responded, looking over both of his shoulders and gesturing to himself with both thumbs, "I wish, buddy! That guy is fuckin' hilarious and probably has a way hotter wife than I do, if you know what I mean," he continued, giving Vincent a knowing bump with his elbow and letting out a laugh that sounded exactly like Tim Robinson's.

"So, you're not Tim Robinson?" Vincent said, unable to reconcile this person's looks, voice, and mannerisms with any explanation outside of the fact that he was Tim Robinson.

"Nah, man. Sorry to let you down. Name's Craig," the man said, extending his hand.

"Vince," Vincent mumbled, embracing the handshake. "Sorry, you just look and sound exactly like him."

"Yeah, I get that a lot. That dude's funny as fuck—when people think I'm him, they laugh twice as hard at my dumb jokes. It's like a weird, stupid superpower."

"Sounds like an awesome superpower to me," Vincent said, quickly warming to this eccentric stranger.

"I appreciate that, my man, but you haven't heard any of my dumb jokes yet," Craig said, breaking into a fit of laughter. "Anyway, like I said, we're at Table Fifteen with y'all, so I'm gonna go find my wife before she meets her second husband roaming around this fancy-ass place. I'll see you over there in a few minutes." Without waiting for a response, Craig turned on his heel, yelled, "Has anyone seen my wife?" and started walking toward the bar.

"Oh boy, this is going to be an interesting dinner," Lisa said, following Craig with her eyes.

"You can say that again," Vincent muttered.

"Did you notice that all the other tables have twelve people and ours only has eight?"

"No. So what?"

"Just kinda strange, that's all. Oh well, at least it's fewer names we have to remember."

"Thank God we're all at the same table," Brandon said, appearing out of nowhere. "I don't know that I could manage at a table by myself. Here, I got you guys a coupla brewskis, just in case it takes a while for the servers to show up with wine."

Vincent and Lisa grabbed the beers and began wandering around the balcony level searching for their table. They had to walk nearly the entire loop before finding it, conveniently located next to a bar and situated near the egress to the outdoor terrace. Craig was nowhere to be seen, but a couple was already seated and chatting with a man that looked vaguely familiar. As they got closer, Vincent became more and more sure that he knew this man, but he couldn't quite figure out how.

"Well, I'll be damned," the man said, standing to greet the newcomers. "Vincent Palmer, is that really you? How you livin', big guy?"

Vincent couldn't believe his eyes. Standing in front of him was an almost unrecognizable Eddie Marx, whom he hadn't seen since college. Gone was the lean middle infielder Vincent remembered, replaced by a big, burly lumberjack. But, despite the drastic physical transformation, Eddie's trademark megawatt smile—now buried underneath a bushy black beard—hadn't changed a bit.

"Eddie!" Vincent exclaimed, before Eddie swallowed him in a hug so tight he could barely breathe.

"What are the odds?" Vincent gasped, desperately trying to catch his breath. "Last time I saw you, you were a fresh-faced kid tossing a mirror into the fire that burned down the Baseball House, and now look at you—you're a grown-ass man!"

Eddie's smile dropped and a look of uncertainty spread throughout his features.

"What do you mean, the fire that burned down the Baseball House?"

The question lingered in the air for a few seconds as Vincent struggled to think up a reasonable response.

"Sorry about my date," Lisa jumped in. "The gummy he ate earlier must be starting to kick in. Feel free to ignore his nonsense."

She gave Vincent a sharp look, making it clear he needed to get it together. But how did she know about the Skittle? Was she guessing?

"She's right," Vincent said, feeling her elbow gently nudge his ribs. "Oh, and this is my wife, Lisa."

"Wife? Only if he plays his cards right," Lisa cracked, shooting him another stern glance. "It's nice to meet you, Eddie. I'm guessing you and Vince played ball together in college?"

"Sure did; those were some good times. Your boy here had an absolute cannon behind the plate. Never could figure out why McGarrity didn't play him more."

"Fuck that guy," Vincent spat under his breath.

"Couldn't have said it better myself," Eddie said, chuckling.

"So how do you know the bride and groom?" Lisa interjected, clearly uninterested in listening to them reminisce about their playing days.

"David and I worked together for a hot minute when I was down in Tampa. It was a seasonal gig running dolphin tours, so we'd spend our days out on the water and our nights out on the town. We always got along great, and I was sad to see him head up this way at the end of the summer. But that's just the way it goes, I guess. Honestly, I was a bit surprised to get the invite because I hadn't really talked to him in a while, but I figured the least I could do was show up for his big day."

"No way! That's kinda what happened with us too. When did you get your invite?"

"Only like three weeks ago, maybe less."

"Same! Such short notice for a wedding."

"Well, let's face it, we're all seat fillers at this table. Am I right?" Craig said, cutting in from behind Lisa as he approached the table.

"I mean, come on, it's so obvious," he continued. "Every other table has more people than us, and we're tucked so far away in this corner that we can't even see the sweetheart table. Plus, we all got the invite like two weeks ago. They needed to meet some sort of minimum, and here we all are, willing to drop everything and head to this beautiful venue to eat and drink for free all night. Well, I tell you what, we may be second-tier guests, but I sure am gonna have myself a top-tier time."

"Um, all right," Eddie replied. "Who are you?"

"Oh shit, I totally forgot to introduce myself. The name's Craig, and this is the light of my life, Alison. Say hi, Ali."

"Hi, everyone—sorry about him. His parents dropped him on his head when he was little so he has trouble communicating appropriately in social situations."

"Well, honey, my head may not work too good, but it's very clear that you married me for my good looks and huge dick."

Brandon spit out his beer mid-sip and started laughing hysterically, causing a chain reaction around the table.

"Hot damn, they better get the food out soon because I'm starving!" Craig said. "Did you all get any of those appetizers at the cocktail hour? They were tinier than David's little baby wiener. Definitely not enough to hold me over when I'm throwing back wedding beers. You know what I'm sayin'?"

"Hell yes!" Brandon cracked. "Man, this is shaping up to be an excellent wedding dinner."

Maybe it was the common bond forged as last-minute invitees, the alcohol, the edible that Vincent had taken earlier, or some combination of the three, but the next hour was hands down the most fun Vincent had ever had during a wedding dinner.

Nobody at the table carried any air of pretentiousness, and the jokes and stories flowed throughout the meal as if this group of eight people had been friends for years. Nothing was off limits, and Vincent had never seen a group of strangers enter this type of situation with such a fluid sense of humor. Even the quiet couple—who never formally introduced themselves—would chime in with the occasional story that had the entire table howling with laughter.

After a bit, Vincent noticed that guests at the tables within earshot were craning around to see what was causing the commotion, many of the women shooting over dirty looks. Vincent couldn't have cared less. If anything, it spurred him on to help keep the energy high—he had finally let go of his earlier anxiety and apprehension, and he didn't want the feeling to end.

Unfortunately, their good time was cut short by the DJ's announcement that it was time for speeches, and he invited everyone to turn their attention to the dance floor on the ground level below them.

"All right, folks, fun's over. Time to listen to some more silly nonsense before we're allowed to have fun again," Craig announced, standing up and heading toward the railing along the edge of the balcony to get a better view of the speakers.

The rest of the table followed suit and arrived at the railing as the maid of honor began her objectively terrible toast. Vincent had strategically grabbed a spot next to Craig, hoping to hear some entertaining commentary, and Craig did not disappoint.

"Jesus Christ, this is the most boring shit I've ever heard," he began. "This lady knows that there are like three hundred people here, right? Did she not practice in front of any of her friends? Somebody give her a mirror, please. It's amateur hour out here."

"Seriously," Vincent affirmed, keeping his comments minimal to encourage Craig to keep riffing.

"I'm no expert or nothing, but a good wedding speech has gotta be touching or funny, or both. And this . . . this is just boring stories about playing softball together. Who cares? Not even one lesbian joke? Not one? It's right there!" he took another swig of his beer and continued.

"Pretty soon she's gonna start talking about how loyal and competitive Rebecca is or some sort of other irrelevant garbage."

"You picked up on the loyalty and competition stuff during the ceremony too?" Vincent responded, happy he wasn't the only one who clocked that peculiarity.

"How could you not? I mean, that whole thing was fucking weird. The *Jurassic Park* music, that old man talking about how a ten-year-old girl was his best friend, the sarcastic vows. Strangest ceremony I've ever seen, and I went to a wedding for a couple of nudists one time. They were full-on naked. Dick, balls, boobies—I'm talkin' the whole nine yards."

Vincent couldn't contain his laughter and felt vaguely aware that guests nearby were shooting him dirty looks. A few angry "Shhs" followed as the maid of honor mercifully wrapped up her speech.

"Will you two keep quiet over there?" Lisa grumbled under her breath. "Let's just get through these stupid speeches so we can dance."

"Okay, okay, I'll keep my cool. I promise," Vincent replied, trying his best to seem contrite but unable to erase the smile on his face, which he was fairly certain was a result of the edible.

"My God, you can't even pretend to keep your cool. Tell you what, go grab us a fresh round of drinks and try to pull yourself together. And maybe if you're lucky, I'll still dance with you tonight."

"Grab me one too," Brandon said.

"Fine, save my spot. I'll be right back."

Unmoored from the rest of the group, Vincent really started to feel the effects of the edible. It was like his inner monologue was in overdrive, but not in a negative way. He felt more observant of his surroundings as he made the short trek, and any self-consciousness he might have been feeling melted away as he sidled up to the nearby bar, which was tucked into the archway leading out to the outer balcony. Once there, he ordered three vodka sodas with lemon garnishes.

To his surprise, the bartender just stared back at him blankly. Maybe it was louder in here than Vincent realized and the guy hadn't heard him? *I'll just order again*, Vincent thought.

"Excuse me, sir. May I please have three vodka sodas with lemon?" he repeated.

The bartender continued staring at him, unable to comprehend what Vincent had just requested.

What the hell? There was no way this guy didn't know how to make a vodka soda, and he had surely ordered loudly enough the second time. What was he supposed to do now? It would be ridiculous to try and order again—

In the middle of his silent, mini-panic attack, Vincent noticed that the bartender was sitting on the barstool behind the bar.

Why was he sitting down? That was curious.

The man continued to stare silently at Vincent, his head tilted slightly upward to meet Vincent's gaze. Slowly, the man looked down at a cutting board in front of him and pointed to a small sign that said "Handmade Cuban Cigars." Without waiting for a response, the man gave Vincent a nod and resumed rolling cigars at a ludicrously fast pace.

"Hey!" a voice called from behind Vincent. "You need help, buddy?"

Vincent executed a 180-degree heel turn and found himself staring at the actual bartender who must have witnessed his previous interaction. Feeling sheepish, Vincent gently pointed a finger at his chest to ensure the bartender was talking to him.

"Yes, I'm talking to you. You're literally the only person over here that's not a staff member. You need three vodka sodas with lemon, right?"

"Oh, yes, please. Thank you," Vincent whimpered.

"Listen, man," the bartender said as he began mixing up the drinks, "this place is very strict about people getting out of hand at the weddings they host here, so consider this your warning. We want you to have fun and get loose, but if you start heading toward incoherence, or stumbling, or just seem generally out-of-control drunk, then I'm gonna have to cut you off. And if that doesn't work, they'll have security give you the boot. Capisce?"

What the fuck? Why is he talking to me like some sort of mafioso? Was the whole staff in on the mobster theme?

"Capisce," Vincent replied solemnly, grabbing the three drinks and carefully heading back to catch the last few speeches.

"What'd I miss?" he asked loudly upon his return.

"Shh! Her dad is still giving his speech," Lisa snapped back.

"Oh sorry," Vincent said, handing out the drinks and turning his attention back to the main floor.

" . . . and we're so thrilled to officially welcome David to the family," Rebecca's father continued. "He's been a real asset to us ever since he moved to St. Augustine. In more ways than one. But I'm thrilled that he's going to be here to take care of my sweet daughter and will be in our lives forever. Because, as you all know, once you're in the family, it's for life. There's no escaping, young man!"

The room erupted into laughter, and Vincent instinctively looked toward David in time to see him force a smile and squirm in his seat.

"All jokes aside, we're happy to create this bond between our families, and cheers to the lucky groom and beautiful bride. Salud!"

"SALUD!" the room roared back, startling Vincent as everyone raised their glasses to the married couple.

"All right, everyone, that wraps up our speeches. Now we'd like to invite the groom and his mother to the dance floor for a very special dance," the DJ announced.

Vincent took this opportunity to squeeze back into his spot on the balcony next to Craig. Something about Rebecca's father's speech felt forced, and he needed to see if anyone else caught the same vibe.

"That was a little strange toward the end, huh?"

"Nothing is ever normal with those people . . ." Craig trailed off, staring vacantly into space.

"What do you mean?" Vincent probed.

"Huh? Oh nothing, don't worry about it. I shouldn't have said that," Craig quickly replied.

Vincent decided not to press him and instead turned to Lisa and Brandon to get their take on the situation that was unfolding. "What'd you guys think of that speech?" he said in a hushed tone.

"Seemed straight out of some mafia movie," Brandon replied, "or maybe some sort of cultlike organization. I don't see too many Italians here, so probably not 'La Cosa Nostra,' if you know what I'm saying."

"Nobody knows what the two of you are saying. What in the world are you even talking about? All wedding speeches are strange. Get over it!" Lisa said tersely, clearly upset with their behavior.

"Jeez, Lisa, relax—" Brandon started to say.

"Don't tell me to relax!" Lisa snapped. "I'm the one who came here to have a good time, and it's you two nuts that—"

"Okay, okay," Vincent interjected. "Lisa, you're right that we're being overly paranoid. Brandon, you're right that this does feel like we've stepped into some sort of strange cult documentary. Is everyone happy now? We all win, and it's almost time to dance."

Brandon and Lisa both locked eyes and gave a nod to acknowledge the truce that Vincent had brokered. Their gazes shifted back down to the main floor, quietly taking in David and Susan's special dance.

As David and his mother swayed to the music down below, Vincent's mind drifted back to the same moment on his own wedding day— surrounded by loved ones and gently swaying with his mom as "Love of My Life" by Sammy Kershaw echoed in the background. He remembered thinking that song was a strange choice—it was a traditional love song after all—but his mom always said the first verse and chorus made her think of Vincent and the gift of motherhood. A tear welled up in the corner of his eye as he pictured her smiling up at him on that day, full of love and proud of the man he had become.

It felt nice to reminisce. He'd spent so much time avoiding the pain associated with his mother's death that he'd ended up burying the good memories along with the bad. But seeing her again had unlocked something he didn't realize had been weighing so heavily on him.

As David and Susan ended their dance, Vincent quickly wiped the tear from his eye and joined in the applause as they ended with a tight embrace. For some reason, he felt compelled to keep watching them as they exited the stage and ceded the center of attention to Rebecca and her father. Vincent could see their moods shift as soon as David and Susan realized they were out of the spotlight and felt like they had some semblance of privacy. There was a stiffness in the way that they were interacting, which struck Vincent as odd. Both stood silently watching the dance, and even from a distance Vincent could see Susan's jaw muscle flexing, as if she were grinding her teeth. David's brow was furrowed, and his right hand was pressed against his leg, balled into a fist. He'd only ever known David and Susan to have a tight, seemingly healthy relationship. But here they were on his wedding day, clearly navigating some sort of turbulence.

His thoughts were disrupted by the sound of the room erupting into applause as Rebecca and her dad finished their dance. He turned to Lisa and saw her holding back tears.

"What's wrong, baby girl?"

"I just . . . it just . . . makes me think of me and my dad one day," she blubbered, followed by a self-effacing chuckle.

Vincent's heart melted as he drifted back to their wedding day and remembered how genuinely happy she looked to live out that moment. Without saying a word, he wrapped her up in his arms and told her how much he loved her as David and Rebecca took the floor for their first dance. Without breaking contact, Vincent transitioned from hug into a slow dance and rocked back and forth with his once-and-future wife while "Maybe I'm Amazed" played in the background.

Their tender moment was interrupted as the song began to wind down, and the DJ invited all the guests onto the dance floor to start the party. Lisa's eyes lit up as she instinctively grabbed both of Vincent's wrists, let out an excited squeal, and made for the nearest stairwell down to the main floor. Vincent had never met anyone who delighted in the silliness of wedding dancing more than his wife. Clearly, tonight would not be an exception to that rule. Instead of trying to hang by the bar all night, as was his typical wedding custom, this Vincent planned to indulge her love of wedding dancing and lean into the party. And lean in he did as the DJ ran through a playlist of hit songs.

———

When there was finally a lull among the dancing crew, Vincent decided it was a good time to break away and find a restroom. He told Lisa where he was going and asked if she wanted to walk with him, but she shook her head. Despite worrying about leaving her alone on the dance floor, she seemed unconcerned about being abandoned.

Vincent suddenly realized two things in quick, successive order: First, he didn't have a clue where the bathroom was, and second, he was very stoned. The clublike lighting on the lower floor made it nearly impossible for him to identify signage or signals pointing toward a nearby restroom, so he decided to return to the calmer atmosphere of the upper level.

At first, he was relieved to distance himself from the strobe lights and pop beats, but that feeling quickly turned to anxiety. Maybe it was the edible, but something in his gut was sending out warning signals. Unable to identify any rational source for this feeling—and feeling as if his bladder was about to explode—he made the conscious decision to ignore his intuition and continue to search for anything that resembled a restroom.

"Vince! I've been looking all over for you, dude!" he heard Brandon call out from somewhere nearby. He quickly scanned the immediate area and noticed Brandon a few yards to his right, chatting with a group of men in tuxedos.

"Come over here and meet these guys. It's David's best man, Charles, and two of his groomsmen."

Vincent walked over, attempting to sober up enough to converse with strangers. After a quick round of introductions, Brandon continued telling a story Vincent assumed had started before he'd interrupted the group. The groomsmen all listened intently, almost in an intimidating manner, and dutifully laughed when Brandon got to the punchline.

"Anyway, David's always been a little bit of a firecracker. Seems like he's carrying that on here in Florida."

The tuxedo men gave one another a look and nodded in acknowledgment, which was apparently all Brandon was looking for in order to keep plowing ahead in conversation.

"Get this, my guy Vince here is convinced there's some sort of mob presence at this wedding."

Everyone stood there in silence and shifted their attention to Vincent, whose stomach felt like it had just dropped through the floor.

Why the fuck would he out me like that? Vincent thought to himself, scrambling to figure out how to handle this uncomfortable predicament. *Doesn't he realize if there's an unseemly presence here, the fucking groomsmen would absolutely be connected?*

"I have no idea what you're talking about," Vincent quipped expressionlessly, calculating that denial was his best path forward.

"What do you mean? You were literally just talking about how convinced you were that Rebecca's dad must be involved in some sort of organized crime. Come on, tell them your theory. I bet they get a kick out of it."

"Brandon, I don't know if this is one of your weird jokes, but I never said anything like that about Rebecca's father," Vincent insisted, trying to telepathically get Brandon to change the subject. "I've never met the guy—it would be crazy to say something like that."

"You're right," Charles, the best man, replied. "It *would* be crazy to say something like that about Rebecca's father."

"Yeah, he's a very well-known figure around here, and these types of rumors can be very damaging. You should be very careful about throwing out accusations," one of the groomsmen chimed in.

"For sure, which is exactly why I would never do that," Vincent responded evenly, trying to figure out how to get away from these people. "Do you guys know where the bathroom is? I'm about to piss my pants."

"Yeah, it's across the way over there. Gonna have to walk all the way around the balcony to get there," Charles said, pointing directly across from where they were standing.

"You, sir, are a hero; thank you so much. Great meeting you all," Vincent replied, seizing his moment of escape.

He waited until he thought nobody would be watching him any longer to release a huge exhale. Cognizant of the fact that he was inebriated, Vincent replayed the interaction in his head, hoping to find a reason to believe he was just being overly suspicious. But there was something ominous about how that conversation had unfolded.

If it was truly an outlandish thought, those guys would have laughed, right? Vincent thought as he scanned the upper level for something, anything, that looked like a bathroom sign.

It wasn't until he had made his way to the opposite side of the room that he spotted a few girls walking out of a semi-concealed hallway, chattering away as if they had just become best friends on the toilet— there *had* to be bathrooms around here somewhere. He didn't see any clear signs but decided to trust his instincts and duck into the hallway, praying he was only seconds away from being able to relieve himself and rejoin Lisa on the dance floor.

But instead of seeing doors boasting clear bathroom signage, he only saw a row of unmarked, old wooden doors. He paused for a second, uncertain of how he should proceed, before making the decision to continue down the hallway trying doorknobs in hopes that one would be a lavatory. It didn't take him long to realize that nearly all the doors were on his right side except for one directly in front of him at the end of the hallway. And to his left was a row of portraits, looking like they dated back to the eighteenth century.

Perhaps it was the THC flowing through his veins, but he got the distinct feeling that the portraits, all of which were of old, mostly white men, were watching him as he hurriedly twisted doorknobs hoping one would magically open. The sounds of the wedding faded away with every step forward and, before he knew it, Vincent found himself standing in near silence staring at the only remaining door, the one at the end of the hallway. He felt a chill run down his spine as he reached his hand out, grasped the brass doorknob, and turned.

Click.

Vincent's heart leapt as he heard the latch bolt retract and the door gently push inward, opening into what looked like a large hotel suite. He froze, holding his breath to see if he could hear anyone else in the room. After a few seconds of silence, he decided to enter and began searching for the toilet.

The suite was deceptively large and featured a huge circular living room with three arched outlets that Vincent assumed led to other rooms. As he surveyed the room, he realized that there were no telltale signs of life. No empty beer cans, no suitcases, no shoes. Nothing. Just an empty room at the end of a hallway full of locked doors. Something felt off; he just didn't know what it was yet.

Pushing his misgivings to the side, he walked to the nearest archway and tried the door. Locked.

Figures, he thought, desperation setting in as he continued to the next doorway.

He took a moment to say a prayer to nobody before trying the knob. To his immense relief, the door swung open, leading him down yet another eerie hallway. There was only one door in front of him, and he trotted toward it as quickly as he could. His prayers were answered once again as the door opened and he found himself in another suite. This time, however, there was a powder room immediately to his left, and he wasted no time taking advantage of the opportunity to relieve himself.

Vincent barreled through the door and began frantically working to loosen his belt and unzip his pants while striding to the toilet. But just as he was in position and ready to let it rip, a loud group of men barged into the main room. He stood completely still—this wasn't a public restroom he had invaded, and he had no idea who these boisterous men were.

He felt extremely grateful for his youthful prostate as he struggled to stay silent and figure out how to get himself out of this bind. Knowing he had mere seconds before his bladder would give out, he lowered himself into a crouch, hovering above the toilet, and angled himself so his stream would only hit the porcelain bowl, hoping that would help mute the noise and give him a chance to sneak out unnoticed.

He heard the men erupt into laughter and used that as a cue to let go, his feelings of fear and anxiety colliding with the absolute euphoria of relieving himself. He couldn't remember any moment in his life that had ever felt quite like this, and after a few seconds he decided he kind of enjoyed the rush. He felt truly alive.

That euphoric feeling quickly subsided as he struggled to hold himself in an awkward squat for what was turning into the longest pee of any of his lives up to that point. The men continued to carry on outside of the bathroom door, and he mustered every ounce of strength he had to stay the course and remain silent.

Finally, after what must have been at least a full two minutes, his bladder completely emptied. He carefully zipped his pants and began working through potential options for an escape. In the rush to find a toilet, he hadn't really surveyed the layout of the suite and had almost no clue where the men might be in relation to the bathroom. But he knew he was only a few steps from the entrance and was sure his relatively fresh legs could outrun most non-athletes with a head start.

Vincent's heart began to thump in his chest. He knew what he had to do; he just needed to wait for the right moment. His hand grasped the doorknob and turned it ever so slowly as he listened for the men's conversation to pick back up.

"You were right, boss—this was the perfect cover," one voice said.

"Yeah, the Feds are going to be so focused on this wedding they'll never realize what we've got going on at the docks," another followed.

"And you fellas had any doubt?" an authoritative voice responded. "Can you imagine the look on that fuckin' cocksucker Stephen's face when he realizes what we pulled off right under his nose? He's gonna be so depressed even his wife won't touch him after this. Not that she does now anyway!"

Rich laughter erupted, and Vincent made his move, throwing his weight forward to make his great escape.

Thump!

He had thrown his entire weight into the door, but instead of opening, the door had slammed into the door jamb, bouncing him backward and silencing the room in an instant.

Fuck! he thought. *It's a pull, not a push.*

In full-on flight-or-fight mode, he yanked the door toward him and burst out of the bathroom so violently he ran into the opposite hallway wall.

"Hey! Stop right there!" one of the men yelled.

Vincent temporarily froze and instinctively glanced to his left to identify the voice. The command had come from none other than Rebecca's father, seated right next to David and surrounded by a cadre of the large "ushers" who had been present at the ceremony and reception.

Vincent locked eyes with David, who looked just as stupefied as he felt, but after a moment, he managed to silently mouth the word "Run!"

Without a second thought, Vincent scrambled toward the entrance, yanked the door open, and took off in a full sprint.

"Don't just sit there—go get him!" he heard Rebecca's father bellow behind him.

Vincent paid him no mind and continued running as fast as he possibly could down the hallway to the first suite. The only sounds he could hear were his footsteps as he skidded to a pause at the next door, yanked it open, and stumbled into the next room.

He'd forgotten that this room had multiple entrances, and it took him a second to regain his sense of direction and find the appropriate exit. He heard multiple men rapidly approaching from behind and quickly sprinted toward the door that he guessed was the exit.

Thankfully, it was unlocked and dumped him back into the long hallway that led back to the main venue. He broke into a sprint, confident that salvation was only seconds away. He heard the men burst through the door behind him, but they were too late. He broke into a slide to slow his momentum, ripped the final door open, and stumbled back into the lively wedding reception. He swiftly gathered himself and headed toward one of the ornate staircases, hoping to blend in with the mass of people on the dance floor. He scanned the floor for Lisa or Brandon, but they were nowhere to be seen. Turning his attention toward the second deck, he spied them both near a corner bar, talking to the "usher" who had taken their picture at the beginning of the ceremony. His heart sank, and he knew two things: From this point on he was on his own and he needed to get out of this building right now!

As he came to this realization, he saw Lisa look down, make eye contact, and point toward where he was standing on the dance floor. There wasn't any time left to mess around. Vincent stripped off his jacket and tossed it aside and began weaving his way through the crowd, hoping he could misdirect as he made his way back toward the staircase and joined a group heading up for cigars. It took every ounce of mental acuity to keep his cool as he slowly made his way back to the upper level. Out of the corner of his eye, he could see one of the large men making his way toward the staircase, but it didn't seem like the man had spotted him quite yet.

Vincent positioned himself so he wouldn't be visible to the man, staying with the group heading to the cigar patio and briskly walking right by the table where the cigars were being rolled and out to the balcony, where a handful of people were enjoying a smoke.

Looking over the railing, he saw it was only a single-story leap into the courtyard. He put both hands on the stone balcony railing and took a deep breath. Though his mind was racing, he remembered that the best way to avoid injury for this type of jump was to start rolling as soon as he hit the ground. He heard someone call out a few yards behind him and sprang into action, hoisting himself over the balcony, dropping into the courtyard, rolling, and ending up on all fours on the pristinely manicured grass surrounding the old hotel.

"Hey!" he heard a voice yell from up top. "Stop right there!"

Not a chance, Vincent thought, and slipped into the darkness of night.

CHAPTER NINETEEN

It wasn't until he felt his legs starting to give out that Vincent allowed himself to slow down and start to take stock of the trouble he'd gotten himself into. His lungs were on fire as he settled into a fast-paced walk and continued to navigate the eerily quiet network of nearby neighborhoods. He was fairly confident he hadn't been followed and finally allowed himself some time to process what had just happened.

Part of him felt vindicated, like his previous apprehension had been justified. He'd felt uneasy from the moment they'd walked into the welcome party the night before, but it was still shocking to think that someone he had once known so well could be involved in some sort of organized crime syndicate. Though the more he thought about what he'd experienced since landing in this godforsaken state, the more things started to make sense.

He considered the chain of events to ensure he wasn't crazy: David's sudden exit from the welcome party, Susan's drinking and odd behavior, the extravagant venue, the shaky lawyer-priest, the intimidating ushers requiring them to identify themselves by adding their pictures to the guest book, the widespread deference to Rebecca's father throughout the evening. Not to mention the conversation he'd overheard in the back room. Everything fit perfectly together, and somehow he'd found himself in the center of it all, simply because he couldn't find the bathroom.

What the fuck was he going to do now?

The question kept ricocheting around his head, and he just wasn't able to land on a good answer.

Assuming his theory was correct, it appeared he was properly fucked. It must have been clear to the men in that room that he was a wedding guest, and if David was a part of their crew—which seemed extremely likely—then he would have immediately rolled on Vincent. So, they knew who he was, where he was staying for the night—since they'd booked a room as part of the wedding block—and they knew he'd come to the wedding with Lisa and Brandon.

Oh shit! Lisa. He had just abandoned her back there. How the fuck was he going to get her out of this?

His mind kept racing as he traversed some of the strangest neighborhoods he'd ever seen. Row after row of one-story bungalows passed him by, none showing any signs of life but all shrouded in a low-hanging fog. There were barely any streetlights, and a ghostly breeze ruffled the leaves of the surrounding palms, giving Vincent the impression that something in the shadows was following his every move. The occasional unidentifiable animal noise would jolt him into a frightened sprint, forcing him to continually have to regain what little composure he still had left. Vincent had absolutely no clue where he was or how he would find his way back to civilization, but he kept walking, certain he was being hunted.

Something brushed his thigh, and he let out a yelp, thinking it might be an alligator or some sort of other Floridian monster roaming the streets. But after frantically spinning around in a circle trying to identify what had startled him, all he could see was asphalt and concrete. It took him far too long to realize that what had startled him was his phone, buzzing in his pocket to signify an incoming call. He dug the phone out, relieved to see that Lisa was the one calling him.

"Lisa! Oh my God, you'll never fucking believe what is going on! Where are you? You need to get back to the hotel as soon as possible."

"Vince? Is that you? What's wrong? Everyone is worried about you," Lisa replied flatly.

"Who's everyone? Actually, it doesn't matter. Listen, we need to get out of Dodge right now. David's got himself mixed up with some bad people, and I'm worried that something terrible is going to happen tonight."

"Honey, you sound crazy right now. Just come back to the wedding and everything will be fine," Lisa said in a nearly emotionless monotone.

The hair on the back of his neck stood up and a knot formed deep in his stomach. Vincent had never heard Lisa speak like this in their twenty years together. "Are you with someone right now?" he fired back.

"No, of course not. Who would I be with? I just want you to come back to the wedding. Everything will be fine if you just come back and join the party. We miss you and we're worried about you."

"What is this tone? Why do you sound like that? Are they with you right now? Have they threatened you? Are you all right?"

"Vince, who are you talking about? I'm not with anybody—I'm just out here on the balcony alone trying to figure out where you went."

"How did you know that I'm not at the wedding anymore?"

His question was met with a tense, uncomfortable silence.

"Hello? Are you still there?" Vincent probed.

"I saw you walk out to get some air, and someone told me that you left. But they didn't know where you went. Are there any street signs around you that might help me find you?"

Vincent stopped walking and tried to make sense of what was happening. Anybody who had seen him leave the venue would not have described it like that. He had jumped off a one-story balcony and ran off into the night, for God's sake. That was much different than just casually leaving the premises.

The only logical answer was that they were using Lisa as bait to trick him into walking right back into their grasp. Which probably meant that Lisa was in danger. Danger that he had brought upon her. The knot in his stomach twisted tighter. He knew he needed to help her, but given the current circumstances, it seemed like his only immediate option was some sort of misdirection.

"Listen, Lisa—I'm sorry to stress you out. I just needed some air. I was feeling a bit lightheaded and took a walk around the block. I'll start heading back now and will see you in ten. Is that okay?"

"Of course. I'll see you soon."

Vincent hung up the phone. It was abundantly clear that he couldn't go back to the wedding venue, and there was no reason to think they didn't have foot soldiers scanning the streets trying to track him down. And now Lisa, his biggest lifeline, was burnt—and potentially in worse danger than he was.

What he needed, more than anything else, was some help.

Then it hit him. If he hadn't married Lisa yet, that meant his cousin Eric was probably still alive. Eric used to constantly get himself into risky, borderline dangerous, situations and somehow always found a way to wriggle away without any real consequences.

He'll know exactly how to get me out of this mess, Vincent thought, scrolling through his phone contacts at lightning speed, his thumb freezing when he spotted the misspelled contact: "Erik Pallmer."

His eyes filled with tears and his heart swelled as scenes from their childhood flashed across his mind, followed by the gut-wrenching sorrow that accompanied the memories associated with the end of their relationship.

It had been so long since he'd last heard Eric's voice, and now, through some otherworldly twist of fate, he might have the chance to talk to his best friend one more time. He took a deep breath and hit the call button, hoping against hope that Eric would answer.

"Yo, dude, what's up?"

Vincent felt silent tears roll down his cheeks and fall to the asphalt. He tried to speak but the words kept catching in his throat.

"Um, hello? Are you there?" Eric asked.

Vincent swallowed as hard as he could, wiped the tears from his eyes, and tried his best to shake off the avalanche of emotions he was experiencing.

"Oh shit. Yeah, I'm here. Sorry, bad reception," he said shakily, coughing to fully clear out his throat. "You have a minute? I'm in a bad spot and need some help."

"Well, you've called the right person," Eric acknowledged with a soft chuckle. "So what're we working with here? Paint me a picture, and then let's figure out how to get you out of whatever it is that you've gotten yourself into."

"Goddamn, I knew you'd be the right person to call," Vincent responded before launching into his story.

Eric listened patiently as Vincent ran through the broad strokes of what had happened at the Alcazar, hoping this rushed explanation would provide his cousin with enough relevant detail to help.

"Man, this is some sort of strange mess you've found yourself tangled up in," Eric said with a deep exhale. Vincent waited with bated breath as Eric took a beat and carefully considered his next words.

"And you're sure they mentioned the Feds? They didn't say the cops or the police?"

"Nope, it was definitely the Feds. I'm sure of it."

"Hmm, well that's not great," Eric opined. "I'm thinking you're right about some sort of organized crime element. But that probably works to your advantage."

"Talk to me. What's going through that mad genius brain of yours?"

"Here's how I see it—if everything you're telling me is accurate, then you're not crazy and you're also in a little bit of danger. But you've already managed to remove yourself from the situation and have made it to relative safety, which is good. The big issue you have to figure out is how to get back to Lisa and Brandon without this Florida gang getting their hands on you. Do you have any idea how to get back to the venue?"

"Not a clue. Ran out of there in a frenzy and made turns at random while cutting through properties with open yards whenever I could. I'm not even sure which direction would lead me back into town."

"And you don't feel like anyone is following you?"

"Not right now, but I'm keeping an eye out."

"All right, good. The first thing you need to do is find north. If you can see the north star or have a compass function on your phone, then I'd suggest using those resources to head in that direction. Not sure that it'll get you back into the town center, but it'll at least keep you from wandering aimlessly in circles."

"Right, that makes sense. I never would've thought to do that."

"These are the things you learn when you live life on the edge, my friend." After a pause, Eric continued, "Lisa's going to call you again. Probably soon, if I had to guess. You've gotta make sure that you're really feeling her out for any signs that she's being coerced. Pay attention to her tone of voice and the words she's using. If any of those give you a sense that she's still with them, you need to hit her with some misdirection. Tell her you're at a bar nearby or something."

"Okay, got it. What should I do if she seems like normal Lisa?"

"That's where this becomes a gamble. If she sounds normal, then tell her you'll meet her in the hotel lobby. Not your room, but the lobby. Where there will be witnesses in case she's not alone."

"Makes sense. How do I get to the hotel?"

"Well, hopefully you run into some sort of civilization and can just hail a cab or something. That's the ideal scenario. If not, I'd think the next best bet is to try to find a house with lights on and ask a stranger for some help. Risky, but it's worked for me in the past."

"Good to know. What if I somehow end up back at the venue or they find me out on the streets? Do I run again? Or is there another option?"

"There's another option, but it's more of a 'break glass in case of emergency' move: Call the cops on yourself."

"What do you mean, call the cops on myself?"

"You call and tell them you got drunk at a wedding and tried to walk home and are now lost. They'll send a car to find you, but there's a fifty-fifty chance they'll arrest you and throw you in the drunk tank. Which sucks but it's better than getting kidnapped by whatever kind of Florida mafia you're dealing with."

"I'll keep that in my back pocket. Hopefully I'll be able to find my way back to the hotel. I'd really like for this to end up being some sort of weird paranoid freakout and not an actual dangerous situation."

"That would be the best possible outcome. Hit to your ego, but no real damage done."

"Exactly," Vincent affirmed as his phone began buzzing. "Shit, it's Lisa calling on the other line. What should I say?"

"Stick to the plan. Tell her you got turned around, but you'll be back at the venue soon. Ask how the wedding's going. Feel her out."

"Roger that."

"I'll be rooting for you, buddy. Call back if you get in any other hot water," Eric said.

"Hey, Eric, before you hang up . . . one thing," he said before his throat locked up and sent him into a coughing fit.

"You all right, bud?" he heard Eric ask.

Vincent forcefully cleared his throat, unwilling to let anything—supernatural or otherwise—prevent him from saying what he needed to say to Eric.

"I love you like a brother and think the absolute world of you and can't wait to see what you're able to accomplish in your life. I'll always be your biggest fan, no matter what."

"Thanks, brother." Eric paused, and Vincent could feel him grappling with this sudden, seemingly random outpouring of emotion. "I feel the same way. Now answer that call and let me know how things shake out."

Vincent felt his shoulders loosen and an invisible weight lift. He had spent so much time compartmentalizing and burying any feelings related to Eric's death, without realizing just how damaging those choices had been to his overall emotional well-being. This felt much better. He now had some closure. Taking a deep breath, he steadied himself and answered Lisa's call.

"Hello?"

"Vince! Oh my God, I'm so happy you picked up! Where are you?"

"Oh, I just got turned around. It's kind of hard to navigate these streets at night. I think I'll be at the venue soon, though. Where are you?"

"I'm just outside waiting for you. You've been gone for a while."

"Is Brandon with you?"

"Yeah. We're both ready to leave, but we don't want to go back to the hotel without you," Lisa replied, maintaining the calm monotone.

Something about her tone made his spidey senses tingle. The Lisa he knew would be furious about the way he was currently behaving. Even if she wasn't outraged, she would at least be worried—he wasn't typically the type to abandon a wedding mid-reception to run through the streets of an unfamiliar city. Why would Lisa have stayed at the wedding instead of heading back to the hotel after their first call?

Something else was going on here; Vincent just didn't know exactly what that something was. He decided to play along, hoping to discover some new information that could help him get them both to safety.

"And there's nobody else with you?"

"What do you mean? Who else would be with us?" Lisa said, her tone completely void of emotion.

Fuck. Something was definitely wrong.

"I don't know," Vincent said, "other people that are leaving?"

"Oh no, it's just us out here. The reception's still going on."

"Okay," Vincent stalled, trying to figure out how to proceed. "I think I'm only a few blocks away, so I'll see you guys soon."

"Wait! Before you hang up, are there any street signs around or anything? Maybe we can come to you?" she said with a desperate urgency, almost as if forced.

Red flag, Vincent thought. *Big red flag.*

"Nothing that I can see right now, but I'll text you next time I see a street sign."

"Okay, I guess I'll see you soon then," she said. "Oh, and Vince, David invited us to his afterparty with the rest of the wedding party. If you hurry, we might still be able to catch the bus that's taking everyone there."

He wasn't totally sure, but it felt like that last part was some sort of signal. Was she trying to tell him to stay away without arousing the suspicion of anyone else who was listening to their conversation?

"All right, I should be there soon," he said. "I love you, Lisa."

As he hung up the phone, his heart started pounding again. Far from putting his mind at ease, that call made him more anxious than ever. Who could he trust? And how he could get himself out of this mess?

He took a deep breath, remembering Eric's advice to head north. Not trusting his ability to identify the north star, let alone follow it, he pulled up the compass app on his phone and pointed it straight ahead. Turned out he was headed westbound with a cross street thirty yards ahead. Not knowing what else to do, he started walking, hoping that a solution would eventually present itself.

When he arrived at the cross street, he turned right and, as he started heading north, he felt relieved to find that this neighborhood seemed unfamiliar. At least he wasn't retracing his steps. But as he kept walking, that sense of relief transitioned into a feeling of uncertainty. The houses he passed were spaced further apart, and after a few minutes' walk, they gave way to a deserted mini-industrial park.

Blinking lights adorning the manufacturing buildings' exteriors provided the sole source of illumination, their sporadic flashing either a malfunction or a calculated deterrent. Meanwhile, a cool breeze picked up, and Vincent could hear the faint sound of wind chimes and dogs barking in the distance. He felt like he was in a scene straight out of a horror movie and momentarily considered cutting bait and turning back. But, despite their occasional differences, he genuinely trusted Eric's guidance and decided to stay the course.

At least I'm alone, and there's no reason for those guys to look for me in this dilapidated part of town.

The thought provided enough comfort for him to continue on, trying to remain unafraid of what might lie ahead.

CHAPTER TWENTY

It only took a few more minutes for Vincent to be rewarded for trusting his cousin's advice. As he continued walking north, the mini-industrial park slowly morphed back into a residential neighborhood. The streetlights were clustered closer together, and up ahead he could hear the welcome sounds of civilization. He picked up his pace, eager to find safety within a larger group of people.

The closer he walked toward the sound of chattering voices and indecipherable musical notes, the more confident he became that he was heading toward some sort of local strip of bars or clubs. He felt some of his stress evaporate and broke into a light jog. From what he could tell, he was about a hundred yards from the well-lit cross street, and he felt like the nightmare was finally about to end. He still had some logistics to work out, but at least now he wouldn't be completely on his own.

Just then he heard a tire screech and glanced over his shoulder to see a car pulling onto the road behind him. His instincts told him that he should stay out of sight until the car passed, and he veered off to the right and disappeared behind the side of a small, unlit bungalow. His pulse quickened as he listened for the car to pass by, on the way to wherever they were going.

After a few minutes, he still hadn't heard anything so he decided to peek around the corner to have a look. As he turned to his left, there was the car, idling a few dozen yards away. At that exact moment, he felt his phone start buzzing in his pocket. Ducking back behind the bungalow he saw that it was Lisa calling him again.

This can't be a coincidence, he thought and declined the call.

Before he could land on any sensible next course of action, he heard a voice he recognized call out: "Hey, Vince!"

Brandon's voice echoed through the block. "You out here, buddy?"

Vincent didn't move. After a few seconds, Brandon called out again, "Come on, buddy, we're worried about you. We know you're out here somewhere—you share your location with Lisa, and her phone says we're right on top of you."

Based on the sound of his voice, Vincent could tell that Brandon was creeping closer to where he was hiding. His phone started buzzing in his pocket again.

"That's me calling you on Lisa's phone. Bro, you're really starting to freak us out. Can you please come out so we can go back to the hotel? It's creepy as shit out here."

Vincent remained hidden, frozen and indecisive. He knew that he could take off running through the network of houses, but that wouldn't do him any good if they were tracking his phone. Plus, his phone was his only lifeline at the moment. There was no way he'd be able to make it out of this in one piece without some means of communication to the outside world.

He'd been operating in fight-or-flight mode for so long that he was beginning to run out of steam—and starting to entertain the notion that he had completely misinterpreted the situation. Maybe Brandon and Lisa *were* worried and just looking out for his best interests.

He took a deep breath and stepped out from behind the side of the darkened bungalow. "Brandon?" he said, feigning confusion.

"Thank God!" Brandon responded, standing directly in front of the headlights of the mystery car. Vincent covered his eyes, trying to get a better sense of the situation and who else Brandon might be with.

"Where's Lisa?"

"She's in the car," shadow Brandon said, taking a few steps toward Vincent.

"Prove it," Vincent barked, walking backward to keep distance between them.

"Prove it? You're being paranoid, dude. Why wouldn't she be in the car? I don't know what's going on with you, but we're here to pick you up."

Brandon took a few more steps toward him. Vincent mirrored them in reverse.

"Stop," he said firmly, uncertain Brandon could be fully trusted. "Don't take another step forward or I'm calling the cops."

"Calling the cops? On who?"

"On myself, if I need to. I'm not letting you take me back to those people that David's gotten himself tangled up with."

"You're out of your mind. There's nothing shady at all about Rebecca's family or David's. That wedding was a blast. *You* were having a blast, until you went crazy."

"Who else is in the car?"

"I told you already. Lisa."

"Who else?"

"Just Lisa and the driver. I swear."

Vincent took a second to think about what he should do next. Before he could formulate a plan, Brandon took a few hard steps forward, forcing Vincent's hand. Vincent took off down the street and dialed 9-1-1, banking on the fact that if the people up ahead wouldn't be able to protect him then maybe the cops would.

Within seconds, an operator answered. "9-1-1," she said. "What's your emergency?"

Vincent blanked, struggling to hold the phone to his ear while running and figure out how to frame his dilemma in a way that didn't make him seem like a lunatic.

"Hello? Is anyone there?" the operator asked.

"Yes, hello. I'm in trouble and need some help," he sputtered, buying some time so he could get to the busy cross street, where there'd be witnesses if Brandon tried to pull anything.

"Okay, what is your location and what type of trouble are you in?"

"I'm not really sure where I'm at right now, but there are people following me and I'm worried they're going to kidnap me."

The operator didn't immediately respond—the delay gave him time to cover the final ten yards into a well-lit, semi-lively area. To his right was a small dive bar where a few people were milling about outside smoking cigarettes, and to his left was a large, nondescript white building. As he turned around, he saw the car had followed him and was idling nearby.

"Sir, do you see any street signs around or buildings that you can describe?"

He looked around and didn't see any street signs, but he did notice a triangular sign hanging off the side of the large white building nearby.

"It looks like I'm right next to the Ashlar Masonic Lodge."

"The big white building? The Freemason's lodge?"

"I think so—it's a large white building with a triangle sign."

"Thank you. I've dispatched a car and they should be there in a few minutes. Please stay on the line until officers arrive. Do you understand?"

"Yes," Vincent replied, keeping his eyes firmly trained on the car in front of him.

"Is anyone with you?"

"No, just the car that has been following me. They keep trying to coerce me to get in. But I don't want to go with them."

"Can you describe the car?"

"I'm not sure. A sedan of some sort. It's in front of me right now, but I can't see much because their headlights are shining directly in my eyes."

Vincent heard a car door close.

"Vince, enough of this!" Brandon shouted. "Get in the car, and we'll head back to the hotel. I really hope you didn't call the cops or else this is going to get really bad for you."

The headlights were bright enough that he couldn't tell which side of the car Brandon got out of or where he was standing now.

"Don't take another step toward me!" he snapped.

"Sir, is there someone else there? Do you know this person?"

"Yes, there's someone here and he used to be my friend. But I feel like he's gotten himself mixed up in a bad situation, and now he's trying to take me down with him."

"Oh my God, you actually called the cops!" Brandon screeched, stepping out from behind the headlights toward Vincent.

"I said stop!" Vincent barked. "The police are on their way, and I don't want you anywhere near me!"

"Sir, we have officers en route. Just stay with me for one more minute. Can you tell me more about this bad situation?"

"Well, I was at a wedding and overheard a conversation that I wasn't supposed to hear, and then I . . . I ran away. My friend followed me and is saying he's trying to help me, but I'm pretty sure that he's trying to bring me back to those people because they threatened him."

The operator was silent.

"Listen, I know this sounds insane. But I'm not crazy. I promise I'm not crazy. Oh, Jesus, that's what crazy people say. I'm just really scared, and I didn't know what to do. And I called the fucking cops on myself. Holy shit, I've just ruined my entire life. Fuck. Fuck! This is bad, isn't it? I'm fucked, aren't I?"

"No, sir, you're fine. Can you see any flashing lights around you? The officers should be pulling up any second."

Vincent looked to his left, then his right but saw nothing. Out of his peripheral vision he noticed Brandon slowly moving toward him.

"Stay back!" Vincent shouted. "Don't get close to me, motherfucker."

"Do you see any lights?" the dispatch officer asked again.

"No, nothing yet. What do I do if they don't get here and my friend keeps coming after me?" He was feeling frantic, like a cornered animal running out of options.

"They will get there. Are you sure that there are no lights around?"

Vincent noticed motion out of the corner of his right eye and quickly glanced to get a better look. The standard blue and red lights that accompanied squad cars were faintly pulsing in the distance, growing brighter with every passing second.

"Yes! I see the lights! They're headed my way."

"Good. Stay with me until they arrive. Okay?"

"Okay."

Vincent kept his gaze firmly trained on Brandon, who had also noticed the squad car and took a few careful steps back toward the sedan. A few seconds later the police car pulled up, blocked Brandon's car and a short, stocky male officer and a petite female officer exited. The male officer bowed his head toward his chest, said something into his radio, and walked toward Brandon while the female officer approached Vincent. He instinctively put his hands up.

"Hello, sir, you can put your hands down," she said, cautiously looking him up and down to evaluate his threat potential. "Have you been drinking tonight?"

"A little, at the wedding."

"So, you're coming from a wedding? How much have you had to drink?"

"Just a few drinks. Five or six, over the course of several hours. I'm not drunk."

"Have you taken any drugs?"

"No drugs," Vincent lied. He wasn't about to tell the cops he had eaten an edible.

"So just alcohol?"

"Yep, just alcohol. Mostly beers."

He peeked over and noticed that Brandon seemed to be having a friendly chat with the male officer.

"So, tell me why you called," she continued.

Vincent launched into his story, leaving out names and key details that could potentially be damaging if the local police were in Rebecca's father's pocket. The officer didn't probe for more details—Vincent could tell that she wasn't buying his story, and now the male officer was walking toward them, his body language giving the impression that he was very frustrated to be dealing with this type of incident. He leaned over and whispered something in the female officer's ear before turning his attention toward Vincent.

"Good evening, sir," the officer stated matter-of-factly. "Do you know that man over there?"

"Yeah, he's my friend Brandon."

"All right, and why would your friend be trying to kidnap you?"

"I'm not totally sure. I just feel like he got sucked into a bad situation, and since I left, he's been trying to get me and bring me back."

"Has he done anything to you personally to make you feel like you're in danger?"

"He's been following me and trying to make me get in the car."

"Where did he say he wanted to take you?"

"Well, back to our hotel. But of course, he's going to say that in order to get me into the car and take me wherever he really wants to take me."

The conversation was not going well. But Vincent couldn't figure out how to reframe the dialogue.

"And where does he 'really' want to take you?"

"That's the point—I don't know. I just know that if I go with him I'll be in danger."

"How much have you had to drink tonight?"

"I already told her." Vincent pointed at the female cop. "I've only had a handful of beers. I'm not blackout drunk or anything like that."

"And drugs?"

"No drugs. I just told her the same thing!" Vincent snapped, frustrated with the officer's condescending tone.

"No need to get confrontational, sir," the officer responded, placing his right hand on his gun. "We need to have a quick conversation. Can you stay here for just a few minutes?"

"Sure. Am I under arrest?"

The officer looked momentarily thrown off balance.

"No, you're not under arrest. Just stay here, okay?"

"Okay, I'll stay right here," Vincent said obediently as the officers walked back toward the squad car.

Shit, shit, shit. He was completely out of moves. The officers were not going to side with him after his chaotic, vague, and incomplete summary of the night's events. He'd blown his trump card, and his fate rested on how the officers decided they should best handle this scenario. He felt sick to his stomach as the officers finished their sidebar conversation and signaled for Brandon and Vincent to join them.

"All right, fellas, we appreciate your patience while we worked this out. Here's the deal—this sounds like a situation where one of you has had a bit too much to drink in an unfamiliar environment. From what we can tell, the best way to handle this is for you," the male officer pointed at Vincent, "to go with him," pointing at Brandon. "Go back to the hotel and sleep this off. There's no need to file a report or cause any issues for anyone." He turned his attention back to Vincent. "How does that sound?"

"Good, sir," Vincent mumbled.

"Excellent. Well, we'll let the two of you enjoy the rest of your night. And be careful with how much you drink in the future."

They headed back toward their squad car, leaving Vincent with no choice but to go wherever Brandon wanted to take him. Without a word, he followed Brandon back toward the sedan, feeling completely defeated.

He remained silent as he entered the back seat and settled in behind the driver. Brandon slid in next to him without saying a word and they sat quietly, waiting for the squad car to pull out and clear a path forward. The driver hadn't yet acknowledged their presence, and Vincent realized he had no idea who was sitting directly in front of him. He leaned slightly to his right, hoping that he'd be able to catch a look at the man's face in the rearview mirror. But it was too dark, and the mirror was angled too severely for him to see any of the driver's features.

The police cruiser shifted into drive and made a U-turn, heading back down the street from which they had arrived. Vincent expected the car to start moving immediately after the cops had left, but it remained motionless; Vincent listened to the engine idle and waited for the driver to make a move. He turned to look at Brandon, hoping something in his friend's expression might calm his nerves. Instead, Brandon was looking down at his lap and mumbling something to himself. Vincent held his breath and tried to home in on exactly what he was saying.

"Can't believe this is fucking happening. Just can't fucking believe this shit. What did I do to deserve this?" Brandon muttered.

At that moment, Vincent had a revelation that made his blood run cold.

"Brandon," he said calmly, "where's Lisa?"

Brandon kept looking down at his lap and mumbling.

"Brandon!" More firmly this time: "What happened to Lisa?"

That seemed to snap Brandon out of whatever trance he was in, and he replied with a simple, "I'm so sorry."

Before Vincent could formulate a reaction, the driver spun around in his seat and pressed a cloth that smelled like chemicals over his mouth and nose. Vincent tried to fight him off, but it was no use. Within seconds, he felt everything go black and slumped over, unconscious.

CHAPTER TWENTY-ONE

When Vincent opened his eyes again, he found himself lying on a bed in a strange, dark room. He had a debilitating headache. He blinked away a few tears and tried to prop himself up to get a better look at his surroundings, but for some reason he couldn't get his body to move. It felt almost as if he was experiencing some sort of sleep paralysis, but the persistent sharp pain in his temples gave him confidence that he was awake.

Unable to get any part of his body to respond, Vincent scanned as much of the room as possible with only his eyes. In his right periphery, he could see a side table with what appeared to be a prescription pill bottle placed next to an alarm clock casting a soft red glow across the table's surface. It didn't seem like there was anything but darkness to his left, and he could hear a faint buzzing coming from somewhere in the room. He was doing everything he could not to completely panic, but he felt his heart rate steadily increasing.

How the fuck did he get here? Everything that had been happening to him seemed like a terrible nightmare, and he had no idea if it was even possible to escape.

Was he in hell?

The thought hadn't crossed his mind before now. It wasn't a stretch to think that some version of hell was experiencing your death over and over again. Like some sort of messed-up Sisyphean time loop that allowed a glimmer of hope before pulling the rug out from under you, throwing you into progressively more fucked-up situations ad infinitum.

After chewing on that thought, he decided he didn't really care if this was hell or not—all he truly cared about in this moment was Lisa. The last time he had seen her, she was talking to some of the bouncers at the wedding, but their conversation didn't look confrontational. Plus, Brandon only had her phone, which he could have nicked at any time. It was possible that she was able to get back to the hotel. It was also possible that she was being held hostage. Or worse.

Either way, she didn't deserve to be involved in this mess. She didn't deserve any of the nonsense he'd put her through over the years. There were so many times she had to carry burdens as a result of his selfishness, so many times he'd abandoned her—just like he had tonight—leaving her to face a cruel and unforgiving world all on her own.

If that wasn't behavior worthy of punishment, he didn't know what was.

Before Vincent could fall too far into his cozy rabbit hole of self-loathing, he noticed a slight, near imperceptible change in the room's lighting. It took him a few seconds to identify what had changed, but once he clocked it, a sense of foreboding washed over him. Peeking through the darkness was a sliver of light emanating from the front corner of the room. It almost seemed like someone had ever so slightly opened a door that he couldn't see. After a few seconds, he heard a faint creaking, and the sliver expanded into a door-sized rectangle.

He could feel a nervous sweat flowing out of his pores, but he was still unable to make even the slightest movement. While his mind raced to process this development, he noticed a human-shaped shadow split the light. As he lay frozen, a primal fear literally gripped him—he could feel its *claws*—and he used every ounce of willpower he possessed to try and get his body to wake up, but to no avail.

Helpless, he watched the shadow make its way into the room until he was staring at the darkened silhouette of a tall, slender figure standing directly in front of him. Vincent wasn't certain, but it looked like the person was wearing a fedora and holding some sort of box in their hand. He could feel the blood drain from his face, and his stomach tightened in reaction to the extreme fear.

Without a word, the figure lifted the box in front of their face and a flash momentarily brightened the room, the extreme contrast temporarily blinding Vincent. The flash was followed by a vaguely recognizable mechanical sound that he couldn't quite place. Before his eyes could adjust, another flash filled the room, again followed by the mechanical sound. He closed his eyes tight trying to get them to readjust to the darkness and opened them just in time to be blasted by another flash, much closer to him than the first two.

Then it hit him—the mechanical sound was a Polaroid camera spitting out instantly developing photo paper. Which meant that this menacing figure was taking pictures of him in his restrained state. Another flash, this time only a few feet from the bed he was lying on. He felt a sharp pain shoot through his chest as the figure made his way closer to Vincent before blinding him with another camera flash. He was now so close Vincent could smell the stink of whiskey on the man's breath and hear his shallow breathing. The next flash felt like it was directly in front of his face.

In the confusion of blinding light, he was transported back to the Aviary and the moment he first locked eyes with Lisa before a final flash inches from his face knocked him unconscious.

CHAPTER TWENTY-TWO

Vincent was startled awake by the sound of three loud whacks and groggily opened his eyes to survey his surroundings. To his immense relief, he no longer seemed to be trapped in the nightmare room. He also appeared to have full control of his facilities, which was a welcome improvement.

Looking around, he realized that he was sitting behind a mahogany desk in some sort of corporate office. Across from the desk were floor-to-ceiling glass windows, blocked by shades pulled all the way down, and a large door—also mahogany—with a shiny golden knob. The setting felt almost recognizable, but he couldn't quite place it.

Before he could investigate further, another round of knuckles wrapping on the door forced him to dive headfirst into this new existence.

"Uh . . . come in?" Vincent weakly rasped.

His greeting was met with yet another, much louder round of knocks. He let out a quick cough to clear his throat and repeated in a more authoritative tone, "Come in."

To his astonishment, it was Amanda Knotts who quickly slid inside the office before closing—and locking—the door. Per usual, she was dressed to the nines, sporting a perfectly tailored, asymmetrical red blazer over a white skirt and ruby pumps, but there was something different about her—Vincent just didn't know what.

"Were you fucking sleeping in here?" she half-whispered through gritted teeth.

"Just resting my eyes," Vincent mumbled, still trying to orient himself.

"You're lucky it was me knocking on the door and not Gil. That twerp would absolutely try to blackmail you if he found out you were sneaking naps in your office during the workday."

"Yeah, I guess you're right about that," Vincent replied half-heartedly. "So, what's going on?"

"What do you mean, what's going on? The whole office is waiting for you to give us permission to clock out for the day and start getting ready for the holiday party."

"Why would they need my permission?"

"Um, maybe because you're the highest-ranking person on the east coast?" She paused and gave him a concerned look. "Are you feeling all right?"

"Yeah, yeah, sorry—I'm just having trouble shaking off the cobwebs. Was having the craziest dream just now. Give me a few minutes to call Lisa, and I'll pop out to rally the troops."

"Excuse me?"

Vincent felt the mood in the room shift but wasn't sure why.

"What'd I say?"

"Did you just say you needed to call Lisa? Your ex-wife, Lisa?"

"Did I?" Vincent spat out, desperately trying to cover his mistake.

"That's sure what it sounded like," Amanda said, her tone bordering on threatening as she placed both hands on Vincent's desk, revealing a massive diamond engagement ring.

"It was something in the dream . . . terrible dream . . . one of the kids was in the hospital and . . . that was why I woke up thinking I had to call." He hadn't had any such dream, but it was all he could think of to try and curb her massive attack of what seemed to be . . . *jealousy?*

"Kids? Whose kids?" Amanda asked sharply.

"What do you mean, whose kids? My kids, of course—Violet and Charlotte."

"Vince, what the fuck are you talking about? Do I need to call an ambulance? Are you having a stroke? Do you smell toast?" she replied, her tone shifting toward genuine concern.

"Do I smell toast? What? No, I just want to make sure my daughters are all right. I had a dream Charlie's school bus was in an accident on the way home from a field trip."

"Vince . . ."

"Yes?" Vincent said, beginning to get frustrated.

"You don't have any kids."

He froze. How was that possible? She said Lisa was his ex-wife earlier, but they'd had Violet within a year of getting married. In what universe would they have decided not to have children? Unless the decision had been made for them . . .

"Jesus Christ," he muttered to himself, feeling his heart break at the thought.

"Jesus Christ is right," Amanda interjected. "What's going on with you today?"

Vincent had to think fast to cover his tracks.

"Honestly, I've been really stressed lately and popped a CBD gummy this morning to help me relax, and it's got me all fucked up. And apparently it makes you have lucid dreams."

Amanda gave him a skeptical look before leaning forward and dropping her tone into an almost seductive-sounding whisper. "I'm going to let it slide, just this once. But that's the last time I ever want to hear the name Lisa coming from your lips." At this point, she was inches from Vincent's face, her overly taut skin making it crystal clear she'd had some recent cosmetic work done. "From now on, the only woman in your life is the one standing right in front of you."

Before he could fully absorb what was happening, but grateful to know that at least Lisa was alive and had not died at the hands of mobsters, Amanda closed the remaining distance between them and locked him in what he considered to be an overly passionate kiss. She then pulled herself away and headed back toward the door, turning before she left to impart one last kernel of advice.

"Make sure you wipe away that lipstick, stud. Can't have any of the underlings getting suspicious about what goes on in this room." She smiled hungrily. "Now hurry up and get yourself together so we can go have some fun!"

With that, she gave him a wink, turned on her heel, and headed back into the bullpen. Vincent was relieved to see her go.

Now that he was alone, he had some time to gather as much information about this reality as he could before he'd be forced to put on yet another show. Looking around the office, he was surprised to see a row of awards lined up on a fancy floating shelf directly behind him. Each award was for a different accomplishment, ranging from individual accolades to upper-level management, and they all had his name on them.

Surrounding the awards were a handful of pictures that, for some reason, mattered to this version of himself. There were pictures of him skydiving, holding a massive marlin on a deep-sea fishing boat, participating in a ski competition, and standing close to Amanda as she held up her left hand to showcase her enormous engagement ring.

Who was this guy? In his previous life, he would have ruthlessly skewered someone who felt the need to brazenly highlight how great their life was going by overemphasizing accomplishments or accolades. He'd always considered those types of behaviors as signs of some sort of deep-seated insecurity. But apparently he wasn't immune from behaving the exact same way in a reality where he was able to successfully climb the ladder within Forrest Dunlop.

Way more concerning was the fact that he was no longer married to Lisa, and they'd never had the girls. While he had always harbored a tiny crush on Amanda, he couldn't fathom a scenario where he would feel more strongly about her than he felt about Lisa. What could have possibly caused him and Lisa to break up? Did he end up doing more than just kiss Amanda at that holiday party all those years ago? Was it because they weren't able to start a family together? Perhaps this version of himself hadn't wanted children? Amanda certainly didn't seem like the matronly type.

There was no way of knowing right now, but this revelation made him feel concerned about who this Vince had become. And who he now had to pretend to be for as long as he was here.

He found an odd comfort in the fact that this was only temporary. Or at least he hoped it would be.

Turning back toward his desk, he caught a glimpse of himself in the black mirror of his desktop computer screen. For the first time in forever, he looked like himself. Well, almost like himself. This version of Vincent appeared to be in his mid to late forties but perfectly coiffed and . . . smoother? Perhaps he was the same age as he had been the day he'd chosen to end it all, but it was hard to tell, considering how different this guy's journey must've been. He looked like a Hollywood version of himself, with wrinkle-free skin, tidier, slicked-back hair, a tan, and—he couldn't believe this one—a set of phosphorescent veneers poking out of his gums.

In the middle of examining his new face, a flash of gold caught his eye and he looked down at his left wrist to see a pristine Rolex peeking out behind a crisp, white, monogrammed double cuff. Moving up his arm, he realized he was wearing a custom tartan smoking jacket colored a festive dark green and red. He looked like money.

For the first time since this otherworldly trip had begun, he felt like he was wearing someone else's skin. *This guy must have lost his way,* Vincent thought.

Or maybe this is the version of me that actually figured it all out?

He shook his head, not wanting to entertain the voice pushing him to play devil's advocate for Corporate Vince.

Truthfully, he'd always wondered what it would be like to derive happiness from money and wealth. He'd had periods where he'd been flush with cash, but he'd always harbored an extreme paranoia that the spigot could turn off at any time. So he played it safe and tried to live below his means, tucking money away for later instead of treating himself and, he hated to admit it, Lisa and the girls. That attitude, paired with the feeling of emptiness he'd experience on the rare occasions when he would buy something nice for himself, caused him to shy away from the bells and whistles associated with modern consumerism. But maybe, just maybe, Corporate Vince knew something he didn't. After all, this Vince was the boss now.

The noise outside his office had risen to a dull roar, signaling that everyone in the bullpen was ready to clock out and blow off some steam. For the first time in his life, he was the one with the power to deliver the good news, and he felt his stomach fill with butterflies at the thought of addressing the full office. In his past life, he'd gone out of his way to avoid public speaking, but he didn't feel like he really had a choice in this setting.

And whatever happened out there couldn't be any worse than what he just went through in St. Augustine.

Comforted by that thought, Vincent pressed both palms firmly on the desk, pushed himself up, and headed toward the door. But when he grabbed the gilded door handle, he stopped, uncertain of what he would say or how he would say it. From what he could gather, Corporate Vince was basically the antithesis of who Vincent had turned out to be. Which meant that he was going to have to take some chances; otherwise, the legion of corporate drones waiting for him to emerge from his office would immediately sense something was amiss. Steeling himself, he took a breath and walked back out into the world.

It took a minute before the people in the bullpen realized that he'd appeared, but a hush descended over the crowd within moments of the first tranche of employees noticing his presence. At least two hundred sets of eyes were laser focused on him, and it took everything in his power to tamp down the feelings of anxiety coursing through his body. He began slowly pacing at the front of the room, hoping that was something this Vince did before addressing the sea of faces staring at him.

"Okay, everyone, I know you're eager to get out of here, but I've just got a few things to say before we close up shop for the day."

He paused, attempting to assess his audience's reaction in real time. Everyone remained focused on him, and he took this as a sign that he was on the right track. He took a deep breath, preparing to channel his best Wolf-of-Wall-Street impression, and plowed ahead.

"For me, this time of year has always represented a time of reflection. As all of you in this room know, it's been one hell of a year. Yes, we've had our fair share of successes—"

He was cut off by overemphatic cheering that started in the front rows and spread throughout the bullpen like a virus. Vincent had been on the other side of these presentations enough times to know that their reaction was inauthentic at best. It was much more likely that their exuberance was driven by some sort of misguided opportunism.

"And I'm thrilled to have the opportunity to celebrate those big wins," he continued, gesturing for the crowd to quiet down. "But we've also weathered our fair share of adversity. In fact, I would bet my life that every single person in this room has struggled at some point during the last twelve months."

Vincent took another moment to gauge the crowd, and this time he noticed some uncertainty in people's faces. He even noticed a few hushed conversations between desk neighbors. His mouth had gotten ahead of his mind, and he needed to buy some time.

"Now, I know what you're all thinking—why am I up here, during the happiest time of the year, talking about struggles and adversity? And that's fair, but just hear me out."

Vincent now found himself in the middle of the office, having walked through the rows of cubicles to better connect with his skeptical audience.

"I'd like everyone to do me a favor and look around this room."

Nobody moved.

"Seriously," he followed with a bit more authority in his tone. "Take a second and really absorb your surroundings."

There was some chatter and a few muffled laughs, but pretty much everyone followed Vincent's directions. He was grateful for the extra time to think and, as he continued pacing, a switch flipped: If he wanted to be inspirational, he needed to connect with the crowd on a deeper, more personal level.

"You see, I consider myself to be one of the luckiest men on the face of this earth because I know just how fucking special this group of people is, and I get to see you in action every day. Most people don't know how tough it is to walk into an environment like this day, after day, after day, and go to war like we do. They can't even imagine the type of grit and determination every single person in this room must possess in order to perform at the level that you all do."

Vincent could feel the volume of his voice rising as his energy was matched by those gathered around him. He'd tapped into something; he could feel it.

"Most people can't fathom what it feels like to operate under the pressures this job requires. They may say their jobs are tough, but we all know that if they worked here, they would break within a week. But you all," he dropped his chin and gently patted his heart, "you all know exactly what it feels like to face real pressure head on and, instead of cowering like 99 percent of the people in this world, you keep pushing forward. That's because this is a room full of warriors who won't take 'no' for an answer and don't stop until they've achieved their goals!"

A smattering of cheers and some clapping rang out across the crowd, and Vincent knew they were hanging on his every word. He dropped his voice and continued.

"But none of us go into battle alone. Every individual's success is built upon the foundation of trust and support we have for each other, knowing that in hard times we have an entire company full of warriors ready to step up and strengthen one another. So, ladies and gentlemen, as we close out this year, I want you all to know, from the bottom of my heart, that I've never been prouder to be associated with the type of winners that are in this room right now. The camaraderie we have in this building is something that deserves to be celebrated. I invite you to take a second, absorb this moment, and let your colleagues know you appreciate them and are there for them when they face tough times, as we all inevitably will."

Vincent was surprised to see that people were actually thanking their colleagues, and some were exchanging what appeared to be genuine hugs. It warmed his corporate heart.

"That's what it's all about right there," he continued somberly. "The people in our lives—you all are what make this job worth it for me, and for that I am eternally grateful."

He bowed his head again and gently patted his chest to show he was being sincere. It was time to bring it home and send these folks off on a high note.

"Now, I've only got one more thing to say," he continued. "I'm proud as hell of what you all have accomplished this year—and especially proud of how you've collaborated to accomplish your goals! So tonight, I want you to come together, celebrate this rarest of kinships, and have the best fucking night of your lives!"

The room erupted, and Vincent ran down the aisle high-fiving any hand he could reach on his way back toward his office. He was almost out of breath by the time he got back to the front of the room but managed a final "See you all at the party!" before ducking back into the cozy confines of his corner office.

He was still working to catch his breath when he heard a faint knock on the door, and Amanda slipped into the room.

"Well, that was quite the speech," she said.

"Yeah? You think they liked it?"

"Certainly seemed like it. Not sure where all that BS about camaraderie came from, though. You usually just tell everyone to make sure they have a ride home and not embarrass the firm."

"Oh well, this year, I felt like they needed a little extra pep. Figured I'd try something different, you know?"

"Sure, but don't make it a normal occurrence. All that lovey-dovey stuff makes you come off as weak. Better that they're so scared of you they won't even think about stepping out of line. You know?"

The last line was delivered in a derisive tone, and Vincent wasn't able to suppress a frown, prompting a quick follow-up from Amanda.

"Aw, I didn't mean to hurt your poor little feelings," she said in a mock-baby voice. "I just wanted you to know that I intend to marry a *man*, not some squishy little *boy*. I am marrying a *man*, am I not?"

Vincent sat there unable to come up with a reply—this entire conversation repulsed him. But there must be a reason why Corporate Vince had chosen to spend the rest of his life with this woman, so he decided to swallow his pride and take the route of appeasement. If he could figure out why he had chosen this path, maybe that would be a key to understanding why he'd ended up here.

"You're right," he sighed, staring at the floor. "It's just tough being the boss sometimes. A lot of pressure and a bunch of idiots I have to keep under control every goddamn day. Must just be the holidays getting to me this year." He looked up, and without breaking eye contact, finished with, "Don't worry, babe. Come Monday, I'll be back to kicking ass and taking names."

Vincent thought it unlikely he'd still be here on Monday, but a little white lie wasn't going to hurt anyone.

Amanda's face shifted into a sinister grin as she sauntered over and draped her arms around his shoulder.

"Now that's the type of man who's strong enough to tame Amanda Knotts," she purred, wrapping him in yet another overly affectionate kiss. "Now, let's go—I need you to drop me off for some pre-party drinks with the girls. I'd rather die than show up to this bogus holiday event sober."

She grabbed Vincent's hand and led him out the door like a puppy dog. Against all his better instincts, he followed obediently while feeling secretly thankful that he would be rid of his new fiancée soon. But he was here for now, and as he continued following her through the lobby toward the elevators, he found himself trying to get a read on this Amanda. Draped over her right shoulder, as a compliment to her candy-cane inspired outfit, she carried a Christmas-themed version of one of those god-awful "high-end" bags made of cheap leather and covered in brand logos—a signal to the public that she was rich enough to throw away thousands of dollars on an ugly, poorly made purse. To top it off, her hair and makeup looked as if they had just been professionally styled, and she strutted through the halls with the confidence of a CEO.

He had always quietly admired Amanda's unabashed flaunting of her success. But what he realized now was that these weren't signs of a confident person. In fact, they were more likely signs of overcompensation. Their previous working relationship had been cordial but very surface-level, which meant he never really "knew" Amanda. But after the conversation they just had, he felt like he'd been granted a window into her soul. And he wasn't thrilled about what that window had revealed. Not because it mattered so much who she was. It was more about who *he* had been when he was so enthralled by her.

When they exited the garage elevator, Amanda strutted toward what looked like a brand-new black Maserati. On the wall above the car was a sign that simply read, "Reserved: Managing Director."

Vincent found himself slightly awestruck by the car. He'd always secretly wanted to drive a Maserati, which was odd because he never considered himself a car guy. But it was a running joke between him and Lisa that if they ever won the lottery, his first purchase would be an Italian sports car.

"You coming or what?" Amanda called, standing by the passenger side door.

Vincent's admiration for the sleek black sedan in front of him had literally stopped him in his tracks. Amanda continued to stare at him impatiently before following up with a snappy, "Let's go, space cadet— the girls are waiting on me!"

Then it clicked. Vincent reached into his right pocket and pulled out a set of keys featuring the distinctive trident and couldn't stop himself from grinning. He hit the unlock button to let Amanda in and giddily made his way toward the driver's seat. He might not have been a fan of many of this Vincent's decisions, but he was determined to savor the opportunity to cruise around town in his dream car.

Amanda immediately buried her nose in her phone and began typing away at what seemed like a series of urgent texts as Vincent took his place behind the wheel. While she was distracted by whatever was happening on her phone, he took a second to appreciate the fine Italian craftsmanship that went into creating the interior. Outside of a test drive, he felt confident that he wouldn't ever get the chance to drive something like this again. After a few seconds of basking, he was ready to hit the road.

"So where are we headed, m'lady?" A part of him cringed at the acquiescence—and at having anyone other than Lisa sharing this experience with him—but what other option did he have? By now it was crystal clear that there was no changing the circumstances within these alternate realities of his.

Amanda continued tapping away at the phone without seeming to register that he had said anything. After a ten-second grace period, he tried again.

"Amanda . . ."

"What?" she snarled, continuing to text. "Can't you see that I'm in the middle of something?"

"Oh, sorry, but . . . I don't know where I'm supposed to go. Could you maybe put your phone away for a minute so we can head out of here?"

"Fine, just give me a second, okay?"

Vincent nodded and waited for her to finish. Finally, after another full minute, Amanda put down her phone and let out a frustrated sigh.

"All right, I'm done. What is it?"

"I just need to know where you're meeting the girls so I can drop you off."

"Oh, we're just going to meet at Sax, up the street."

"Sax? Like the bar three blocks from the office? That Sax?"

"Of course, what other Sax is there?" Amanda snapped.

Vincent let out a chuckle. "It probably would've been easier for you just to walk, don't you think?"

"Walking is for poor people. I'm not going to walk when you can drop me off and keep me from getting dirt on my red bottoms."

"Noted," Vincent replied, glad he would soon be rid of this beast woman.

Apparently satisfied with the way the interaction had played out, Amanda returned to her phone, and Vincent pulled out of the garage.

Much to his relief, Amanda remained hyper-focused on her phone during their brief trip down the street. Normally this type of behavior would have irritated Vincent—he seemed to be the only person bothered by the ever more routine act of phone snubbing—but the silence was a welcome respite from Amanda's elitist musings. In fact, she was so engrossed in the screen that it took a full two minutes before she realized that the car was stopped in front of their destination.

"Oh, are we here already?" she said.

"Sure are," Vincent replied. "Hey, when do you think you'll be heading over to the holiday party?"

"We'll probably make our way over there in an hour or two. Depends on how chatty everyone is feeling tonight. By the way, did you hear that Becky and Greg are getting a divorce?"

Vincent had no idea who Becky or Greg were, but figured it was best to play along.

"No way! What happened?"

"I'm not sure yet, but I heard that Greg got fired recently, and they had to get rid of her Porsche. Don't worry, though, I'll get all the details. I just hope she's got a good lawyer and can squeeze some sort of cash out of that deadbeat."

"Oh, wow, I'll be curious to get the full scoop," he said. Playing along with someone as basic as Amanda was easier than he expected. "By the way, can you remind me of the name of the place that's hosting our party?"

"Ugh, you've asked me at least ten times. We're starting at Pamplona and probably going to Heist for the afterparty."

"That's right," Vincent said, doing his best to feign recollection. "Now I remember. Guess I just need to figure out what to do before I head that way."

"I thought you were heading over to Alton's with Toby and Gil and a handful of the other guys to pregame?" She gave him a look that wavered between concern and disgust. "What is going on with you today?"

"Oh, right. I just spaced. Long day, right? And . . . it's super distracting to have such a gorgeous woman sitting next to me."

As he spoke the placating—and nauseating—words, Amanda leaned in, planted a hurried kiss on Vincent's cheek and opened her door, turning back to impart some unsolicited advice.

"Just make sure you pick up the tab. It's the holidays, and I don't want anyone thinking my fiancé is stingy. See you soon!"

It wasn't until Amanda was out of sight that Vincent realized that his entire body had gone tense. He let out a deep exhale and felt his shoulders loosen. Corporate Vince might want to spend the rest of his life with Amanda, but he could barely stand being around her for more than five consecutive minutes.

He decided to head toward Alton's, hopeful that a few drinks with the fellas would help him loosen up—and maybe learn something about why he was here, in this reality. As he drove, Vincent's thoughts darted toward Lisa and what could have happened to cause their split. A universe where he would have chosen to leave her behind just to end up with someone like Amanda was unimaginable. He needed to find out more.

As soon as he hit a red light, Vincent grabbed his phone and started rifling through his contacts, hoping that he still had Lisa's number saved. He sifted through a list of names, most of which he didn't recognize.

Lenny Raffle

Lindsay Stephens

Lizzie Brown

His wife's name was nowhere to be found amid the litany of strangers.

Vincent's stomach sank. Of course Amanda would have demanded he delete Lisa's number from his phone as soon as they started dating. Or maybe it had been his choice to delete her number?

He took a second to chew on this theory. It wasn't that outlandish to think that part of his evolution into Corporate Vince would involve severing ties with those that didn't share his ultra-capitalist, alpha-male ideals. But something about that didn't feel quite right.

Not ready to give up, he pulled up the dial pad and began typing out Lisa's cell number from his original reality. He could feel his pulse in his throat as the line caught and he listened to the steady drone of the dial tone trying to connect to the other line.

After what felt like a lifetime there was a click and Vincent's heart skipped a beat, praying the next sound he would hear would be Lisa's voice.

And it was.

"Hi, you've reached Lisa! So sorry to have missed you but I must be out saving the world or something, otherwise there's no way I would've let this call go to voicemail! Please leave a message at the beep or, better yet, just shoot me a text, and I'll get back to you as soon as I finish my meeting with the U.N. Cheers!"

The line beeped and Vincent quickly hung up the phone, unable to think of any message he could leave that would make any sense. He let out an exhale and committed to calling again before meeting up with Amanda at the holiday party.

For now, it was enough to know that Lisa was still out there somewhere and not tangled up in whatever he'd left her to deal with in St. Augustine. He had her number, and that at least gave him hope that he might be able to find his way back to her.

The light turned green, and he tossed his phone in the cup holder, allowing himself to feel cautiously optimistic that he could somehow make things right with the love of his life.

CHAPTER TWENTY-THREE

Alton's was an upscale cigar bar located in the heart of the business district that routinely attracted local executives and ambitious ladder climbers. From what Vincent could recall, it was the epitome of the old-school, boys-club establishments glamourized by elder states-men and maligned by the modern workforce. He'd been there a time or two during his tenure at Forrest Dunlop, typically at the invitation of some visiting bigwig, but it wasn't his normal scene. Even still, he couldn't pass up the chance to see how different Gil and Toby turned out in this reality.

He was surprised to hear the valet welcome him by name as he handed over his keys and made his way toward the front door.

I guess this Vince is some sort of regular here, he thought. *But I can't even remember the last time I smoked a cigar.*

The personal greetings continued as he made his way through the lobby, past the bar, and toward a secluded corner booth in the back where Toby, Gil, and a few other team members were excitedly chatting away.

"Chief! You made it!" Toby called out, waving Vincent toward their booth.

Vincent weaved through the crowd and said his obligatory hellos before taking the seat next to Toby. Within seconds, a female server had snuck up beside him and in a sultry voice breathed into his ear, "It's good to see you again, Mr. Palmer, and welcome back. We've taken the liberty to handpick a cigar from your personal humidor and prepare a glass of your favorite tawny port, a perfect pairing for an evening with friends. Would you like us to bring those out or would you prefer something different on this occasion?"

"That sounds excellent, thank you," Vincent replied, doing his best to go with the flow.

"As you wish. I'll have a staff member stationed nearby in case there is anything else we can help you with tonight."

"Very much appreciated," Vincent said, then remembered Amanda's departing advice.

"Actually, there is something you can do for me," he continued, dropping his voice. "Could you make sure anything my friends order ends up on my tab?"

"Absolutely, sir, we'll ensure everything is charged to your membership account."

Without another word, she disengaged and was immediately replaced by another member of their staff carrying a tray with his cigar and a glass of port wine. He recognized the signature black-and-yellow label associated with a genuine Cuban Cohiba cigar.

As Vincent plucked the stick off the outstretched tray, he took a moment to admire the perfectly smooth, caramel-colored Habano before leaning forward to allow the waiter to help him light up. He'd never smoked a real Cuban before.

A cloud of dense white smoke filled the air in front of Vincent's face as he took his first few deep pulls. He didn't think he'd enjoy this ritual, but there was something about the atmosphere in the lounge that Vincent found surprisingly alluring. The calculated combination of low lighting, hazy cigar smoke, and smooth jazz playing in the background quickly lulled him into a state of relaxation. He closed his eyes and allowed himself a moment to appreciate the life of luxury he was inhabiting.

Corporate Vince really doesn't cut corners when it comes to treating himself, he thought, giving the waiter a nod to subtly signal that he was no longer needed.

Oddly, the cigar wasn't nearly as satisfying as he expected. Lisa had always complained about the smell anytime they were stuck near someone smoking one, and an endearing image of her wrinkling her nose popped into his head. Taking another pull, he shifted his focus back to his immediate surroundings and realized their entire group had been watching him with intense, borderline-creepy interest. Toby was the first to break the ice.

"Man, that looks like one hell of a cigar, bossman. Is it a genuine Cuban?"

Vincent slowly examined the wrapper, "It would appear so," he replied, taking another pull for emphasis.

"There's really nothing in the world like a good Cuban cigar," Toby replied, then turned his attention to the rest of the group. "Have I ever told you guys about the time I went down to Havana? That was an absolutely wild trip . . ."

Toby then launched into a story that Vincent knew was almost certainly fabricated. Like any stereotypical sleazy salesman, Toby had a story locked and loaded for any and all occasions. In transactional or superficial situations—like most sales calls—it was a great tactic, but after spending years sifting through Toby's bullshit, Vincent couldn't help but get annoyed anytime he launched into a new tale. He felt himself disengaging from Toby's rambling and started to take stock of the people around him.

They were sitting at a semicircular booth with Vincent at one end next to Toby and Gil seated directly across from him on the other end of the booth. In between Toby and Gil sat two fresh-faced twenty-somethings stifling coughs and doing their best to pretend they knew how to smoke cigars.

Vincent guessed they were a pair of recent college grads that Toby or Gil had flagged as "Rising Stars" within the firm, and it was clear they were hanging on Toby's every word. They laughed at all the telegraphed jokes, and their rapt attention kept Toby engaged—and unaware that Vincent was no longer listening. Gil, however, remained relatively quiet, his eyes darting around the room like a predator searching for his prey.

Gil had always been somewhat of a mystery to Vincent. Like many of the higher-ups within the firm, he had started his career on a sales desk and managed to work his way into an executive-level role. But, unlike many of the other bigwigs, Gil didn't seem to possess the charm or charisma one would expect from a high-performing salesperson. Instead, he had somehow managed to climb the ladder through a combination of shrewdness, ruthless pragmatism, and an unflinching ability to look out for his own self-interest.

In Vincent's past life, Gil had been one of the more intimidating people he'd had to interact with, wielding his corporate power with impunity and outwardly disgusted by anyone who showed the slightest hint of weakness. More than once, he'd told Vincent he was too soft to ever advance within the company. But in this present reality, Vincent had somehow found a way to achieve a status within the organizational hierarchy that exceeded Gil's previous role as regional director. He was Gil's *boss* now. Nevertheless, Vincent was skeptical that this Gil would be any less ruthless than the man he knew to rule with an iron fist.

"So then this guy asks me, 'Do you want to meet Castro?'" Vincent heard Toby say. Gil had perked up, focusing his attention on Toby.

"And of course I say 'yes,' so this guy I just met tells me to follow him out back and he'll take me to Castro's mansion."

"Bullshit," Gil chimed in. "This is the most made-up story I've ever heard."

"Oh yeah? How would you know, Gil? You have some sort of private eye following me twenty-four-seven?"

"No, I just know that Castro lived in the penthouse of the Havana Hilton. Come on, we both know you're making this entire story up. Just admit it, and we can move on."

"You know what? If you're going to be like that, then fuck it, you don't get to hear the rest of this story."

"Wow, whatever will I do with myself now that I'm not able to hear the rest of your fake story about meeting a dictator?" Gil responded, each word dripping with disdain.

Vincent could feel the tension ratcheting up between the two and decided to do something he never would've dared in his previous life: intervene.

"Knock it off, Gil," he said firmly. "You've made your point, but we'd like to hear the rest of the story. Isn't that right, fellas?"

He paused and watched the two young guys in the circle nod in agreement.

"Proceed, Toby," Vincent said, leaning back and taking another pull on his cigar. Toby gave him a slight nod of appreciation and launched back into his story while Gil visibly disengaged and resumed scoping out their surroundings.

Part of Vincent was astounded by how easy it was to get the people around him to follow his orders. The other part was trying to reconcile this experience with his former life. It was hard to square how differently Toby and Gil were treating him with how similar their personalities were to his former corporate overlords.

Were people so influenced by job titles and perceived worth that they would honestly treat another human *that* differently? Had they naturally adapted to the corporate hierarchy to the point where unquestioning obedience was now the default setting for their relationship with Vincent? Or, had the success that Corporate Vince experienced warped the way he treated the people around him to the point that he was feared by his subordinates?

Toby finished his story to a round of laughter from the rookies. Vincent faked a laugh, but his mind was far from the conversation happening around him. With the story over and the tension broken, the group fell back into their normal banter, but Vincent was unable to focus on anything being said.

He found himself much less comfortable with this alternate reality compared to the others. Perhaps the nostalgia he felt during the other experiences provided a sense of comfort, even possibility. Maybe, deep down, he had hoped he might get a chance to reshape the path his life would ultimately take. Or maybe he was simply happier during those phases of his life and was glad to return to the good old days. But things were moving so quickly that it was difficult to know what, if anything, he wished would happen next.

The final moments of his life—his real life—flashed across his mind.

If only he could find his way back to that reality, then he'd have the chance to make things right.

For now, though, laid out in front of him was the opportunity to experience a lifestyle that had always seemed out of reach. Instead of standing on the outside of the gate and looking into the country club, he was now lounging in the clubhouse with the type of upperclass people he simultaneously despised and admired. He was running the show at the firm where he'd spent his entire career and apparently making enough money to open doors he wasn't previously aware existed. But as he looked around at the faces of his colleagues, he felt a familiar emptiness.

Sure, he was the big boss he'd always secretly wanted to become, but with that success came paranoia. Everyone smiled and showed deference to him, but he knew he couldn't trust that those behaviors were authentic. Did these people even like being around him? Or was it all just about power?

These thoughts continued to float around in his head while he politely engaged in conversation with his subordinates. He even took a risk and told a few of his old sales stories, hoping to avoid any suspicion. He was able to not only fly under Gil's bullshit radar but ended up encouraging Gil and Toby to share some old war stories of their own.

As they all finished their cigars, Vincent started thinking about his next move. Without realizing it, he'd downed at least three glasses of port wine, which, in combination with a full cigar, had him buzzin' like a bee. There was no way he could drive himself, or anyone else, to the party in his current state. Glancing around the room, he was able to catch the eye of the waitress who was watching after their table and gently nodded to call her over. Within seconds she was crouched by his side.

"Hello again, Mr. Palmer," she purred. "How may I help you?"

"Would it be possible for you to help me reserve a car for my friends and I?"

"Of course. Would you like one car or two?"

"Oh, I guess one SUV would be fine for all of us."

"Excellent. And before you leave, would you like us to assist with deodorizing your clothing?"

"Sure . . . is that extra?"

She paused, and Vincent could tell she was having trouble processing his question.

"I mean, can I put that on my membership bill?"

Her face lit back up. "Of course, sir. As always, we're able to charge your account for everything you've enjoyed this evening."

"Excellent. Sorry, it's been a bit of a strange day. Could you let us know when the car's arrived?"

"Absolutely, Mr. Palmer. We'll be sure to build in time for the deodorizing process to ensure a seamless transition. Will that be all for now?"

"Yes, that'll be all. You've been really great; thank you."

"My pleasure. Please enjoy the rest of your evening," she said before disappearing into the rhythms of the lounge.

CHAPTER TWENTY-FOUR

Members of the office were beginning to trickle into the party by the time Vincent and the others pulled up to Pamplona, a trendy Spanish tapas restaurant that was always busy. Forrest Dunlop had apparently reserved the entire space for their holiday party, which must have cost a pretty penny.

While Gil, Toby, and the newbies giddily filed out of the SUV, Vincent decided to stay put and take advantage of what might be his last opportunity to call Lisa before Amanda reentered the picture. He quickly typed her number into the dial pad and pressed the phone to his ear, his knee anxiously bouncing up and down as he waited for the call to connect. His heart thumped loudly in his chest as the first dial tone started to play.

Vincent took a deep breath to steady himself as the second dial tone began, but before the dial finished its lazy drone the line dropped and he was met with the same lighthearted voicemail greeting from before.

He felt like he'd been punched in the gut. Less than two rings before getting sent to voicemail could only mean one thing: Lisa had declined his call.

Dejected, he slumped in his seat and stared down at the phone, trying to determine if a second call in a row would help his cause. His finger hovered over the call button, but before he could follow through, a hard knock on the door stole his attention. His driver rolled down the window to reveal a valet who politely requested that they clear the drop-off area in front of the restaurant to make room for other cars.

Not wanting to cause any issues, Vincent slid the phone back into his pocket, took a deep breath, and reluctantly stepped out of the SUV to join the rest of his colleagues inside.

He wasn't sure what this Vince had done to screw things up so badly with Lisa, but he could get to work repairing the damage later. Tonight he had a company event to host and, given his newfound stature within the firm, he intended to right a few past wrongs and throw the type of celebration his colleagues deserved.

The holiday parties had always been a bit of a mixed bag. Early in his career, they had become notorious for the inevitable debauchery that resulted from combining an open bar with a large group of outgoing salespeople. But, as the company became more aware of their liability for any misdeeds that occurred during these events, the parties had been scaled back from raucous free-for-alls to tame cocktail hours. Tamping things down was met with spirited resistance among employees as the holiday party devolved from one of the most anticipated nights of the year to a lackluster obligation. People yearned for that one night a year where the company would pay for them to let loose and feel comfortable enough to swap their work personas for their authentic selves. It made up for at least some of the bureaucratic bullshit they all had to swallow on a regular basis.

As the years went on, many people no longer remembered—or hadn't been around for—those free-flowing events. What was once an annual highlight faded into a forgettable, pseudo-mandatory chore. But this year, Vincent was determined to use his newly acquired authority within the company to change that.

It was still early, and Vincent wasn't quite sure what lay ahead for the evening, so he figured he might as well have a drink while the rest of the staff made their way to the venue. He sauntered up to a bartender who couldn't have been more than twenty-three years old and asked the kid for an old fashioned.

"Sure thing, sir. That'll just be one drink ticket," the boy replied.

Vincent just stared at him.

"Um, that'll be one drink ticket. Please?" the kid said a little louder while extending his hand.

Vincent continued to stare as his brain worked to put the pieces together.

"Wait, we have to use tickets to get drinks? How many does everyone have?"

"Typically, for parties like these, everyone gets two."

"What happens if they want a third drink?"

"They can have as many drinks as they want. They'd just need to pay for them once they run out of tickets."

"Seriously?" He couldn't believe what he was hearing, "I just told these people we were going to have the night of our lives, and I get here and find out that it's basically a two-drink max?"

He could tell that the young bartender wasn't sure how to handle the situation.

"Is that a rhetorical question?"

"Not really. I'm actually trying to understand what kind of debacle I'm about to host."

"Sir, it was your company that requested we do it this way to limit costs."

"This was *our* idea? Is there a manager here I can speak with?"

"Um, what kind of manager?"

"Don't worry, I'm not gonna get you in trouble. I just want to talk to whoever can change this to an open bar."

"Oh, great. Yeah, let me go grab Kristina, and she can help you out."

"Thanks," Vincent said as the bartender started walking away. "Oh, and hey, kid?"

The boy stopped in his tracks and looked at Vincent apprehensively.

"How about that old fashioned before you grab Kristina?"

"Yes, sir," he replied, turning on his heel and heading back to his station.

When the bartender summoned Kristina, Vincent made a point to let the manager know that nothing was off limits to his employees except the option to order full bottles or more than one drink at a time. Vincent figured that was enough of a hedge against any outlandish behavior, and as a bonus, it allowed everyone the chance to try whatever top-shelf alcohol they preferred. Plus, he didn't really care what the tab was at the end of the night—he had no idea how long he'd inhabit this reality anyway.

For the next hour, Vincent positioned himself off to the side of the bar and held court. Word quickly spread that he was the reason the drink tickets in their pockets were now worthless, and everyone was eager to kiss the ring. At least that's what it felt like from his perspective, which he did worry was getting warped.

As a way to temper his ego, Vincent made it a point to be as engaged as he possibly could during any interaction, no matter what his counterpart's role was within the firm. All that really meant was that he needed to listen to whoever he was talking to and ask semi-thoughtful questions. It was so easy, yet it was something his previous bosses consistently neglected to do, opting instead to dominate conversations with lavish stories that highlighted their own personal wealth. Which was a shame for them, because Vincent was genuinely enjoying getting to know more about the people he worked alongside.

In fact, he was having so much fun that Amanda's absence hadn't even crossed his mind. That blissful existence was shattered when he heard someone shout from across the room:

"Where's my feeee-ahnc-ayyy?"

It was loud enough to break Vincent's concentration and turn his attention toward the entrance where he saw Amanda, shadowed by two of her girlfriends, marching directly toward him.

Evidently, she had changed outfits since he'd dropped her off at happy hour and was now wearing a low-cut, bright-red dress that might as well have been painted on. It was immediately clear that every set of male eyes in the room was trained on her, wishing they were the ones she was walking toward, but Vincent found himself wishing the opposite. A sense of dread washed over him as he watched her part the sea of people between them, and he suddenly felt a strong urge to ditch the party and track down Lisa.

"Am I late?" she slurred. "I didn't think everyone would be here already. I was hoping you and I might have some time for a quickie in the bathroom."

Amanda tried to wink but ended up blinking instead. It was clear that she was completely shitfaced. Not just tipsy, but three-sheets-to-the-wind drunk.

"Oh wow! Looks like you girls had more than a few drinks at happy hour. Have you had anything to eat? I'm pretty sure there are still waiters floating around with hors d'oeuvres."

"Pssssh, I'm fine," she replied with a loud hiccup. "I just need a martini to settle my stomach a bit."

"Water might be the best move for you, champ. Would you like me to grab one for you?"

"Oh, you think you can tell me what to do just because we're engaged?"

"No, that's not what I—"

"Well, you can't tell me what to do." She hiccupped so intensely that the involuntary movement caused her to take a step back. She steadied herself before lifting a wobbly finger and wagging it in Vincent's face. "I'm a strong, independent woman, and I don't need no man."

Not terribly sure what to expect from a semi-confrontational and clearly inebriated Amanda, Vincent did his best to keep things from escalating. He knew firsthand how quickly things could spin out of control when alcohol was involved.

"Well, I'm not going to tell you what to do," he said calmly, "but I'd strongly suggest pacing yourself a bit. Otherwise, we might not make it to the afterparty later."

"Ugh, you're such a buzzkill sometimes. Don't worry, I've got a little helper to get me through the night." She tapped her nostril with her index finger.

"Jesus!" Vincent yelped. "Please don't get caught with that here. That's the kind of stuff that just invites trouble."

He must have startled her, because she just stood there silently swaying in place. Then he saw her face scrunch up and was certain she was about to make a scene. She took a deep breath, ready to unleash hell, but before she could get started, Vincent was saved by one of their coworkers.

"Mandy! Where have you been, girl?"

Amanda's expression instantly softened as she greeted the woman with a hug. She looked to be roughly Amanda's age and also seemed quite drunk.

"Oh my God! Are you having the best time?" Amanda asked.

"No lie," the woman responded, "this is the best holiday party I've been to in years. Apparently, they opened the bar up, and I've been drinking Clase Azul on Forrest Dunlop's tab this entire time."

"What? How did that happen?" Amanda said, turning to Vincent for answers.

"Um, yeah, that was me."

Amanda's jaw dropped. "That's exactly the type of move I'd expect from my future husband." She gave him a seductive look. "You've earned something special later tonight."

"All right, lovebirds, enough of that," the woman interjected while grabbing Amanda's wrist. "Come on, Mandy—it's time we get a drink in that hand and go see the rest of the girls. Sorry, boss, I've gotta borrow the future Mrs. for a little bit. Don't worry though, I'll bring her back in one piece."

"Not if I have anything to say about it!" Amanda screeched. They both erupted in laughter and headed toward the bar without a look back at Vincent.

He let out a deep breath, relieved that he was spared from having to continue to interact with Amanda. His relief was followed by a sudden, sharp pain in his chest—he missed Lisa and the girls. He wished more than anything that he could snap his fingers and find himself curled up on the couch with the three of them, eating popcorn and watching whatever cheesy rom-com had recently been released on Netflix.

Before he was able to dwell on that thought, a younger associate nervously approached him, and Vincent settled back into some friendly banter with his coworkers. All around him, he could tell that the energy in the room was beginning to change. People were starting to loosen up, shedding their work masks and legitimately having fun. From what he could tell nobody had been overserved—yet—and the Pamplona staff had even cleared some tables to create a small dance floor, which was quickly becoming a hit. Everywhere Vincent looked, he saw people letting their hair down and having a great time.

In a way, he felt vindicated. In his past life, he'd constantly had his ability to lead questioned by empty suits who confused ruthless corporate bullying with leadership. But as he looked out at the crowd and saw people connecting and appreciating one another's company, he knew that his style of management would have resulted in greater successes than the stale, rigid bullshit he'd endured for the last decade. It didn't take a genius to figure out that people performed better when they were treated like human beings instead of numbers on a spreadsheet, but apparently all his previous bosses had missed that memo.

———

The next hour went by in a snap as Vincent made his rounds and talked to what seemed like everyone in the office. It reminded him of his wedding day in a weird way. Before he knew it, Pamplona's manager was at his side, giving him the thirty-minute warning that the staff would soon be opening their doors to the public for the rest of the evening. He noticed Toby walking toward the bar and grabbed him by the arm.

"Hey, watch it, man!" Toby snapped, before realizing who had grabbed him. "I mean, what's up, bossman? You need a drink?"

"I'm good, thanks. But I do need a favor—can you help me out?"

"You know it!" Toby slurred excitedly, his eyes focusing on Vincent's face as best as they could.

"Awesome. Listen, the open bar is going to close in thirty minutes, so I need you to spread the word that we're headed to Heist for the afterparty. And Toby . . . make sure everyone you talk to gets another drink before the bar closes down."

"Aye-aye, captain!" Toby saluted and disappeared into the crowd.

Now he just needed to find Amanda; as much as he didn't want to find her, it did seem like the right thing to do within this reality. Hopefully she was still somewhat functional.

Vincent took a deep breath and dove into the crowd of dancing people. Try as he might, he couldn't seem to find Amanda anywhere, but he was impressed by how many people already knew about the afterparty. Toby had apparently taken on his assignment with vigor, and Vincent was optimistic that their transition would go smoothly. However, he couldn't spot Amanda anywhere, which, given her choice of outfit, was quite surprising.

He decided to grab one more drink before the bar closed and keep an eye out for her. The nice thing about how much talking he'd been doing over the last few hours was that he now felt almost completely sober and all clear to order something stiff before closing the tab.

The moment the bartender handed him a Sazerac, the manager was at his side with the bill for the evening. She looked nervous as she extended her hand with the receipts for him to review and sign. Vincent nearly spit out his drink when he saw the total.

"Twenty-four thousand dollars? That can't be right, can it?"

"Trust me sir, we have a top-of-the-line system that ensures accuracy. And I should mention, the total does not include any gratuity you'd like to leave."

Vincent stared at her for a moment before bursting out laughing. He knew the tab was going to be fairly expensive, but in no way had he thought this night would cost as much as a new car. Thanks to his laughter, the manager, who was at least a decade younger than him, visibly loosened up.

"So, how much would you recommend I tip on a tab like this?" he asked, careful to convey a friendly tone.

"Twenty percent?"

"That's it? Are you sure there isn't some sort of 25 percent minimum for parties of this size?" he said with a wink. It took her a moment to catch on.

"Twenty-five . . . oh, you're absolutely right, sir! We do have a minimum gratuity of 25 percent for parties of more than fifty people."

"Excellent. And all of this tip goes directly to the staff, right? You've been extremely accommodating, and I don't want your bosses taking credit for all that work."

"Everything goes directly to me and my staff at the end of each night. I'll make sure of it."

"That's what I like to hear," Vincent finished, signing off on a thirty-thousand dollar tab he was definitely not authorized to pay.

There was a small chance he'd have to deal with the consequences of those decisions, but for now it felt good to be generous.

After he'd settled the bill, Vincent hung by the bar and scanned the crowd. Slowly at first and then with increasing speed, he noticed that the faces he recognized were being replaced by members of the general population. Feeling more than ready to turn in for the night, he stifled a yawn. Suddenly he realized he had no idea where this Vince lived, so he waited by the bar, hoping Amanda would finally reappear. He wasn't even sure if they lived together, or if they'd made plans to go home together at the end of the evening. He looked down at his watch and saw it read 11:05.

I'll give her another ten minutes, and then I'm probably safe to head out, he thought. Worst-case scenario, he'd book a room at a hotel nearby.

He was beginning to think she had left him at the party, which was perfectly fine with him. Vincent was getting the feeling that Amanda spent most of her weekends in these types of environments. In a past life, he used to envy his colleagues who were able to freely attend a spontaneous extended happy hour or spend their Saturday nights out on the town, but now all he wanted was to be home with his family.

Vincent again found himself thinking about Lisa and the kids. Where were they? What were they doing? How much time had actually passed since the night he'd died? Had Lisa found another partner? Did Violet and Charlotte prefer him to Vincent? Did Lisa hate him?

The last thought sent a chill down his spine.

He would have continued spiraling if it weren't for the sound of high-pitched giggling nearby. He shook his head in an attempt to physically snap out of his funk and saw Amanda and her friends emerging from the bathroom laughing and engrossed in a friendly but extremely loud conversation. He watched from afar to see if she would notice that all her coworkers had left the venue. Maybe she wouldn't see him, and he would be free to book that hotel room and spend the rest of his night alone.

At that moment, almost as if she could read his thoughts, Amanda spotted him and announced very loudly to nobody: "There's my FEE-YAWN-SAY!"

The women she was with let out a collective "Whoo!" and started heading his way as if they were being pulled by some sort of invisible magnetic force.

So much for spending the night alone. Vincent took a deep breath to prepare for the human hurricane headed right for him.

Once she was close enough, Amanda wrapped him in an over-the-top hug, kissed his cheek, grabbed his chin with one hand like a grandmother would grab a toddler, and turned to her friends.

"Isn't he just the cutest man you've ever seen?" she said.

Vincent was not at all amused by this type of insultingly affection-ate behavior. But Amanda apparently expected him to lean into her performance. "Oh, Mister Bossman is so serious today," she mocked, continuing to squeeze his cheeks. "Mister Bossman better lighten up if he wants to get lucky tonight."

Her followers broke out in supportive laughter as she mercifully released his chin from her grasp. Never before had Vincent wanted so badly *not* to be touched by such an attractive woman.

"Have you seen Taylor? I have the funniest thing I need to tell her," Amanda said, turning her attention back to Vincent.

"I'm not really sure," he replied. "She probably headed over to the afterparty with everyone else."

"The afterparty? There's no way it's time for Heist yet. It can't be any later than nine-thirty."

"It's almost eleven-thirty."

"Get out of here!" She slapped his chest. "We were only in the bath-room for a few minutes! There's no way it's already eleven-thirty. Are you lying to me right now?"

Vincent felt the mood shift from playful to paranoid, and he had the sudden realization that at some point Amanda must have snuck off to the ladies' room with her crew and indulged in a little Bolivian marching powder. It explained the long disappearance, newfound pep in her step, and borderline erratic behavior she was exhibiting now. This wasn't surprising, but it certainly didn't motivate Vincent to tag along for whatever type of night these girls were gearing up for.

"I'm not lying to you," he calmly replied. "Check your phone. I've got no reason to lie about something like that."

He could tell Amanda wasn't happy with his measured response, but his confidence seemed to relax her suspicion.

"No, no, you're probably right," she said. "Well, I guess the only thing to do now is meet up with everyone at Heist!"

Before Vincent could say anything, she grabbed his hand and they marched out of the building. Every fiber in his being was telling him to break off and go home—wherever that was—but he knew that suggestion would receive hard pushback from Amanda so he agreed to push through for a little longer. At least he wouldn't be walking into a club full of strangers.

CHAPTER TWENTY-FIVE

Only a few blocks from Pamplona, Heist was one of the more mysterious nightclubs in the city. Its entrance was tucked away down a back alley, and the only signage was a pair of double doors with a handle in the shape of a longhorn skull. On busy nights, the alleyway would be filled with people waiting in line for their chance to see what all the fuss was about. Vincent was relieved that tonight the alley was empty, apart from a few loiterers sharing joints and paper bags.

Amanda guided Vincent and the girls through the double doors and led them down a flight of stairs toward the pulsing sounds of club music, growing louder with every step. At the bottom they were greeted by a large bouncer dressed in all black, not unlike the ushers at David's wedding. Above the bouncer's head was a TV that seemed to be live-streaming closed-circuit coverage of what was happening both inside the club and in the alleyway. The bouncer initially eyed them with suspicion but within seconds of speaking with Amanda, they were being graciously welcomed inside.

"It never hurts to have an attractive woman by your side when trying to get into a busy nightclub," Amanda informed him, seeming pleased with herself. Vincent rolled his eyes, following Amanda as she stepped inside the basement club.

The main area was extremely dark—the only exception being some sparse uplighting and backlights behind the bar—with mirrored ceilings that couldn't have been more than eight feet high and music loud enough to cover any noise the crowd was making. It felt claustrophobic. He hadn't been in this type of environment since his twenties and felt completely out of place.

Amanda, on the other hand, seemed to be in her element. She skillfully weaved through the crowd to commandeer a spot at the bar, and greeted the bartender as if they were long-lost friends. As she placed their drink orders, Vincent scanned the crowd, looking for friendly faces. It was hard to make out much in the darkness, but all he saw were random clubgoers. The crowd demographic skewed a bit older than Vincent would have expected. Instead of a mass of drunk twenty-somethings, it seemed as if the people surrounding him were all in their thirties, forties, and beyond. Everywhere he looked, he noticed designer clothes, naked ring fingers, and searching eyes. It was like being in a room full of people who were trying desperately to fit into a lifestyle from which they should have graduated long ago.

Maybe it was an unfair observation, but it seemed like Heist's patrons were all there hoping to find something—or someone—that would eventually make the need for frequenting these types of establishments a thing of the past. Something he'd been lucky enough to find a long time ago. If only he'd realized that when it still mattered.

"Here you go—I got you a tequila soda," Amanda said, handing him a drink and pulling him away from his heady thoughts. Vincent hated tequila.

"Oh, thanks, but I don't really like tequila. Do you think one of your friends wants it?"

"What do you mean you don't like tequila? I thought we talked about this. Everyone knows that tequila is 'in' right now, so that's what we drink when we're in public."

Vincent was flabbergasted. He could not imagine ever having that type of conversation, let alone agreeing to drink something he despised simply because it was considered "in."

"Just drink it and be happy that you get to take home the hottest girl in this club tonight," Amanda said, followed by a patronizing pat on the cheek.

Vincent took the drink and decided his best course of action would be to order something else when she wasn't paying attention. He looked back at his watch and saw that it was almost midnight. At most, he only had to endure a couple more hours of this nonsense, and in the morning he could figure out what to do about this untenable relationship.

"Bossman! You made it!" he heard Toby's voice say from behind him.

"Oh, hey, Toby—glad you guys made it out."

"Are you kidding? This is the most fun we've had at a holiday party in at least a decade! Follow me—I've got a primo table in the back for our people."

Before Vincent had a chance to say anything, Toby had thrown his arm over his shoulder and was shepherding him through the disorienting, constantly shifting mass of human body parts toward their table. Vincent looked back, attempting to catch Amanda's eye, but she was fully engrossed in a conversation with the bartender and someone who appeared to be his manager. Thankful to be removed from her company, Vincent decided to roll with the situation—Amanda would end up at the Forrest Dunlop table at some point soon enough.

———

Their table was positioned in the back corner of the club next to a hallway that led to the restrooms, and Vincent was pleasantly surprised to see there were about twenty team members still out and sticking together.

He was even happier about the fact that their table seemed to be positioned in an acoustic dead zone that made it significantly easier to hear his colleagues over the club music pumping through the speakers.

After working through the compulsory greetings, he noticed a bottle of vodka sitting in the middle of the table with carafes of orange and cranberry juice. He poured himself a vodka cranberry and discreetly discarded his tequila drink among the various empties scattered on top of the table. Feeling a bit more autonomous, he settled in and did his best to try and enjoy the conversations happening around him, hoping it would help pass the time before he could head home.

He wasn't sure how long he'd been anchored at the table, but when he went to pour a refill, it dawned on him that he hadn't seen Amanda since they walked into the club. He felt slightly guilty for abandoning her and decided to keep a better eye on the dance crowd.

It didn't take long before he spotted her standing off to the side of the DJ booth, still talking with the bar manager and what appeared to be a member of the DJ's crew. Her friends were nearby but fully engaged in flirtatious exchanges with a group of younger guys dressed like wannabe Narco drug lords. For some reason this really annoyed Vincent—if not but for Amanda, he would have skipped the afterparty entirely—yet here she was, spending all her time hanging with random club rats? It wasn't his job to babysit her. He'd had it.

Without a word to anyone, he shot out of his seat and started wading through the crowd toward the DJ booth. It was around this time that he realized he was undeniably drunk. He felt like he was walking on an airplane as he tried to squeeze through an endless crowd of people. Their reaction to his sloppy attempts to navigate his way through the dance floor made it very clear that he wasn't going about his mission in the most efficient manner, but he didn't care. All that mattered was that he got to Amanda so he could get out of this ridiculous basement and put an end to this exhausting day.

But by the time he finally pushed through the last group of people huddled in front of the DJ booth, Amanda was nowhere to be found. Vincent scanned the dance floor for any sign of her, but it was too dark to see anything in the pit. Before he gave up, he decided to pop up on the balls of his feet and cast his gaze toward their table in the back. Maybe they had inadvertently missed each other during his journey to the front.

He didn't see any new faces at the table, but out of the corner of his eye, he did see a man and the shadow of a red dress turn the corner down the hallway leading to the bathrooms.

Vincent immediately latched on to the worst-case scenario and started clawing his way back through the crowd toward the bathrooms. He couldn't believe how blatantly disrespectful she was being—not even this Vince deserved to have his fiancée treat him like this. His temples started to throb, and he was only vaguely conscious of the people he was pushing aside. It didn't really matter how he felt about Amanda— something inside him was ready to snap, and he wasn't sure he would be able to control himself if things got rocky. Maybe this wasn't the best place to dump his fiancée, but he wasn't sure how much more of this woman he could take.

He burst through the crowd and was barreling around the blind corner toward the bathroom when he slammed into a large man's chest. Vincent had been moving so quickly that the force of impact bounced him back slightly, giving him a second to confirm the man wasn't who Amanda had absconded with.

He muttered a half-hearted apology and tried to sidestep the man but found himself once again buried in this giant's chest.

"Could you move?" Vincent snapped.

"No can do, boss," the man replied flatly.

"What are you, some sort of bathroom bouncer or something?"

"Bathroom is on the other side of the club, bro. Only VIPs allowed in the lounge."

Vincent opened his mouth to respond but needed a second to process what the man had just said.

"Well, my fiancée is back there, so I'll just go grab her and we'll be on our way," he replied, again trying to sidestep the bouncer, who threw an arm out and stopped Vincent in his tracks.

"Sorry, boss, gotta be on the list to get back there."

"I just told you my fiancée is back there. Was she on the list?"

"What's her name?"

"Amanda Knotts."

The bouncer didn't break eye contact.

"Nope, not on the list."

"Oh, come on! She just walked back here in a red dress. I know you saw her. Just let me pop my head in, grab her, and I'll be out of your hair."

"Now that you mention it, there is a girl back there in a red dress. Pretty gal." He let out a low whistle.

"Well, uh, thanks, I guess. So, you'll let me go get her?"

"Nah, can't do that, boss. I'm pretty sure that's Mo's girl for the night."

Now, this was really the last straw. "Listen up, motherfucker, that's my goddamn fiancée, and you're going to let me through right fucking now!"

The man smirked and calmly cracked his knuckles, as if trying to see if Vincent was serious about escalating the matter. Before Vincent could make his next move, a bald head popped out from around the corner.

"Hey, is this where the bathroom is? Oh shit, hey, Vince! We thought you left already," Toby said, completely oblivious to the tense circumstances.

The bouncer shifted his attention toward Toby for a split second, and Vincent took his shot, hitting the bouncer with a swim move and sprinting toward the door of the lounge. The hallway was only about twenty feet long, and he had enough of a head start to get to the door before the bouncer could follow in pursuit. He gripped the handle, yanked the door open, and was greeted by an image that left him momentarily stunned.

In front of him was a small, dimly lit room that appeared to be covered floor to ceiling in a dark-red velvet. There were two plush semi-circular couches inside, each with a circular, gold-framed glass table directly in front of them. On the couch nearest the door, Amanda was sitting on the lap of the man she had followed back to the lounge. His hand was gripping her partially exposed backside while she leaned over to blow a line of coke off the glass table in front of them.

"Amanda, what the fu—" Vincent yelled before a hand aggressively grabbed his collar and unceremoniously pulled him backward away from the door. The last thing he could see before the door closed was the guilty look on Amanda's face.

"Okay, fella, I've had enough. It's time for you to go," the bouncer said, grabbing the beltline of the back of Vincent's pants and perp-walking him back toward the dance floor.

"Get your hands off me!" Vincent yelled, flailing his arms and trying to get the man to release him.

"All you big shots always think you got such loyal women. But if you had loyal women, they wouldn't be taking you to places like this. They'd be making you take them to dinner at the Olive Garden or some shit. Best you figure this out now before she can take half your money and run. Really a blessing in disguise, if you think about it," the bouncer said.

He was right. There was a reason Vincent and Lisa stopped going to places like this as their relationship matured. What was he so mad about? Why should he care if Amanda was doing blow and hooking up with some guy in the VIP lounge?

"You've got a point," Vincent grumbled, still struggling to get himself loose.

"I know," the bouncer responded. "Now why don't you stop fighting me, and we can take you out of here the easy way?"

Vincent considered the offer, temporarily relaxing his arms before a devilish thought popped into his head. "Here's the deal," he said, "I'm here with a bunch of my employees, and it's the tail end of our holiday party. For the sake of their entertainment, it'd be great if we could make this look like a real struggle. If you don't mind?"

Vincent knew that for a holiday party to be considered truly great, something singularly outlandish had to happen. Forevermore this would be remembered as the holiday party where the boss got thrown out of the club.

"Man, you rich folks really are crazy," the bouncer chortled. "Sure, man, we can make it look real—not that it's really gonna matter. You couldn't stop me from throwing your ass out if you tried."

"Oh, yeah?" Vincent said playfully.

"Not a snowball's chance in hell," the bouncer confirmed.

"I'm not buying it." Vincent was starting to have fun. "What do I get if I do manage to slip your grip?"

"If you can get loose, I'll let you walk out of here on your own two feet."

"And if I can't?"

"I guess we'll just have to see how things play out," the bouncer dead-panned, shoving Vincent toward the crowd at the end of the hallway.

He didn't love the sound of that and immediately began flailing and twisting with all his strength as they burst onto the dance floor.

Try as he might, Vincent couldn't seem to do anything to shake the bouncer's iron grip as the mass of people began parting to open a lane for them to pass through. He had the distinct feeling that this type of ceremonial exit was a common occurrence at Heist.

By the time they had made it to the top of the stairwell, Vincent was completely out of gas—the bouncer's confidence was not misplaced.

"All right, you win," Vincent gasped. "Now what?"

"Now you gotta go for a ride, my man," the bouncer said as the door opened from the outside. "I've gotta make a show of this, nothing personal. Just part of the job. Sorry, bro."

Before Vincent had a chance to respond, the bouncer yanked him backward, pulling him completely off the ground, and tossed him out of the club, roadhouse style. Vincent heard the rip of fabric as he was forcibly introduced to the filthy pavement lining the alleyway. He was lucky enough not to have hit his head too hard on the ground, but he immediately felt something warm running down his right arm and lower legs.

It took a moment for him to readjust and pull himself up to his knees. He looked down and saw two small puddles developing under each knee and could tell blood was flowing from his right elbow down to his hand, slowly dripping to the ground. Nothing felt seriously injured—they were only flesh wounds.

After taking stock of the damage, Vincent gradually made his way back to his feet and was surprised to see that the alley was now filled with people waiting in line to join the party. A few good Samaritans came over to offer assistance, but Vincent waved them away. He knew he needed to figure out his next move, but the alleyway was so loud and distracting that he was having trouble gathering his thoughts. There also seemed to be some sort of commotion happening toward the back of the line that kept drawing his attention.

Vincent's appetite for additional confrontation was nonexistent, so he decided to start walking in the other direction. He'd only taken a few steps when he heard Amanda shout from the club entrance. "Vince, where are you going? Wait for me!"

Without looking back, he waved her off and kept walking, faintly aware that the noises from the back of the line were getting louder. Seconds later he heard the clip-clop of high-heels approaching from behind him, and Amanda's hand grabbed his shoulder.

"What the fuck, Vince? I can't believe you just embarrassed me in front of all our coworkers like that!"

He spun on his heel, unable to contain his disdain any longer.

"I embarrassed *you*? Are you fucking crazy or something? In what world was I the embarrassment tonight? Do you have any clue why I was just ejected from this stupid fucking overhyped basement bar? Do you?"

"Wow, you're acting insane right now. You know that, right?"

"Jesus Christ, can you just leave me alone? You clearly have no interest in being with me—and I have very little interest in you—so just go back to that lounge and continue on with your drug-fueled bender."

"Honey, I haven't done any drugs tonight. I can't believe you would even say something like that. We've been basically attached at the hip this whole time. You're going to wake up tomorrow and feel really stupid about how you're acting right now."

This type of gaslighting would normally send him into a tailspin, but at this point all Vincent could do was laugh. Her claim was too audacious to take seriously.

"Are you fucking kidding me?" he said in between chuckles. "I literally just saw you in there sitting on some guy's lap blowing lines of coke with your ass out."

With the wind knocked out of her sails, Amanda came back with a half-hearted "That's not what was happening in there . . ."

Instead of dignifying that falsehood with a response, he just stared at her. He could sense her wilting under his gaze, recognizing in real-time that she wouldn't be able to manipulate the situation to her advantage. A part of him pitied her.

Taking a deep breath, he started to say, "Look, let's just get out of here." But before he could get the words out, the crowd lit up with screams and began running toward them.

BANG! BANG! BANG!

Gunshots rang throughout the alleyway as dozens of people stampeded toward the feuding couple. Amanda took off without a passing glance backward, but Vincent felt glued to where he was standing.

Another shot went off, and as the crowd made its way past him, Vincent could see that the loiterers from earlier were now engaged in a full-on gunfight with a rival group. He'd never seen anything like this, despite spending a solid portion of his adult life in densely populated cities. He wanted to run, but his body would not listen to his mind— his sympathetic nervous system had apparently decided the best thing to do was freeze.

Time felt like it was slowing down while Vincent watched the violence unfold in front of him. One of the loiterers had been hit and was struggling to find shelter, bleeding profusely from his stomach. A member of the rival group was lying motionless in the middle of the alley. The rest had sought refuge behind various dumpsters and parked cars and continued to exchange volleys. For the first time, Vincent realized that the other end of the alley was a dead end. In order to escape, they would need to head his direction.

On cue, the people positioned nearest to Vincent made a break and began sprinting toward him, firing indiscriminately over their shoulders as cover. They were about ten yards in front of him when a large man stepped out from behind a dumpster and took aim. Vincent recognized him immediately—it was the Big Man who had fired the shot that had started all of this.

As if in slow motion, Vincent watched the Big Man steady his aim and pull the trigger. The last thing he saw was the flash of the muzzle, and once again, his world went dark.

CHAPTER TWENTY-SIX

The first thing Vincent noticed was the sound of birds singing. He kept his eyes shut and took in the gentle chirping for a few seconds, afraid of whatever new reality awaited him once they opened.

The noise reminded him of early springtime when the sun began rising earlier and the days stretched out well into what was previously nighttime. He used to hate the sound of the birds outside his window. They always managed to wake him up right before his alarm, depriving him of those last few precious minutes of semiconscious bliss before having to wade into the day ahead. But right now he didn't feel anything but gratitude and appreciation for the birds and their songs.

The next thing he noticed was the temperature—or rather, the climate. The air around him was a bit warm without being uncomfortable, and a cool breeze blew through every few seconds. The airflow almost made him feel like he was outside, but if that was the case, he'd surely have felt the heat from the sun beating down on him from above.

He kept his eyes shut, terrified that when he opened them, he'd be thrown right back into some strange scenario from his past or future. Of course, he deserved whatever misery awaited him. He owned the mistakes he'd made and had no choice but to accept the consequences.

The funny thing was . . . he didn't even recognize the version of himself that had decided to end his life. How could he have been so foolish as to not appreciate how great things had been? What was he so upset about?

Vincent took a deep breath and exhaled, hoping that would help his mind reset. All this self-pity . . . it didn't serve any purpose. The only thing he could control was the way he dealt with whatever was in front of him in this reality, and all he could hope was that things worked out for the best. He took one more deep breath and opened his eyes.

In front of him was the inside of a small, single-room log cabin containing only a large potbelly stove, small kitchen area, and the cot that he was lying on. He was sure he'd never been here before—or in any log cabin, for that matter—but for some reason this place felt familiar. He rubbed his eyes, wanting to guarantee that he wasn't dreaming. When he reopened them, he was greeted with the same scene, but this time he realized the door was left open, letting a soft breeze waft throughout the small dwelling.

Despite having only three windows—two on either side of the doorway, one on the opposite wall above the kitchen counter—the room was flooded with natural light. The sunlight pouring in from the open doorway seemed to beckon him outside, and without a thought, Vincent got to his feet and walked toward the unknown.

Once outside, he found himself looking down on a weathered front porch underneath a small overhang. To his left was an empty rocking chair, and to his right was a homemade bird feeder hanging from the ceiling with a diverse collection of birds hovering around and helping themselves to an easy snack. The air smelled fresh and reminded him of childhood. Everything about this place felt simultaneously novel and nostalgic—like a reminder of a past he hadn't lived or a future he didn't yet know.

Vincent closed his eyes again and basked in the stillness of the moment. Trees rustled in the background. They sounded like gently crashing ocean waves when the breeze picked up. Without opening his eyes, he took a step forward and felt the warm embrace of the sun. He tilted his head toward the sky and extended his arms outward, fully appreciating the sublimity of his environment.

Slowly opening his eyes, he noticed a smooth dirt path leading to a picturesque lake, surrounded by a forest of thick, tall trees. At the end of the path there was a small dock jutting out into the water and an old man sitting on a rocking chair tending to a fishing line. Again, without hesitation, Vincent felt himself walking along the path toward the dock as if guided by an invisible magnetic force. His steps felt effortless and his shoulders felt lighter than usual as he rambled up behind the old man, hopeful that he may have some answers.

Stepping onto the dock, Vincent realized he had no idea how to start this conversation.

It turned out he didn't have to. "Beautiful day, isn't it?" the old man said, welcoming him while keeping his gaze firmly fixed on the fishing line.

"Um, yeah, best day I've seen in a while," Vincent replied.

The old man nodded and began gently rocking back and forth in his chair. After a few seconds of silence, Vincent continued. "Do you know how I got here?"

"Must've finally woke up," the old man quipped. "That's how it typically works."

The old man gave a lazy wave to invite Vincent to join him at the edge of the dock. Vincent obliged and instantly felt comfortable enough to take a seat and drop his feet in the lake. The water was the perfect temperature.

"What is this place?" Vincent said with quiet wonder.

"Some people call it heaven." The old man chuckled. "But I just call it home."

"Am I dead?"

"Do you feel dead?"

Vincent thought for a second. He felt a little strange—in a good way—but not dead.

"No, I guess not. But I haven't felt alive for quite some time."

He wasn't sure why he was being so honest with this stranger.

"Why is that?"

"I just . . ." Vincent faltered, unsure of how much he should share. "I just always thought my life was going to be different. I pushed for years and years trying to make something of myself, and after a while I finally gave up. I still held out hope that maybe fate would intervene and something would happen to set me on the path I was meant to follow. But then I realized nothing was going to happen. Every day felt more miserable than the one that came before, and eventually I couldn't even remember what it was like to feel joy. My life was behind me, and I'd never live up to whatever potential I'd once had. Then one day I got fed up and . . . and I decided to do something about it. Something so incredibly stupid, and hurtful, and selfish, and gutless. And now I'm here."

Vincent realized he had started crying.

Instead of hiding his tears in embarrassment, he let the floodgates open. Everything he'd been holding on to for decades was bubbling up to the surface.

The old man sat in silence and let him take as much time as he needed to return to the conversation.

After a few minutes, Vincent's sobbing began to die down, and he felt his breathing return to normal.

"You know," the old man interjected, "you look like someone with a lot of life ahead of you. What if this big, life-changing event you're searching for hasn't happened yet? Or what if it already has and you just haven't had the time to live through the full reverberations?" He paused, staring at the water. "Never really can tell what's good or what's bad until it's behind you. Could be that the only way to truly know is to see things through to the end."

"But what if it's too late?" Vincent asked.

The old man took a beat, turned toward Vincent, and, for what felt like the first time, made eye contact. They had the same eyes.

"It's never too late, kid," the old man replied, turning his attention back to the fishing line, which was now dancing across the water. "All it takes is a little bit of patience," he continued, reeling in his fresh catch.

Vincent noticed golden streams of sunlight poking out between the leaves of the trees and realized the world around him was beginning to dim. A shiver ran down his spine. He turned to the old man and nervously asked, "So what's next?"

The first thing Vincent noticed was the sound of birds. No, that wasn't right. The tone of the chirping was too harsh and evenly spaced to be birdsong. It sounded more like . . . hospital monitors?

Here we go again, he thought. *I wonder how old I'll be this time.*

Keeping his eyes firmly shut, Vincent took a second to gather himself before jumping into yet another new reality. He was lying on an uncomfortably firm bed, positioned at an angle—not quite sitting up, not quite lying down—and covered in crisp, papery sheets. There was something putting pressure on his right index finger, but not enough to cause any pain, and it felt like something was taped to the back of his left hand—it felt itchy. He felt no pain whatsoever, but the air featured a faint, chemical scent that all but confirmed his suspicions.

Vincent took a deep breath, held it for a second, and let his eyes flutter open as he exhaled. He was right—it was a hospital room. The bright sunlight flooding in from the window to his right mixed with the harsh fluorescent lighting overhead caused his eyes to water, preventing him from fully taking in his surroundings.

Finally, after what felt like a lifetime, he blinked away the last of the moisture and was confronted by an image that left him stunned. Sitting on two faded vinyl seats at his bedside were Violet and Charlotte, curled into one another and fast asleep. Vincent quietly absorbed the scene in front of him—Charlie, with her halo of wild curls, had her head tucked against Violet's shoulder, who leaned ever so slightly toward her—as if protecting her baby sister, even in dreams.

They were exactly how he remembered them, and he was powerless to stop silent tears of joy from streaming down his face. Watching the two of them awakened a love that he'd believed was beyond revival.

They looked so peaceful that Vincent found himself hesitating to wrest them from such a tranquil slumber. He so badly wanted to call their names and wrap them in the tightest hug he possibly could, but he couldn't shake the nagging thought that, despite their appearance, these weren't really the daughters he left behind. He didn't think he had the emotional strength to handle that outcome. So he continued to wait silently for events to unfold on their own, come what may.

He didn't have to wait long. Only a few moments later, he noticed movement in his peripheral vision and turned his attention to the doorway. He saw Lisa stopped in her tracks, both hands pressed against her chest and undoubtedly feeling the exact same loving joy Vincent did. He kept his gaze fixed on this Lisa, trying to discern if she was really *his* Lisa. She certainly looked like the Lisa he remembered—a bit more disheveled than usual, but still managing to radiate the same attractive, positive energy that had caught his attention all those years ago. Despite the unflattering light and circumstances—whatever those were exactly, he wasn't quite sure, but they weren't great—she looked even more beautiful than she had in St. Augustine. He'd missed her—he missed her right now, though she stood only feet away.

As she crossed the threshold and stepped into the room, Lisa turned her attention to Vincent and froze. Before she could say a word, Vincent raised an index finger to his lips with one hand and waved her over with his other. He could sense the trepidation behind her emerald-green eyes, but she quickly shook off any doubts, glided around his bed, threw her arms around him, buried her face in his chest, and started sobbing. Vincent wrapped his arms around her and whispered, "I'm so sorry."

She lifted her head off his chest and managed to say, "Oh, honey, what are you talking about?" between stilted, heaving breaths.

She placed a gentle hand on his face, and the light pressure caused him to flinch, revealing a tenderness underneath his left temple.

"You have nothing to be sorry for. *Nothing.* I'm just so happy we didn't lose you for good. The doctors weren't sure you'd make it—or if you'd even be the same person if you did—but here you are. The same Vincent I fell in love with on that rooftop. I can tell it's you behind those eyes. You made it back to us."

Vincent found himself unable to do anything but gaze into his beautiful wife's eyes and pray that she was right. He wanted to tell her everything that had happened since he'd walked out the door on his birthday, how stupid he had been to take this life for granted, but the words wouldn't come.

"Dad?" a groggy Violet mumbled. "Is he awake?" she asked, shifting her attention to Lisa.

"He sure is, sweetie," Lisa said softly.

"Charlie," Violet said, forcefully shaking her baby sister. "Wake up! Dad's awake!"

"What?" Charlie muttered, rubbing the sleep from her eyes. "He's up?"

"I'm up," Vincent announced, smiling wide enough to cause another twinge of pain under his left temple.

The girls wasted no time sprinting to his bedside and collapsing on top of him, hugging him so tightly that it made breathing uncomfortable. Vincent didn't care. He hadn't felt this happy, or whole, since they were babies.

"Be gentle, girls," Lisa cooed. "Your father's been through a lot, and he's still recovering."

The girls reluctantly peeled themselves off the bed but found ways to stay connected, Charlie resting a small hand on his knee and Violent taking his right hand in hers. Even these small gestures seemed to transmit an unmistakable energy into Vincent's body. They had to be his daughters; he could feel it at a cellular level. But . . . he had to know for sure.

"How—" he started, but the words got caught in his windpipe.

Not this time, he thought, clearing his throat and willing himself to get the rest out.

"How old am I?"

Their optimistic expressions shifted to concern.

"Told you he'd have brain damage," Violet whispered to her sister, who began to tear up.

"Violet!" Lisa chastised. "Don't scare your sister like that! Charlie, your father is going to be just fine. He's just shaking off the cobwebs after a long nap. Isn't that right, honey?"

"Uh, yeah, of course," Vincent replied, playing along and doing his best to mask the concern rising within his body.

"See?" Lisa continued, satisfied with his response. "Now why don't you two go down the hall and grab your dad a Gatorade? It sounds like his throat is a little dry."

"Do we have to?" Charlie whined.

Lisa's eyes narrowed, and she jerked her head toward the doorway. The girls exchanged a quick glance, realized this wasn't going to be a fight they could win, and scurried out of the room. She waited until they were out of earshot and dropped the tough façade.

"How are you really feeling?"

"Honestly?" he said, uncertain of how much he should—or could—share. "I'm just really confused. How did I end up in the hospital?"

"Well . . ." Lisa paused, and Vincent could tell she was calculating how much she should disclose. "You're in the hospital because someone shot you. In the head."

Vincent's heart froze. Maybe he *had* made it back home. But how was there any way to know if this was all real and not just another head-fake? He was pretty sure he couldn't handle even one more of those.

"How did I . . . who would . . . what?" he sputtered.

Lisa took his hand in hers and started lightly stroking his forearm. "Easy there, big fella. No reason to get worked up over something that's in the past. Deep breaths."

Her soothing tone and gentle touch calmed him. He took a few cleansing breaths and tried again.

"What happened?"

Lisa pursed her lips and furrowed her brow in concentration, a look that Vincent knew well and meant that he was about to hear news that he wouldn't like. "They're not exactly sure," she said. "Based on the police report, it sounds like it was some sort of carjacking gone wrong."

"Carjacking?" Vincent probed.

"That's their best guess. They found you unconscious in your car, window smashed in, glove compartment empty, no wallet, keys, or phone on you . . . and you were covered in blood."

"Jesus. I don't remember any of that," he said, hoping he sounded convincing enough to allay any potential suspicions.

"It sounded like a pretty gruesome scene. At first, they thought you had . . . that you were . . ." She couldn't bring herself to say the word. "But you still had a faint pulse, so they called the EMTs and rushed you here. Apparently, the bullet grazed your head, right below the temple. The impact was enough to knock you out but not enough to . . . well, you know. It was touch and go for the first few days, but eventually you stabilized, and you've been lying here in a coma ever since."

"How long have I been here?"

"A week, I think. The days blur together in this place, but I think today is either the twentieth or the twenty-first."

"So, this all happened on my birthday? Helluva present," he joked.

Vincent was happy to see Lisa crack a reluctant smile. He'd really put her through the ringer.

"Do they know who shot me? Were there any witnesses?"

"None," she said, her smile disappearing. "It happened in the Broadlands late at night. Nobody in the neighborhood saw a thing." She hesitated before asking, "Do you remember why you were out there in the first place?"

A flicker of guilt stirred in Vincent's gut, but he let it fade. He knew exactly why he was out there, but he wasn't the same person who had made those decisions.

"It's a little foggy, but I remember Toby making us work late, leaving the office, and then having to take a detour because of road work. After that everything gets hazy."

He was relieved to see that she accepted his truncated retelling of that evening. All things considered, he felt it was best she didn't know the true motivations behind his trip through the Broadlands. At least not yet.

"Lis," he continued, "I'm so sorry for all of this."

"Oh, stop," she replied, giving his arm a playful slap. "None of this is your fault. We're just happy that you're all right and going to make it out of this mess without any lasting injuries. Well, except for the brain damage."

Vincent couldn't help but laugh. One of the many things he loved about Lisa was her ability to effortlessly bring levity to almost any heavy conversation. She was giving him an off-ramp, but he still had more to say before he would feel comfortable leaving this in the past.

"Eh, I can handle a little brain damage," he began. "But seriously, Lisa, it's important that you know how much you and the girls mean to me. I know that I haven't been the best version of myself recently and—"

"Only the last few years," she interrupted, her tone ice-cold.

"Well, yeah, the last few years haven't been my best," Vincent admitted. "You deserve better than that, the girls deserve better than that, and

I'm going to do better, be better, for you all. I know it shouldn't take something like this happening for me to realize what's most important in life, but I'm so grateful I've been given the chance to make things right. Or try to, at least. If you'll let me."

Vincent wasn't sure when they started, but tears were once again streaming down his face. Lisa took his head in her hands, gently brushing away the wet streaks on his cheeks.

"Vincent, we're not going anywhere. No matter what. Sure, these last few years have been rough, but that's life. It ebbs and flows, but that doesn't mean that our love does. Unless I find out the reason you were in the Broadlands was because you were cheating on me—then all bets are off."

Vincent cracked a reluctant smile.

"I'm serious," Lisa continued, valiantly trying to suppress a grin of her own. "But outside of that, we're all in this together. We'll lift each other up when things get tough, celebrate when things are going well, and be here to support one another for all the moments in between. That's the deal."

He'd never loved his wife more than he did in that moment. She was a far better woman than he deserved, one that he would never take for granted again.

Charlie came bursting through the door before he could get a response out, followed closely by Violet, who was clearly frustrated with her little sister.

"Here you go, Dad!" Charlie said, sidling up to the side of the bed and handing him a yellow Gatorade.

"I told her your favorite was orange, but she insisted that it was yellow and hit the button before I could stop her," Violet said with a sigh.

Vincent was smiling so wide his cheeks were starting to hurt. He felt cracked open, in the best kind of way. Somehow, the world had shifted back into place.

"Thank you," he said. "This is perfect."

Charlie beamed and stuck her tongue out at her sister.

"But you're both wrong," he continued. "My favorite is light blue."

Charlie's smile drooped, and it was Violet's turn to return the gloating gesture.

"Whatever," Charlie said, before changing the subject. "Hey, Dad," she probed.

"Yes, sweetie?"

"What was it like to die?"

"Charlie!" Lisa gasped.

"It wasn't that different than being alive. Time worked differently; sometimes it was scary, sometimes it was fun, and sometimes it was just *strange*."

"He didn't die," Lisa reminded them. "He *almost* died. It's like the doctors told us; he's been in a really deep sleep for the last week. The 'death' your father is describing is just a long dream."

"Whatever you say," Vincent replied, giving Charlie a wink. "Either way, I spent the whole time wishing I was back here with you all. I've missed you more than you would believe. I'm just so, so grateful that I get another chance to be the father and husband you deserve. You're my whole world, and I'll never let myself forget that again. I love you all to the ends of this universe and into the next."

Violet, ever the teenager, rolled her eyes. But Vincent could tell that his message landed, especially with Lisa, whose eyes were welling up with tears.

"Now, what do you all say we get out of this hospital and go have some fun?"

"I don't know about that," Lisa said. "Shouldn't we wait for the doctors to give you the 'all clear'?"

"We could. Or . . ."

Vincent let the words hang in the air for a second.

"Come on, Mom," Charlie chimed in. "Let's get out of this place! We've been here for a full week, and Dad seems fine."

"I hate to agree with Charlie, but it would be nice to get out of here sooner rather than later," Violet concurred.

They all turned to Lisa, who stood with her arms crossed, seriously weighing their options.

"I don't know," she murmured. "What if they still need to monitor him or something? I'm thinking we should wait until the doctors tell us we can leave."

The girls deflated, but Vincent wasn't ready to give up that quickly. "You know," he said, "I've already lost a whole week with my family, and I don't intend to waste any more of the precious time we have left."

Lisa's expression softened a bit, but she still seemed torn.

"Listen, I feel perfectly fine. So good, in fact, that I think we should blow this joint and head straight to the nearest lake for a week. We've got some time to make up, and if the weather outside is any indication, it looks like we might get lucky and run into a false spring. What do you girls think about that?"

Violet and Charlie exchanged looks and quietly nodded in support—careful not to get their hopes up before Lisa weighed in.

"Let's do it, Lisa. There's nothing stopping us," Vincent softly pleaded.

"What about work?"

"What about it?"

"Don't you think they're going to want you back for all the merger stuff?"

"Ha!" Vincent barked. "I couldn't care less—I'm done with all of that. Life's too short to waste my time working for assholes."

"So, you're going to quit your job—and then do what?"

"Don't know," he replied, "but I'm sure I can figure something out. Honestly, I think it'll be kind of fun to try something new. Hell, maybe I'll flex my creative muscles and try writing a novel or something."

Lisa scoffed under her breath, but she wasn't pushing back.

"That's all stuff we can figure out later. Back to the order at hand. Everyone who thinks that we should ditch this popsicle stand and go have some fun, raise your hands."

Vincent threw his right arm in the air and both girls immediately followed suit before turning their attention to Lisa, whose arms remained stubbornly folded across her chest. She maintained a neutral expression as she looked around the room and finally settled her focus on Vincent. He raised an eyebrow and saw the corners of her lips curl into a smile as she slowly raised her arm to the ceiling.

The girls instantly broke into cheers and began jumping up and down in celebration. Lisa joined in, and before he realized what was happening everyone had fallen onto the bed, burying Vincent in a loving dogpile. He wrapped his arms around his girls and was overwhelmed by a feeling of pure bliss.

He couldn't wait to start living the rest of his life.

ACKNOWLEDGMENTS

You know, my memory is really hit-or-miss. There are things that I've done, or that have happened to me around witnesses, of which I have absolutely no recollection. Recently. Like, I'm talking within the last few weeks. It's not that I think people are lying to me when they "remind" me of something I was allegedly present for—those moments just didn't stick.

Yet there are other moments I can picture so vividly that I'm almost able to reinhabit my past self whenever my mind wanders backward. I can only imagine those memories remain so clear because somehow, in some way, those were moments that would have an outsized impact on the course my life would take.

For example, I remember typing the last sentence of this manuscript (running through a brief editorial rewrite, no doubt subconsciously trying to stretch the moment), sitting quietly on my rooftop, and feeling like I'd actually accomplished something of significance for the first time in my adult life. And I clearly recall walking into my house on a gorgeous spring day, holding a freshly printed draft that I'd picked up at UPS on my way home from work and thinking, *I've done it, the hard part is over.*

Boy, was I wrong.

That's not to downplay the difficulty of getting the original ideas on the page, but I had no idea how much more thought, effort, collaboration, planning, and decisiveness would be required to turn that manuscript into the book you're holding in your hands right now. So, without further ado, I'd like to spend a little time giving props to the people who made that second step possible. Feel free to check out if the acknowledgments aren't your thing, but stick around if you'd like to know who the real heroes are behind *Everything You Leave Behind*.

First and foremost, I have to thank my wife, Alex, for not only supporting my seemingly random desire to write and publish a novel, but also for serving as the inspiration for all of Lisa's positive qualities. If you liked Lisa's character, you'd love Alex. Just as important to this journey was my mother, Wendi, who was equally supportive and, you guessed it, served as the inspiration for Vincent's mother in the novel. I'm incredibly lucky and grateful for their love and encouragement.

I'd also be remiss if I didn't mention two other brilliant women who had a profound impact on the finished product: Lindsay Starck and Ava Jaylee. As a first-time author, I cannot adequately stress how important it is to work with talented editors whose wise guidance and unflinching honesty can transform a rough, unpolished manuscript into something that you feel excited to share with the rest of the world. I feel enormously fortunate and deeply grateful for their help—this book wouldn't have been nearly as readable or interesting without their input.

While we're on the subject of working with top-notch people to produce a novel you're proud of, it's only fair that I recognize the team at Greenleaf Book Group and River Grove Publishing. Their professionalism, responsiveness, and flexibility rival that of any company I've worked for, or with, in my corporate career, and I'm thrilled that I've had the opportunity to partner with such an amazing group of people throughout this process.

In addition to all these remarkable people I'd like to personally thank Kenny Porpora, whose advice and willingness to connect me with industry professionals were integral to my success in getting this book published. He might not know it (yet), but I owe him a debt of gratitude I'm not sure I'll ever be able to repay. Thank you, Kenny.

I'd also like to provide a special shout-out to my brother Forrest, who is responsible for creating the incredible cover art for this novel. He's an unbelievably talented artist and clearly the more gifted sibling—I'm extremely grateful for his help and support.

Finally, I'd like to acknowledge all my friends and family members who have had to listen to me ramble on about publishing a novel for the past few years and responded with nothing but positivity and support (even if they secretly thought that I was crazy). Without them, I wouldn't be the person that I am today, and there are no words that can adequately convey my appreciation. I love you all.

If you've made it this far, I'll close with a sincere thank you and I hope you enjoyed the story. Until next time . . .

ABOUT THE AUTHOR

Born in Tucson, Arizona, Weston currently lives in Washington, DC, with his wife, Alex, and their dog, Stella. When not writing, he enjoys composing original instrumental music, traveling internationally, and finding occasions to enjoy a nice cigar and port wine. *Everything You Leave Behind* is his debut novel.